Underperforming Underworld

Andrew Harrowell

First self-published, July 2020

ISBN 9798666578766

Find out more about the author at
andrewharrowellwrites.co.uk

For Spud

Always follow your dreams

Chapter 1

"What do you mean I'm dead?"

Minos, Final Judge of Souls, took in the confused soul that stood before and, just for a moment, enjoyed not having to worry about any of the managerial responsibilities that came with his role.

After a morning of reviewing budgets, approving rotas and completing periodic data reports, the Underworld's chief arbitrator had managed to slip past his tiresome Personal Assistant, Gronix, and dive down to the Judging rooms where his vast army of demons processed the recently deceased. Despite the centuries that Minos had spent as one of Hades' right-hand men he still felt uncomfortable with the management side of his duties. The demi-god despised all the board meetings and paperwork that he was required to complete to keep his department running.

For Minos, there was nothing more rewarding than a day spent assessing the sins that the ex-mortals had committed during their lives, before deciding how they would spend the rest of eternity. The judge relished dishing out punishments that reflected the transgressions committed. As often as he could, the demi-god would slip away from his overloaded 'In' tray and get stuck in with the day-to-day work of his team.

Today, the short demi-god had volunteered to help clear the backlog of souls that the more junior members of his department had been fighting against.

Well, Minos told himself he had picked this spot because he wanted to help his overloaded demons. In truth, he'd thought he'd caught a glimpse of Gronix's spikey shadow coming down the corridor, suggesting that the perpetual thorn in his side was already on the prowl with some Purchase Order or Annual Leave Request that needed approving.

"I...errr...still don't understand this," stammered the overweight dead man, oblivious to the fact he was being dealt with by the best in the Underworld judging business. The soul's greasy hair was matted to his sweaty forehead, while the black tie wrapped around his meaty neck bobbed up and down as he spoke each word, "Can someone please explain what's going on?"

Behind his desk, Minos adjusted his faded toga, before leaning back in the tired swivel chair, the springs softly protesting at his 'middle-aged' (although this was a rather relative concept for an immortal being) spread. He enjoyed a second basking in the soft light cast by the kingdom's perpetual mist, the odd brightness of the haze shining through the large void where the rear wall of the room should have been. The gloom reflected off the tired rustic marble of the other three walls (which were still in their rightful place). If it had been a clear day, the demi-god would have been afforded a glorious view of the many ancient offices where Hades' loyal workers toiled to keep the business of death running. But that wouldn't happen – the fog rolled across the land constantly, a permanent reminder to souls, demons and their masters of the sombreness of death.

"I'm not sure which part of the process you're not following, Mr..." Minos' piercing green eyes glanced down at the file in front of him, "...Strodman. You died. My team have processed you, and now I decide how you spend your afterlife."

The Adam's apple of the soul dipped up and down, hefting the frayed collar with it. Before Strodman could respond, the room's large oak door squeaked open and the hairy head of Pasdong, the Judging Rooms' Office Manager, poked through. The shaggy blue creature locked eyes with his superior and squeaked,

"Sorry to disturb gaffer, but have you got a moment?"

Minos looked from the demon to Strodman and back again, exasperation painted across his elderly features.

"I'm in the middle of something here, Pasdong. Whatever it is, it will have to wait!" Minos hated being interrupted when he was judging souls. He despised it even more than working out his quarterly 'Soul to Punishment' ratios.

"But, boss – it's quite, well, urgent, really…"

The furry mouth ran out of words as it registered the annoyance in Minos' eyes. The head ducked back behind the door, which then slowly eased shut.

The judge momentarily brushed his long fingers through the white tufts of hair which framed his bald head, before he composed himself, "Sorry about that – you can't get the demons these days! Where was I?"

"You said I was dead," whined the soul, "People keep saying that, but it can't be right. I feel as fit as a fiddle and look – I'm all here." The man waved his arms back and forth, as if drawing attention to his girth added to his argument.

Minos sighed and pulled at the white hairs on his chin. This was the main challenge for any judge – helping new souls accept what had happened to them. He knew that he should probably have the admin team do a bit more to prepare the souls, but if he tried to introduce something like that the demons involved would no doubt resist and start demanding extra pay (creating more paperwork and meetings for Minos, which was an extra burden he just didn't need). The wizened demi-god stared down at Strodman, trying not to get too distracted by how oily and repellent the soul's appearance was,

"Of course you feel alright – that isn't your body. You left that behind in your coffin. The worms are already eyeing you up as a nice feast..." *More like banquet*, Minos thought but choose not to voice that particular observation. "You now exist just as your soul, the same as every other mortal who arrives here after death."

"But I can't be dead," wailed the leftovers of Strodman, his face becoming redder. "There was nothing wrong with me. I wasn't ill!"

Minos pointlessly double-checked his notes,

"That's not what it says here. And let's be honest – you are in the Underworld.

"Look," the judge waved his slim fingers around, "It's perfectly normal to feel a bit disconcerted when you arrive. You just have to accept it."

Strodman stood quietly, then confirmed to Minos that humanity wasn't missing anything following his demise, as he asked,

"So, I'm dead?" The judge chose to do nothing more than nod his bare head up and down. "Really truly dead?" The demi-god sat silent, letting the soul process his new place in the universe. "Aw man – that sucks!"

Strodman's brow wrinkled in confusion, then he threw his hands up despondently, before his top lip started wobbling, "But, but – I had so much I wanted to do...things to see..." The man started pacing backwards and forward, his large hands wringing at his tie, "And – oh god – I'll never get to finish the 'Game of Thrones' box set!" The soul ground to a halt, his head turning, as he stared at the judge, "I don't suppose you have a streaming service, do you?"

"Come on Mr Strodman – of course we have TV and all the good shows! There's still plenty of life in the afterlife!" The demi-god always enjoyed throwing in that little play on words to lighten the mood. Unfortunately, it fell on stony ground today.

"So how does this work – sitting on clouds, eating grapes, surrounded by vestal virgins?" Strodman's beady eyes seemed to grow rounder at this thought. Minos, surprised that the rolling mist behind him hadn't given the soul some clue of what the Underworld was like, shook his head from side to side,

"No, no. That sort of malarkey is the preserve of the gods on Mount Olympus. We don't do those things here..."

"But – does that mean I'm in hell?"

The judge glared at the soul with a look that would have killed Strodman, if he hadn't been more than six feet under already.

"Not that word again," Minos barked, his short tongue cracking against grim teeth. "You humans and your heaven and hell! There's no such thing, only the Underworld!"

"Oh – so it doesn't matter what I've done?" Strodman's inability to have comprehended anything he'd been told by Minos' team so far caused the judge to scrap his hand down his face in despair.

"Look, there's no heaven. No hell. We just made that stuff up to try and make you lot understand right from wrong. It's all a bit of a metaphor really. Someone should have gone over this already, but let's try again."

The judge took a deep breath, trying to calm himself. "There are three places you can spend eternity. We have the Island of Elysium, where anyone who did a noble deed lives in luxury for the rest of their days. Then the Asphodel Meadows – it's a sort of middle ground for those who have clean balances. You know," Minos held his palms out flat, juggling them up and down to imitate a set of scales, "those individuals who have lived a life which is neutral. They didn't do anything exceptionally good or bad."

The demi-god momentarily paused, as a tiny creak emanated from the room's door. Once again the Office Manager's fuzzy face peered round the wooden surface,

"Guvnor," Pasdong whimpered softly, "Are you sure we can't borrow you, just for a few seconds?"

Minos slapped his wrinkled hand down on the desk,

"Pasdong – I'm with a soul! I'm busy! Whatever it is, it must wait!"

"Yes chief," stammered the fur as it started to recede out of the room, stopping momentarily as the demi-god called,

"And Pasdong – if you or anyone else disturbs me again, I will chuck you in the River Phlegethon and you will burn in its fire for the rest of this year!"

The little blue face yelped and disappeared, almost rattling the door off its hinges as he slammed it. Minos sucked in a breath, moved the papers from Strodman's record back and forth and tried to remember where he'd been before the interruption. "Ah – yes," he resumed his explanation, "Then there is the fate that we save for people like you, Mr Strodman. The naughty ones, who break the rules."

The soul blinked several times, fear and uncertainty fighting across his features.

"What rules?" Strodman finally blustered, "No one told me about anything like that!"

Minos cocked his head to one side in mock surprise,

"Seriously? You mean to say you have the concept of heaven and hell, yet don't recall the Ten Commandments? Because I can quite clearly see hundreds of visits to church on your record. Although," Minos added, "I notice that towards the end you spent a lot of that time trying to catch a look between the buttons of the vicar's wife's blouse.

"But that sort of behaviour was always your downfall, wasn't it, Mr Strodman? The sin of coveting thy neighbours' wife. And in many cases, his girlfriend, sister and even mother."

Strodman's lips flapped up and down, trying to find some words, as Minos continued, "Plenty of examples here of you letching on women. Doing your best to film up young ladies' skirts with your phone when travelling on the tube," the deity shook his head in sad despair as he continued reeling off offences, "I can see over 10,000 hours of leering at pornography websites, and of course the wicked things that followed that…" He moved on, not wanting to dwell on that awkward thought. "Good grief man – there's even one case of you climbing the tree in your garden so you could watch the wife of the man who lived next door undress. I mean that is almost the literal definition of the rule!"

"But what about my charity work? I donated money to good causes. And I always went and checked my Granny's smoke detector!" protested Strodman, snivelling and sniffing at the judge, almost in tears. "I didn't think you had to follow those Commandments. I just thought they were…errr…" the soul struggled, trying to come up with some sort of feasible excuse. "…good advice. I mean it's not like they featured throughout the whole bible or anything. Aren't they just one small part of the whole story?"

Minos did concede that Strodman had put in effort for other people and while some of it was commendable, the judge's focus was on the sin. Rather than addressing this, though, he preferred to share his views on Strodman's second observation – a source of constant annoyance to the judge.

"To be honest I can't argue with you about the bible. The chap who we got in to write all the different religious texts, well, he did gild the lily a bit." Minos winced as he recalled the dubious young man Hades had employed for the task. "But I suppose that's what we get when we don't really have a marketing budget. You do things on the cheap and you end up with mixed messages and ambiguity. I mean, if we'd got a proper writer in, he wouldn't have put together most of the damn books so they featured him! I get that he was trying to make a name for himself, and avoid following in his father's footsteps as a carpenter, but he really could have done something a bit more imaginative with the characters.

"That's beside the point though," Minos returned to the reason why Strodman and he were there (well Strodman, anyway – the judge was really just avoiding a stack of paperwork he didn't want to do), "You knew that your behaviour was wrong. That's why you always deleted your internet history.

"Now, it wasn't one of the bigger rules you broke – you didn't murder anybody and I don't have to sink you up to your neck in the Pit of Despair. However, I will have to do something with you to make amends..."

"Please, no," tears streamed down the soul's fat face, as he sagged down onto his knees. From the ground he clasped his hands together, praying up at Minos. "I can be better – give me another chance. Send me back and I'll make amends..."

"Mr Strodman," Minos raised his voice. "This is not a Hollywood film. You don't get another chance. You've had your life and you chose to break one of the rules. As a result, you must atone."

The judge paused for a moment, as a little smile tugged at his lips. He knew exactly how the dead man would spend his afterlife.

"Gavin Stanley Strodman," Minos felt wonderful as he summoned up the stern tone he reserved for judgements. "You spent your life doing everything you could to demean women and catch a glimpse of their bodies. Since you like flesh so much, I am condemning you to an eternity of bearing it yourself!

"You shall work in one of our strip clubs. From scantily clad waiter you will progress your way up to pole dancer before going on to offer private viewings."

"Strip club?!?" screamed the soul, "I can't do that! Look at me! Who would be interested in this?" he grabbed one of his many fat folds and shook it, much to the revulsion of Minos.

"My demons," explained the demi-god, averting his eyes from the flab that continued to be wagged at him. "After all, they've got to get their jollies somehow!"

Strodman let out a wail and stammered between big sobs,

"Please – I can change. I can be better…" Minos tuned out the pathetic wretch, as he clapped his hands.

In response to the sound, two Kers glided through the hole at the rear of the room in absolute silence. The winged harpies' short, stocky bodies were pure black, their fiery red eyes burning as bright as the passion they brought to their role in the Underworld's security team. As the demons flew forward, they opened their mouths, rows of white pointy teeth coming together in terrifying sneers.

Strodman fumbled backwards, dragging his mighty girth away from the creatures, as they landed on the floor. The pair clicked their spindly talons across the hard marble before roughly grabbing the soul under each arm and hoisting him up into the air. Despite the man's protests, and weight, the threesome simply then soared out of the room.

Sentencing was complete.

Minos couldn't help but feel pleased with himself. It felt good to be dishing out punishments to wicked souls. It was what the judge loved most in the Underworld.

Before the judge could afford himself any more delight at a job well done, Pasdong slipped into the room. The fluffy fur which covered the Office Manager's short body swished this way and that as he bounded over to Minos,

"Thought I'd heard you finish with your last client, boss..." he locked his lips together registering the annoyed look he was getting. Before Minos could launch into one of his speeches about the sanctity of the judging process, and how Pasdong should know better, the little creature slipped a sheet of paper onto the desk.

Sensing the judge's confusion, the demon pushed forward his advantage, "I really do think you need to see this, chief. It's caused quite a stir with the lads." Minos glanced down, trying to anticipate what sort of storm in a teacup was trying to ruin his afternoon.

The first thing that caught his attention was the official seal of the Underworld's ruler adorning the top of the page. Other words started to clamour for the judge's attention and he scooped up the document, trying to take in the most bemusing message he'd ever seen.

FROM: Hades, Ruler of the Underworld

TO: All staff

Colleagues,

It is with regret that I have to inform you that the Underworld is on the verge of collapse. Our finances are way off target and we are experiencing a serious cash-flow problem.

In the best interests of us all, I have engaged the services of the London division of the mortal management consultants Schneider, Schneider & Patterson, who will be helping to turnaround our fortunes. Non-dead representatives from the firm will spend time with each department looking at how we can improve efficiency. I expect all staff to afford the consultants their full support.

I need to be clear with you all – the way we work must change in order for us to survive.

I look forward to us achieving the success we all deserve.

Yours faithfully

Hades

Minos stared down in disbelief — nothing about this had ever been discussed during any of the board meetings. As the judge looked over the memo again, he felt a knot tighten in his stomach, a sense of panic and uncertainty ran through him.

Change?

The demi-god's mind recoiled at the word. There was nothing wrong with the Underworld or how everything worked (besides the reams of annoying paperwork Minos had to process, but that was part and parcel of the job).

Hades has to be over-reacting...

As Minos' mind reeled, he tugged at his small beard, each hair pinging through his fingers and curling against the bottom of his chin. The judge was astonished that Hades was reacting in this way. That the god was allowing living mortals into the kingdom. It just wasn't done.

What sort of right do they think they have to come into the afterlife and tell us how to run things?

"Honestly Pasdong," the demi-god stormed, as he rushed for the door. "This is extremely serious for all of us — why didn't you bring this to me sooner?"

The judging room's door crashed loudly behind the demi-god and the small demon sadly shook its head, as it observed,

"Damned if I do, and damned if I don't, in this place."

Chapter 2

It was widely accepted that any day in the Underworld started badly.

The oppressive fog-covered continent, situated deep in the Earth's core, was home to billions of souls, and many had not accepted the punishment they had been sentenced to with anything close to dignity or reserve. Tortured, unrepentant individuals would spend every minute, of each day, wailing longer and louder than a whale who had signed five consecutive recording contracts. The squeals of the damned ran the entire range of emotions from despair to self-loathing, along the way stopping at elaborate threats and, in some cases, very graphic suggestions about what the soul would do to the mother of the demon in charge of their punishment.

As day turned to night, and the general hubbub of the afterlife faded away, the howling of desperate souls would lessen, as the tormented snatched a few winks between punishments (even if it required the steady counting of the souls of sheep, just to help them settle down). It never felt like long though before the morning shift of demons clocked on, at an annoyingly early hour for all concerned, and the anguished screams were renewed, waking the rest of the kingdom to an unfortunate dawn chorus.

After millenniums of dedicated service in the Underworld, Minos had accepted the conditions of the land. The low warble of regretful souls was now white noise to him. Equally, the judge has grown accustomed to the fog induced gloom of his home. What he had never quite learned to cope with was the rush hour commute, and, today, the traffic was doing little to improve the demi-god's already dark mood.

As the most senior legislator in the realm sat in his much-loved Ford Prefect on the U1 road, stuck with all the souls and demons trying to get somewhere before nine o'clock, he felt the creases in his forehead setting even further into a deep scowl. The traffic stretched along the side of the River Phlegethon, it's red surface broiling and bubbling, the strong smell of sulphur stinging at the demi-god's nostrils. In the misty distance, dark silhouettes of towering trolls created small booming earthquakes as they pounded at the souls of those who had borne false witness. Minos ignored the usually calming sights of his homeland, his attention focused on his final destination: the Palace of Hades.

More specifically the judge was thinking about the boardroom, where his superior waited to discuss the disturbing memo that had been distributed the afternoon before. Despite the warmth being thrown off by the Phlegethon, the demi-god shivered.

As the glittering disco of red brake lights flashed ahead, Minos shifted uncomfortably, trying to focus his attention on the many cars around him. This just depressed him further, as he was confronted by a host of more modern vehicles than his own, including copious amounts of Volkswagens (after the emissions debacle of 2015, no self-respecting demon would be seen without one of the rotten gas spewing monstrosities). Why demons needed power steering, heated seats or rear parking sensors, Minos didn't know. The Prefect was perfect for Minos. It had not let him down in the 75 years he had had it already and he imagined it would do ten times more than that before he needed to even start thinking about another automobile.

The legislator took a moment away from crunching the gears between neutral and first, and back again, to adjust the snake belt he had squeezed round his considerable waist. The green lizard accessory was Minos' smartest item of clothing, yet today the creature seemed intent on devouring its own tail and squashing all the air out of the demi-god. A quick tap on the creature's head reminded it who was boss, and Minos managed to take a few much-needed breaths as the coil relaxed around his large frame.

With a momentarily sense of relief settling around his middle, the judge once more surveyed the traffic, watching as demon drivers bounced up and down, roaring at each other. Metal ground, as tempers flared, and car bodies were scrapped together. In some cases, this was just a friendly greeting from one worker to another. For others, it was pure road rage, excessive insults shared between demonic drivers. Minos sighed deeply as he resigned himself to the reality that by the time he made it to the palace, the queue at the overly popular coffee franchise would be horrendous and he would not have time for an caffeine fix. It might be overpriced, and all too complicated for Minos' liking, but he certainly felt like he needed a little something extra this morning.

Not for the first time in the last few centuries, the judge reflected how life in the Underworld used to be. He had loved the early period when everyone had been running around on horseback, slurping grape juice to get them through the hours of work. Sadly, the thought of the good old days – when there were true heroes to reward, and punishments had to be created for mortals who attempted elaborate sins like trying to steal Hades' wife – made Minos even more down in the mouth. The words from Hades' letter continued to swirl past the demi-god's eyes. He tugged at his little beard – his displeasure pulling out a number of white hairs without him noticing.

The situation the Underworld found itself in felt so sudden, unexpected and, just, ridiculous. There was nothing wrong with the way the afterlife worked and the old judge couldn't understand why Hades felt it necessary to bring in a bunch of wet-behind-the-ears mortals to tell the gods how to run the business.

Not being one to normally sit and stew, Minos had tried to get answers as soon as he'd read the memo, but no one in Hades' office would answer the phone. The only helpful piece of information Minos could glean was from Gronix, who had relayed that all of the department heads had been summoned to a 9am meeting the next day.

The small green pest had suggested that there might be more information on Minos' email account. Whilst suspecting that this was just Gronix's ploy to get his boss to check his many unread electronic messages, the judge could not resist the bait and set about trying to work his computer. After 30 minutes waiting while the battered laptop updated its software, the demi-god had then suffered 15 more of pure frustration as he tried to remember the password for his hot-mail account.

"Maybe I should have taken up Steve Jobs on his offer to sort out our computers before sending him off to the Island of Elysium." Minos grumbled out loud, knowing full well that even if he had been interested in this sort of thing, Hades would never have spent out on new devices. The thought jarred the judge, making him wonder how long the financial issues had really been going on. Had Hades had concerns for a lot longer than he had been letting on?

The demi-god's musings were broken as he finally reached the slip road, allowing him to get the car up to second gear, and make some real progress on his way to the grand palace.

The regal home of Hades was vast, stretching across many acres of land. What the god did with all the rooms he possessed in the palace, Minos had no clue. The judge knew there was a mind-boggling assortment of pottery, pieces of art and paintings scattered across the enormous spaces. For a brief moment, some glee returned to the judge's face as he recalled sentencing two servants, who had been extremely light-fingered in life, to clean every item in the building. Of course, the sheer volume of nick-knacks in the palace meant that the old maids from Crete had a never-ending task.

As the car approached the structure, the tired knots in the demi-god's ancient neck popped as he tilted his head back to admire the palace's many spires, which disappeared up into the kingdom's grey gloom. Minos' attention was drawn to a handful of Kers, their bleak blackness contrasting against the faded white ivory of the towers they circled.

The demon workforce had always indulged in various rumours about the spires of the palace, suggesting everything from the tips being so tall they stretched all the way up to touch the ground underneath the mortal's feet, to the idea that most of the structures had remained unfinished due to Hades realising that no one would ever see them. Minos, for one, had no interest in what was up in the tall towers.

Since his appointment to the Underworld, the demi-god had always associated the palace with the dull meetings, including tedious objective reviews and budget setting, he was forced to endure as a member of Hades' top team. Minos had quickly convinced the kingdom's ruler to abandon the idea of public trials at the foot of the palace, instead taking over the building his team now occupied – well out of the way of the rest of the Underworld operation. The demi-god preferred to keep his distance from his managerial responsibilities, and being out of sight, happily kept him out of mind. He was overlooked for projects or extra tasks and this suited the elderly judge perfectly. On any given day of the week, he was keen to avoid the palace – and that sense of foreboding was even more pronounced today.

Minos pulled up in the car park, situated at the base of the magnificent stairs which led up to the opulent entrance of the palace. As he exited his old Ford, the judge paused momentarily to take in the sight of the ridiculously long queue outside the small beverage outlet set into the side of the building. He was vexed by how there could be such a small collection of cars around him, yet an insanely long line for frothy coffee. The demi-god sighed deeply, as life felt more depressing than ever.

Suddenly, Minos was struck from behind, and had to grab at his car's raised wing mirror, to save himself from falling over. Before he could cry out in anger, he felt a wet tongue running repeatedly up his cheek. Saliva stuck to the demi-god's face as he pushed against the large form of Cerebus, the Underworld's Chief of Security.

"Down boy," Minos finally managed to wheeze out, between long sloppy licks, as he pushed against the chiselled human torso of his good friend. The large dog headed figure stepped back and stood quite still staring at the judge, a moist tongue hanging slightly out of his mouth.

If Minos was at Hades' right hand, the lead of Cerebus was firmly attached to the god's wrist. The loyal creature had been Hades' faithful companion since before anyone could remember. Given his fearsome appearance, the 'hound of Hades' (as the monstrous demi-god had been affectionately nicknamed back in the early days) had been the natural choice to head up the arrangements to keep souls in the kingdom. Since day one, Hades had become completely focused on increasing the numbers in the Underworld and in Cerebus he had the perfect best friend to ensure that the numbers were never going to decrease.

As Minos steadied himself against the bonnet of his car, he took in the full sight of the head of security. The creature's dark muscled chest seemed even more toned that usual, while his tree trunk-like legs, covered only by his short ceremonial skirt, rippled with power. The snake, which prodded out of the creature's back, swished this way and that, as the black bull-terrier head continued to gaze expectantly at the judge. Taking the cue, Minos reached out his hand and scratched under the dog's chin.

A look of happiness spread over the faces of the dog and the snake. Minos thought he detected the hint of a powerful leg twitch as he rubbed his fingers through the short hair. "What's up lad?" he enquired.

"You've seen the memo, haven't you?" muttered the hound gruffly.

"Do you know anything more?"

"Nothing – I haven't seen Hades for days." Cerebus stepped back, his fiery eyes fading to a dull glow. A forlorn expression spread across his hairy face, while the snake head sunk lower, "I sent my best Kers over to the palace last night for a poke around, but they couldn't find out anything more. It's like whatever the master is doing, we're all being kept away from it."

Minos knew that using the Kers to sneak around was considered one of the perks of the Chief of Security's role, however he had never heard of the practice being used against their leader. The judge realised how concerned Cerebus must be if he was utilising the more unhand tactics of his job against the god he trusted more than anyone else in the Underworld.

A thought crossed Minos' mind, he weighed it up for a moment, and then decided to voice it,

"You do not think he is considering retiring, do you?"

Cerebus shook his head so violently great globs of drool swung out of his mouth, spraying everywhere.

"No way – he loves this place. You know he's determined to make a true success of it. There isn't a hope in hell of him doing anything else."

Minos winced at the dog's use of the 'h-word' but had to concede his friend was right. The Ruler of the Underworld had never seemed to wan in his enthusiasm for their work. The judge nodded towards the stairs leading up to the palace,

"Come on. Looks like this meeting is the only way we are going to get any answers."

*

Inside the building, Minos was disconcerted to find the usual buzz replaced with an eerie silence. Although the protests of souls being punished for the sin of coveting thy neighbour's animals resonated deep in the background, the entranceway was otherwise devoid of activity. Not a single soul queued to appeal their punishment or waited patiently in line for the start of the next scheduled ten-day tour of the palace.

It's like the whole Underworld knows that's something is wrong, Minos mentally observed, realising that while rumours would have spread like a case of the clap through the demon population, they shouldn't have made it to the souls at this stage. *And it shouldn't have dissuaded people from coming here*, his mind added.

Without a word, the judge and Cerebus crossed the gigantic hall, barely registering the array of paintings that covered the walls showing Hades at work, rest and play. The pair passed vast depictions of the god tossing souls into the River Phlegethon, lounging on a large sofa reading, and even throwing a frisbee into the jaws of Cerebus. They then ascended the cold stairs, made from elephant tusks, towards the office space set aside for Hades' senior team. Minos winced with every step he took, his sandals slapping loudly against the hard floor, the noise resonating through the empty space.

As the demi-gods climbed, the judge noticed his companion starting to grind his fangs together, acute pain washing across the dog's features.

"What is it?" Minos asked, genuinely concerned for the creature's wellbeing.

"Just wait," came the curt reply.

As they arrived at the carpeted reception area for the offices, with a large sign that welcomed them in whilst requesting they leave all swords, scabbards and axes with the receptionist (who was nowhere to be seen), Minos ears were assaulted with the too-high, too-tinny sound of something that was meant to approximate music. Cerebus was now pawing at his ears with his human hands, doing his best to pin the flaps down to block out the racket.

As the music resonated more terrible notes, Melinda, wife of Hades and Head of Facilities, suddenly skidded out of the furthest office. The beautiful, lithe girl rocked her raven hair back and forth as she sang into the business end of a stapler,

"Oh yeah – dinner by the sea.

"I say, dinner by the sea."

Melinda energetically rocked along to the music, the edge of her powder-blue dress swishing around her slender legs as she kicked them out. A few times she came close to whipping the short, gold-embroidered hem of the outfit so high it would reveal more than she should, but in each case, she would cut in a small movement that demonstrated her youthful energy, as well as her ladylike grace.

The demi-goddess sang more lines of the crude pop tune, concluding enthusiastic dance moves with the stapler held out in front of Minos' mouth, her gaze clearly expecting him to join in. While the music crashed on, the judge stood still, simply staring down at the young imp.

"Come on Minos! At least do the chorus," Melinda squealed, thrusting the inert piece of stationery up against the old deity's chin, it's black plastic disappearing into his tufty beard.

"Afraid I don't know this one, Melinda."

"Oh, come on – you must have heard it! All the mortals love this one. I got it on my last expedition up top, the month before last."

Minos had always considered that there was something laughably ironic in the marriage between Hades and Melinda.

The young demi-goddess of vegetation had been stolen from the Earth by the Underworld's ruler, with the intention of him making her his wife (despite them being second cousins – although that sort of thing was much more acceptable back in the old days). She had initially resisted the god's advances, yet as time wore on their relationship blossomed into friendship and finally romance.

However, given the poor health of Melinda's parents, and her role in the bringing of Spring to the mortals, Hades had to accept that his wife was often required to leave the Underworld. The god, who insisted everyone stayed in the kingdom, had always had to make an allowance for the woman he loved. Minos concluded that this spoke volumes about how much the god really did adore his wife, however much they often disagreed during board meetings.

The judge's thoughts were disturbed as Cerebus started to barf and gag,

"Disgusting! Why anyone would want to leave this place is a mystery to me!" The dog spat a ball of orange phlegm into the corner of the corridor, making his contempt quite clear. In the background, the music died in an altogether too spirited final crescendo.

"Oh – is 'man's best friend' jealous because I can go places he can't?" Melinda cruelly teased, as she gave Minos an odd wink, that he hoped was nothing more than her acknowledging her latest attempt to wind up the dog.

It was well known that Cerebus hated the Earth. The last time he had been taken up there, as part of Hercules' great (and many in the Underworld considered, evil) Labours, the Chief of Security had been physically sick and out of action for more than a week after.

"You think I'm bothered because you can come and go as you please? Not at all. Go to Earth as much as you want. Maybe stay. Permanently, next time!" shot Cerebus, his fiery eyes narrowing.

For as long as Minos could remember there had always been animosity between Cerebus and Melinda. The judge could never fathom whether it was a result of the pair constantly vying for Hades' attention, the fact that

Melinda's flitting in and out of the Underworld flew in the face of everything the security department stood for or just a simple case of one not being a dog-person and the other not being a people-person. Deciding, as he often did, that he did not want to get involved, Minos cut in between the verbal sparring.

"I think the others are waiting for us," he grumbled as he pushed his girth between the feuding pair. With the first salvo of squabbling still ringing in his ears, Minos was looking forward to the board meeting less and less.

*

Minos couldn't work out which of the two figures in the boardroom he was least pleased to see. He was still unhappy that one had dragged him to the palace for a situation that threatened his way of afterlife. While the other individual was someone he always wanted to avoid.

At the far end of the room, more imposing and rock solid than the granite table he was stood behind, was the Ruler of the Underworld. As Hades' deep blue gaze swung across the arriving threesome, a huge hand thoughtfully caressed his beard, which had only recently started to show flecks of grey. The god's bare chest rippled with muscles and dark hair, contrasting against the white chinos and loafers he wore. He radiated the sternness which had made him such an imposing figure in the Great War, many millennia ago.

Hades had never asked for, or, many suspected, ever wanted, the Underworld. After the illustrious crusade where he and his older brothers, Zeus and Poseidon, had led the charge against the old guard of deities, the victors had bickered over which of them would rule the three different realms. With the world's most important decision hanging in the balance, the siblings decided to solve the squabble in the only way brothers can – playing 'rock, paper, scissor'. Whether there was a fix or not, the results had not really surprised anyone.

Hades, for his part, had taken the outcome on the chin, and whether it was his first choice or not (he always dodged this question, no matter how drunk his team got him), he was determined to make the most of it. Over the millennia, the god had ruled his domain with a firm hand, his focus always on swelling his numbers, leaving Zeus and Poseidon to worry about matters like art, architecture and who had the cleverest inhabitants (Minos knew which flippered mammals he'd back in a pub quiz).

Across from the Underworld's boss sat the man Minos was glad he had not seen so far that day (and was happy to bypass any other, for that matter). Thantanos, Chief of Death, was by far the most mundane member of the senior team. His gaunt, pale face made him look like he had only recently passed away himself, and it didn't help that he was dressed in the drabbest black suit anyone, alive or dead, had ever seen. Even the supposedly-white shirt was dull enough to blend in with the boring figure that Thantanos cut.

"And I'm telling you it's a good idea," whined the Chief Recruitment Officer at his manager, most of the sound squeaking from his long, slender nose.

"Once again," Hades' voice rolled like a storm across the table, "I will give no consideration to coming down and involving myself in the recruitment role-plays you organise, Thantanos. Your team may be bringing in good demons, but they do not need to see me prancing round pretending to be a soul."

"I just thought that..." Thantanos' wrinkled lips clamped tightly shut as Hades' gaze narrowed, the look just daring the embodiment of death to argue with him.

Picking up on the topic of conversation (it wasn't a new niggle between Hades and the man he charged with workforce planning), Cerebus clapped Thantanos on the back, making the frail figure jump,

"Don't worry – I'm sure you can still find someone to inspire your troops," a low snigger emanated from the dog's snout, ensuring, as always, that everyone knew that the dull demi-god was the butt of the joke. The snake head, swaying behind the security chief's back, let out a soft wheeze as if it were joining in the gag.

"It has nothing to do with that," complained the washed-out face, waving his slender and shrivelled hands around. "I just felt that having our benevolent master join in with the team's efforts would give them a boost. And remind you lot how important our work is."

"Hasn't delivered great results in my team," snorted Minos from the other side of the table, "Last lot of newbies you sent me all took ages to break in. I had one who thought the right punishment for coveting thy neighbour's possessions was a jolly good telling off!"

"Don't go blaming me if the induction and training you provide to new team members is not sufficient. If you check the inter-departmental agreement, page 177, subsection six, paragraph three, you will clearly see that..."

Thantanos got no further in his argument, as a deafening noise, louder and more menacing than any clap of thunder, boomed out from the head of the table,

"Quiet!" Hades voice was as thick as gravel, silencing every member of his team. "I did not call this meeting to discuss recruitment practices or other trivial matters from your departments."

Minos and the others slid into their usual seats, not daring to meet their boss' steely gaze. As always, the god was flanked by his wife and Cerebus. Minos and Thantanos sat opposite each other at the far end of the table.

A moment of complete quiet passed across the ensembled group, no one daring to speak. Each of the demi-gods found something more interesting to look at, most concentrating their attention on the paintings that were dotted around the walls, depicting the Underworld's colourful history. From the arrival of Hades and his first sentencing of a soul, all the way through to the punishments doled out to Pirithous and Theseus – the two scoundrels who had tried to steal Melinda away from her husband. "That's better," the ruler finally harrumphed, "Now, we are all here because the Underworld is facing the greatest threat it has ever seen."

Placing a petite hand on her husband's arm, Melinda was the only one brave enough to point out,

"They have all seen the memo, darling."

In response, Hades bent down, settling into his ornate chair at the head of the table. The large seat the god inhabited was constructed from cooled magma, its blackened surface punctuated with little holes where air pockets had existed as the boiling rock had cooled. To Minos the chair looked thoroughly uncomfortable, but the ruler made it look like a natural extension of his huge body.

"I know they have seen yesterday's note dear, however I was trying to underline the seriousness of the situation." Hades shot what looked like an imploring look at Melinda as he spoke. Minos was certain the woman would have already heard what the god had to say, and would have helped him refine his words behind the closed doors of their private chamber. The ruler refocused his gaze on the others in the room, "Gentlemen, we are on the brink of a catastrophe, the likes of which we have never known. The consultants predict that we may not even have enough gold to keep the operation running beyond the next two months. And I don't have to tell you what happens then..."

Hades voice trailed off, expecting a reaction, however, the team just shared blank expressions between themselves.

"Surely it isn't that bad?" eventually Cerebus asked, his hairy head swishing around, "What do we need money for, anyway?"

Hades eyes widened, as those around the table shifted nervously in their seats, not trying to give away the fact that they had all been thinking the same thing,

"What do we need money for?" indignation crossed the god's hard features, "Everything! To pay the demons! Feed and clothe the souls! The Sports package on the TV in your Kers' mess room doesn't come free, you know..." Hades glared around the table. "I mean, do any of you actually know what it costs to keep a soul for a year, let alone the millennia that some of them have been here?"

There was a combined, and slightly fearful, shaking of heads, "Well…errr…neither do I. And that's sort of the point," recovered Hades, looking just a tad sheepish that he couldn't answer his own question. "Sandra from the consultancy says the first thing we need to understand is our…ummm…fixed and variable costs, alongside our predicted income."

Minos noticed that the last few words had to be read from crude scribbles on Hades' palm. Although the god had never been one for public speaking, he was usually confident addressing the boardroom. The fact the god was referring to notes demonstrated to the judge how out of his depth he felt with what was going on. "Things need to change," the ruler continued, now free of his aide memoir, and puffing out his chest as he met everyone's gaze. "We have less than sixty days to get our costs under control, bring in more money and make sure that the Underworld doesn't fold. Which means go bankrupt. Not, I'm told, bent in half – in case any of you were wondering." No one said whether they were or not, so Hades made his final point, "I need you and your teams ready to adapt, to help us survive. This is not going to be easy. It may be the hardest feat anyone has attempted since all that Hercules nonsense."

Minos watched as Cerebus visibly winced at the mention of the one mortal who had beaten him in a fight. For the sake of the canine's pride, the judge tried to move the conversation on,

"But what do we have to change?"

"That is what the consultants will work out," explained Hades, his deep voice grating across the table, "They will meet with each of you and assess your departments. They will report back to me and I will have to make some tough decisions."

"Like what exactly?" Thantanos now spoke up, his beady eyes darting around, "You don't mean – getting rid of people, do you? We've never had to process redundancies before. There isn't a policy for it." If the prospect of losing his job made the demi-god go pale, it didn't show.

In response to this new, and very strange, concept, Minos tried not to squirm too much in his seat. He didn't want to lose his job, and he definitely didn't want to get rid of any of his demons. He'd approved the appointment of each and every one of the demons in his department. He'd known some of them for centuries, shared in their successes, supported them during difficult times.

They were almost like his family.

It was the same for all those seated around the large table. Well, everyone except Thantanos. Minos wouldn't even consider him as a weird uncle, twice removed.

Hades sucked in a deep breath, glanced at his palm, and continued,

"I have to make it clear that no one is exempt from this process. The consultants will review everything and present their findings to me. You must all be prepared for the worse."

Suddenly the big god found his feet very interesting.

The next second felt like it stretched into a millennium, before anyone reacted.

Then everyone did at exactly the same time, Minos Cerebus and Thantanos launching into questions, worry etched into each face,

"You can't be serious?"

"What about my Kers?"

"Will we get time off to update our CVs? Mines great – I'm just thinking about the others…"

Melinda intervened at this point, her husband continuing to keep his gaze down,

"Gentlemen, please don't think my husband takes any of this lightly. He wants nothing more than to make this kingdom a success.

"Unfortunately, over the decades we have all become…sloppy. Myself included," she added the final words as Thantanos opened his mouth, "We all want what is best for our souls and demons. For each other."

She reached out and took Hades' hand, "We need your support. If the Underworld goes bankrupt, we won't be unable to look after the souls we do have. And if that happens, we won't get anymore. The humans will become immortal and that is really going to cause problems for all of us gods.

"We need to resolve this, and fast – whatever it takes…"

Chapter 3

"Do you think I'm doing the right thing?"

As the Underworld's ruler spoke, he shifted uncomfortably on top of the flowery duvet covering the four-poster bed in his marital chamber. Through the large window at the end of the room, dusk was settling on the kingdom, a small army of demons roaming the streets, intent on their task of extinguishing the many lamps and candles.

Hades adjusted the small reading glasses perched on the end of his nose and finally put down his copy of 'God Monthly', resting the publication on top of his blue and white striped pyjama trousers. He had reread the same sentence in an article about the best ways to mount a cloud several times, his mind unfocused, insisting on making him replay the trauma of the day.

Straight after issuing the ominous news to his team, the god had instructed them to head out to speak with their own departments, reiterating the key messages he had been told that they had to pass on. The god had then retreated to his office with the pair of consultants for the rest of the working day, and many hours after. The mortals had poured over the kingdom's governance documents, reviewing and questioning Hades on everything from strategy to delegated financial authority (although he had to confess, he still wasn't sure what that was).

By the end of the intense session, Hades had found himself exhausted – more so than after any of the battles during the Great War. After a day of slicing and dicing his enemies the god's every fibre would ache, but his body would course with adrenaline, keeping him wired and alert. Now he just felt drained. He could almost sense his brain wanting to trickle out of his ear, and, given its current insistence on forcing him to relive the probing questions and stupid answers he had stammered out, he would have gladly let it.

How could I have been so stupid to tell them that I don't know how much it costs to run the annual Christmas party? It's somewhere in the Purchase Order system! Why couldn't I remember that at the time? His overworked brain once more chastised.

As Melinda strode into the room from the en-suite, Hades tried his hardest to just enjoy the view of his wife. Her tiny figure was shrouded in a delicate, almost see-through, nightie, that left little to the god's imagination. Sadly for the god, the expression on the woman's face was making no attempt to reflect the mood she had been trying to create when she'd slipped into the garment.

"Not this again," the demi-goddess complained in response to the question her husband had released on their evening. "You have been brooding ever since we agreed to bring those consultants in."

"Yes...but...well..." Hades trailed off, suddenly not knowing what he could say that hadn't already been covered in the long talks with his wife over the preceding days. He nervously rubbed at his hairy chest, his rough fingers creating a sound not dissimilar to course sand paper on old wood.

"Yes, but nothing!" Melinda snapped, her nightie softly bouncing up and down as she took each step across the room. "We've gone over this and we simply do not have the ability to tackle this situation by ourselves! We agreed this was the only course of action open to us." She climbed onto the bed and curled up by her husband's side, nuzzling into the soft covers, in an attempt to rescue the moment that she had wanted between them. Without a word, she shooed Hades' hand away from his chest hairs, and locked her dainty fingers around her husband's meaty palm. Melinda's other hand stretched up to stroke at the god's bushy beard. Hades relaxed a little, breathing in the sweet fragrance of his wife's perfume and allowing her soft touch to sooth his worries.

The moment didn't last, as the god's mouth engaged before his brain did,

"I know we have to do this, but did you see the looks I got this morning. The whole team hates me," the god whined, a look of sheer misery crossing his features. "I don't know how it got this bad. I thought we'd be fine and this place would really take off."

Melinda's beard stroking upped its pace, as she cooed,

"Darling, you have become a victim of your own success. If we didn't have so many souls, we would not have experienced this situation," she continued rapidly, not giving Hades a chance to interrupt with his usual preachy protest about needing to increase the Underworld's numbers. "We both know the underlying point – we have to bring more souls in. That's a given. We just need to make sure it is sustainable.

"And that's what we will do. You and I, together."

She leaned up and kissed her husband, deeply and passionately. Well, that was what she offered. Hades response was lukewarm, his heart, and lips, not in the embrace.

"I just feel so terrible," he continued, oblivious to the scowl his whinging was creating on his lover's face. "The team! The guys who work for them. Some of those demons have been with me since the start. They've been so loyal – and this is how we repay them? I may seriously have to give them something called a P45, which means they don't work here anymore. Can you imagine?"

"Shhhhhh," Melinda moved her hand up to massage her husband's ear lobe. Hades looked further conflicted. His wife spoke more softly, "It's all for the greater good of the kingdom. I'm sure everyone will understand.

"Besides," she added, upping the speed at which her hand caressed the lobe, "the suggestions by the consultants will set us back on the path to success." Melinda knelt on the bed, before using her palms to ease Hades forward. With ease she slipped behind the god, sitting down so that her little feet poked out either side of his body. She then dug her hands into her husband's shoulders, clawing at the muscles, trying to loosen them.

Hades' head lolled back, losing himself in how good his young wife's hands felt as they attacked his tension knots. Melinda, grinning in response, continued speaking, in a soothing tone, "Perhaps the consultants can also help you change things around so all the pressure isn't on you anymore. Maybe you could just become top executive or something like that. Let someone else take the reins and worry about all the day-to-day matters.

Then, you and I could really start focusing on other things...like having a little Hades."

"Trust you to bring that up now!" roared the god, leaping to his feet. Melinda, looking crestfallen, immediately snatched at the bedding, pulling it up to afford her exposed body more cover. "Why must we keep coming back to this issue?" groaned Hades, marching away from the bed. "We have tried. And we keep trying! But I can't just give up my job in the hope that it will help you have a baby."

"Us!" wailed Melinda, jumping up and bouncing on the soft mattress. "Help *us* have a baby! I thought you wanted to have a little son or daughter as much as I do. Has that changed?"

It was now Hades' turn to look deflated,

"Of course I want a little god," his voice took on a calmer tone, as he recalled the disappointments the couple had already endured. "Nothing would give me greater pleasure than to have the sound of little god's feet running around the palace." As Hades' mood melted, he climbed onto the bed, and shuffled on hands and knees towards his wife. In response, Melinda jumped down to the floor.

"Well you don't show it, do you. You never do! It's all about running the Underworld. You are always more worried about being a god than being my husband! What about me, Hades? What about my needs?" She retreated away from the bed, as the god crawled over the covers. "When are you and I going to spend some quality time together? Really throw off the stresses of this place and concentrate on having a family? You keep saying to me, 'in a few months, dear', but that time never comes.

There's always something else out there that needs your attention." She thrust her arms towards the window, wildly gesturing at the dark structures, the sad look on her face almost breaking Hades' heart. The god rubbed at his own eyes, trying to make it look like there was something in them.

"It's not like that," he implored, moving off the bed to follow his wife as she stalked towards the room's large door. "It's just there's always so much going on. It's not easy being in charge. I have so many people relying on me." He tried his best to flash her a loving, and, he hoped, reassuring, look, "I don't mean to neglect you. It's just I have a lot to look after."

"Wrong!" countered Melinda, anger turning her face a dark shade of red, "You have one thing to look after – me! I should be your number one priority, before all that lot."

They had now reached the door and she unlatched the mighty slab of wood, a low protest emerging from its hinges as it swung open. She turned on Hades again, "How long have we been trying? Three, four years? I'm the goddess of Spring! Fertility, new life – this stuff should come easy to me."

"I know it's frustrating my dear, but it will happen for us. Just give it time."

As soon as the words had escaped his mouth, Hades knew he had just lobbed in a metaphorical grenade.

"Time? Give it time?" Melinda exploded. "How much longer do I have to wait? When are you going to stop making me play second fiddle to everyone else?"

Tears rolled down her smooth cheeks, as she narrowed her eyes, "Why don't you have some more time – by yourself!" With a deft movement, she slipped round Hades, giving him a soft poke in the ribs. Out of surprise, at Melinda's harsh tone and the jab, the god became slightly unbalanced and took a few steps forward, crossing into the dimly-lit corridor. Hades immediately spun round, only to find the door slamming in his face. "Enjoy your alone time!" squealed Melinda from the other side of the dark timber.

With a desperate sigh, Hades' head dropped. He scuffed a large foot through the hard carpet on the floor, before he turned to skulk off to the spare bedroom.

"Great," he muttered to himself, "Now everyone in the Underworld hates me!"

Chapter 4

Minos grudgingly stared across the large boardroom table at the pair of mortals that, he had already concluded, would have tried the patience of Saint Peter.

The judge rubbed wearily at the bridge of his long nose, feeling the start of a full-blown headache bubbling below the surface of his mind. He had suffered from a dull brain ache ever since his last visit to the room. It was unbelievable to the judge that not even 48 hours had passed since the horrific meeting with Hades and the others.

Most of Minos' time since that depressing get-together had been spent dealing with a range of questions he couldn't answer, as well as facing down endless criticism from his team of demons.

A great ripple of uncertainty and fear had stretched its way across the judge's department by the time he had returned to his office. Thanks to Hades' memo, and the awkward message Minos was meant to convey, the usually respected demi-god had had to try and handle constant panicked interruptions to his work.

Minos had been flabbergasted by the manner in which his demons had reacted during the relatively short period. The legislator had always tried to do right by his team, but he certainly wasn't feeling that level of support reciprocated now. He'd actually stopped using the third-floor toilets, as he had been genuinely shocked by the hateful, and very personal, graffiti that had scrawled on the cubicle walls. The judge had also received over two dozen resignations. In many cases, these were from some of his best people – demons it would be hard to replace.

Worse than the worriers, felt-tip warriors, and turncoats, in Minos' opinion, were all the plotters. While his good team members seemed intent on running, more dubious demons appeared to have eyes on using the situation to climb up the greasy pole of management. He was being repeatedly bombarded by enquiries from overly ambitious underlings with an eye on taking their boss' job, whether it would soon be vacant, or not. And although nothing had been said to his face, the demi-god was very concerned about the rumours that suggested his own deputies, Rhadamanthus and Aeacus, had the same thoughts.

The exact way Minos would be bumped out of the way seemed vague in the tales which reached his ears, and every version he heard seemed more ludicrous than the last. The suggestions ranged from the slightly scary idea that the old deity could be stuffed in a sack and returned to the Earth, all the way through to him being fired from a large cannon (why someone would do that to him, Minos honestly couldn't work out).

As the judge let the hand that had been fruitlessly massaging his nose fall to join the other in his lap – his whole demeanour making him look like a naughty school boy called in to see the headmaster – he wished he could go back in time. He so desperately longed for the simple life of just passing judgement on souls. He really didn't want to be sat there talking to the undead.

Seemingly oblivious to the fact she was doing something few living mortals ever got to do, Sandra Sparkes, asked the judge the next question in what seemed like a never-ending barrage of pointless enquiries,

"Tell us about your vision, Mr Minos." The woman's curvy figure was stuffed into her white blouse and slimline black skirt. She sat ramrod straight, her fingers interlaced on the dark table, and batted long eyelashes at the judge. Minos couldn't help but reflect on how familiar he was with the woman's type.

In the demi-god's experience, women like the one sat before him were always involved in the breaking of the 'no adultery' commandment. He suspected she spent most of her time either screwing around to progress her own career, or boffing her underlings in exchange for the promise of exciting work projects. Many a man would be judged by Minos' demons (if there was any left after all this silliness) as a result of the extra marital activities they engaged in with Sparkes.

In response to the woman's enquiry, Minos shrugged his tired shoulders, fiddled with his snake belt (which, again, was trying to cut off circulation to his legs) and explained,

"My vision's ok, I suppose. Of course, it's not what it was, but I can still make out all the writing on your colleague's little name badge."

'Kevin Branaghan, Tactical Analyst' were the words the demi-god could see on the small square of plastic attached to the patterned shirt of the second member of the consultancy team. The young man, who seemed to scribble twice as much on his notepad as Minos said, appeared to be the total opposite of his colleague. His dark brown hair was swept over in a style reminiscent of souls which used to arrive in the Underworld in the 1940s and 1950s, yet the youngster hadn't so far displayed any of the charisma from that period. Pausing from his writing for a moment, Branaghan slipped off his glasses and used the, oddly stained, bottom of his dark tie to clean his coke-bottle thick lenses. Without the eye-wear the analyst's round freckled face seemed even more diminutive and child-like.

Minos' attention was pulled away from the determined glass cleaning by Sparkes loudly clearing her throat,

"That's not what I meant, Mr Minos" the demi-god resisted the urge to correct her, again, about the fact his official title was 'Final Judge Minos', "What's your plan and objectives for your department?"

Minos responded with a deep frown, unsure how his eyesight was connected to the follow up question. In an attempt to get out of the room at some point this ice age, he decided not to try and link the two and simply ploughed on with what he thought the woman wanted to hear,

"We judge souls."

Sparkes' deep red lips pouted out so far her face almost resembled an anteater.

"No, no. We know what you do but what's your aims for the department?"

Minos sat and looked blank, unsure what to say other than,

"We judge souls."

Branaghan's pen seemed to hit light speed at that moment and, not for the first time, the judge tried to crane his neck and read the black scrawl the analyst squeaked onto the white ruled page. Sparkes, meanwhile, looked Minos up and down, as she spoke in a low voice,

"I'm not sure you understand the severity of the situation, Mr Minos. If nothing changes then in six weeks the Underworld is finished. Finito. End of. You rattling off what you think are cute answers does not move us forward in our work to help you and your colleagues." Without giving the demi-god a chance to respond, she snapped, "Let's try a different tact, shall we? If I said to you how could we save 20 percent of your budget, what would you tell me?"

Minos blinked a few times as he considered the question. His let his gaze momentarily drift up to the large portraits around the room, however they offered very little other than to ratchet up his annoyance level a couple of degrees.

How can Hades do this to all of us? There's nothing wrong with the Underworld – whatever these two say.

The judge was certain the obvious answer to Sparkes' question was to sack a fifth of his demons, but there was no way he was going to put forward that suggestion, irrespective of recent behaviour. The judge dug at the deepest corners of his mind, trying to find for an answer. He needed something safe, avoiding his people.

"Well," he mused, shifting around in his chair, attempting to wake his round backside up. "I've always thought that we could consider turning a number of the judging rooms into larger administration spaces. That way we would have more space to handle the new souls before processing. I guess if we connected these then we could save on the heating and cleaning." He forced a positive look across his face, even though he knew what a pathetic answer it was.

"And how much do you think it would cost to do that?" rasped Sparkes at him, her fingers tapping out her annoyance on the table's surface. Branaghan flipped over a page in his notebook, pausing briefly to blow his nose loudly on a red spotted handkerchief. It sounded like a mini foghorn filled with mucus.

Doing her best to ignore the phlegm clearing at her side, Sparkes let her digit drumming end, as she leaned forward, "Let me put it another way – how would you cope if a third of your team didn't show up for work?"

Ah, Minos beamed, *that's an easy one.*

"We'd get on with the job. Process the souls as best as we could."

"And what about the third of souls you couldn't see."

"Well we'd leave them until the next day. Perhaps in some sort of new waiting area..." Minos' face brightened, pleased that he'd found a way to loop back around to his first point. His every fibre tingled at the hope he might soon be on the home stretch and could then escape back to the sanctuary of his own office. Or a pub, with copious amounts of beer.

The look on Sparkes' face suggested the answer was not what she wanted to hear. It was that or she'd suddenly taken up professional lemon sucking.

"So, the next day you come in and your demons still haven't turned up. You've got a third more work to do, plus the leftover souls from the day before – anything you'd do differently?"

Trick question, considered Minos.

"I'd get onto the absentees and find out when they were going to be back. That would help. And I'd offer overtime to the demons who came in. That always makes them happy. Pop a couple of packets of digestives in the mess room and they'd be ecstatic."

Sparkes slowly nodded her head up and down, but not in a positive way. Branaghan noisily flicked over another page, his pen having been in overdrive with Minos' latest suggestions.

"I think it's best we leave it there. We will visit the department soon and undertake some observations, time and motion studies, that sort of thing."

The demi-god beamed from ear to ear, relief at the opportunity to flee washing over him. He stood and nodded at the pair,

"I'll be off then."

Sparkes met Minos' proffered hand (he had been taught it was always the polite thing to do) with a dead eyed stare,

"Thank you for your time, Mr Minos. It's been..." the woman took the proffered digits, gripping them loosely, her indifference unapparent to the judge, "Well...it's been. Hasn't it?"

Minos tried to extend his hand to Branaghan, but the man was again caught up in a loud nose blowing contest with himself. The judge turned the outstretched palm into a wave and darted for the exit, walking straight into the first of many unexpected surprises he was going to have to deal with.

Chapter 5

Minos was moving out of the boardroom quicker than a large lady who has been told the all-you-can-eat buffet closes in five minutes, so he did not see the stack of ring binders until it was too late. The sharp edges of the cardboard delivered a spikey burst of pain to the demi-god's torso, but the yelp died on Minos' lips, as the multi-coloured folders tumbled to the floor, revealing the person who had been holding them.

"Rhadamanthus, what are you doing here?" Minos puzzled out loud, as he automatically squatted down to retrieve the various pieces of paper that had become disgorged from the files. The sheets were scattered across the dark floor, in a similar pattern to the patches of white in the hair of the judge's deputy.

"The consultants said they wanted to see me," drawled Rhadamanthus in the French accent he had long ago adopted to make him sound more 'continental'.

If Minos could pin point any period in the Underworld when he had considered life to have been truly perfect, it was the first few decades when he had overseen judging alone. However, as more souls arrived, Hades had insisted that the demi-god brought in extra staff to help oversee the operation. Although Minos hadn't liked the idea, he'd towed the line, seeking out individuals to specialise in punishing the sins committed by the Europeans, as they raped and pillaged their way across the world, and their cousins in the East, who regularly stuck craven images into orifices they shouldn't (and ate monkey brain, which wasn't covered a sin, but was something that Minos thought was really gross).

Appointing the dapper Rhadamanthus as the Judge of Westerners, had quickly turned out to be a mistake. While the deity gave a good interview, in practice he was lazy and self-obsessed, wanting nothing more than the status afforded by his position, without actually doing any of the work.

Bent down as he was, Minos couldn't see the nervous look that now crossed his subordinate's slender face. A manicured hand slicked back long hair, before the demi-god uncomfortably adjusted his tailored suit jacket. He kept silent as Minos began to hand paper up to him. This quickly stopped though, as the judge straightened, a look of confusion crossing his face.

"What's this?" he demanded, waving typed pages at his second-in-command. The words 'Objectives', 'Recovery Strategy' and 'Five Year Plan' flapped this way and that.

"Just a few thoughts for the department," waved off Rhadamanthus with a waft of his wrist, his attention remaining a few inches above his boss' head. His expensive cologne drifted unpleasantly into Minos' nose, assaulting the judge's nostril hair with its repugnant smell. "The message I received said that I should come prepared to talk about the future direction of our area."

Minos stood in disbelief, thumbing through the comprehensive pages he found in his hands. He couldn't believe the graphs, statistics and policies he saw outlined across the various parts of the document. Minos had never seen the smooth-talking figure work out so much as a bar bill, let alone a bar chart, before.

"You haven't suggested any of this to me!"

Rhadamanthus shrugged lightly as he took the paperwork back and stuffed it away into one of the binders.

"It is not much – just a few, roughly scribbled thoughts, to help with what is going on," Rhadamanthus oozed, his silky accent rising a few tones, "I'm sure I've discussed these with you over the years. I just wanted to get them down on paper, in case it helped the mortals. You know what they are like." The deputy judge puffed out his cheeks, as if it was nothing significant.

"Ah – Mr Rhadamanthus. So good of you to join us. Do come in." The voice of Sparkes slinked over Minos' shoulder as the woman beckoned his subordinate into the boardroom. The judge spluttered, but before he could string together a protest, Rhadamanthus' smooth voice was wafting a greeting of 'enchante' to the mortal.

"I wasn't told to come prepared..." Minos wailed as the door slammed shut, disbelief and despair making the judge shake. His head whipped around, but with no one to garner any sympathy from, the judge stalked off, planning elaborate ways he was going to teach Rhadamanthus a lesson for showing him up.

"I'll teach him to suck up to the mortals," he mumbled under his breath, completely unaware he was heading towards an even bigger upset.

*

Minos' thoughts were becoming increasingly churlish as he reached the palace's grand entrance hall.

"I'm certain no one's cleaned out the file storeroom in a few decades," he muttered, "Seems like a very responsible job, that only someone of Rhadamanthus' seniority can handle…"

Once a soul had been processed, and allowed a few decades to appeal, the associated paperwork was archived. The Underworld had been in business so long, it now required a room that rivalled the warehouse at the end of Indiana Jones and the Raiders of the Lost Ark (one of Minos' favourite films, even if the depiction of the Ark of the Covenant was way off base) to keep all the files. No one had been to certain parts of the storeroom for such a long time that there would be more than enough dust laying around to ruin Rhadamanthus' precious suits. Despite his brooding, Minos sniggered to himself – that would teach his underling to try and upstage him.

"Good morning, Final Judge Minos." The old creaky voice barely registered on the demi-god as he continued to plot against his subordinate.

The judge took a few more steps before the words cut through his thoughts, a flicker of unexpected recognition crossing his face. He swung round, taking in the features of Astraea Calisto's soul, the wrinkled skin of the old woman's face pulling together in a slightly embarrassed look, "You do not remember me, do you." It was more of a statement, than a question, as brown eyes gleamed with a wealth of life experience (which, of course, the soul wasn't technically adding to these days).

Minos beamed – he may not know every soul in the Underworld, but he remembered this particularly naughty woman, all trussed up in her old maid's uniform, feather duster and spray polish brandished in either hand.

"Astraea! How are you, my dear?"

Normally, Minos hated bumping into those he had sentenced, but at that moment the elderly soul offered a glimpse into the heyday of the kingdom. She felt very much to Minos, like a physical symbol of him at his judging best.

"I am well, thank you" the diminutive lady eased out. She paused for a moment and then added, "You are very wise, Final Judge Minos. This punishment – it is right for me and my friend." She gestured around the grand hall with the tools of her punishment, indicating the many statues, pots and artefacts. "Our new life here, it fits the wrong we did before."

"How is the cleaning?"

Astraea leaned closer to Minos, her tone becoming secretive,

"It is better these day – easier than years ago. There's less to worry about," her voice was barely above a whisper as she eased away from the judge. "But that's ok. We know the wrong that we did and this is a fitting punishment." Her eyes shone kindly in the dim light.

Minos didn't hear the soul's words as he was distracted by the sight of two large demons, their rippling muscles bulging against overalls that appeared two sizes too small for them, hefting a large oil painting across the room. The judge had never seen the pictures moved and his attention was particularly caught as the piece bouncing across his vision was one of his favourites: the scene of Hades and Cerebus frolicking together.

"Where are they going with that?"

Astraea glanced over her shoulder, her eyes lingering on the stocky demons and the sweat glistening off their biceps,

"Oh – everyone thinks it's best." Minos stared at her in confusion. The maid picked up on his look and softly took his hand. "You have not heard?"

"What?" With all the silliness going on Minos suddenly felt very worried. His stomach lurched like it had become a heavy rock, a dead weight beneath his lungs.

"The doggy, well, he's not here anymore," stated Astraea, once more taking a long glance at the demons.

"What?"

"Yes, everyone says it happened today. He went upstairs and then he was done. Something to do with red dungarees."

Minos rolled the words around his mind,

"Do you mean redundancy?"

The woman nodded,

"Yes – that's it. The doggy is redundant. He doesn't work here now."

The demi-god let out a soft, slow groan, and covered his eyes with his hands.

For a moment Minos just enjoyed the darkness of his little sanctuary. He wished to himself that he could stay tucked away in the black, avoiding what was beyond it.

If Cerebus had been fired, then no one was safe.

Recollections from the meeting Minos had just left tumbled through his mind. How much trouble was he in with those stupid mortals?

What did it mean for him, and his whole way of life?

"Where did Cerebus go?" Minos demanded of the shrivelled woman, as his eyes refocused.

"I'm not his keeper," Astraea shrugged back, "Maybe you can ask someone else. Was nice seeing you." Minos missed the soul's final words, as he crashed out of the palace's exit, hoping he could track down the now-former security chief.

The fear of losing his own job sunk down the judge's insides, like a fat dumpling in a thin stew, as he broke into an uncharacteristic run.

Chapter 6

If Minos had been thinking rationally, he might have considered the possibility that there was little he could do for Cerebus. He may have realised that his time was better spent trying to trump Rhadamanthus, with an even better plan for dealing with the changing landscape of the Underworld.

But the judge wasn't thinking clearly.

And he prided himself on being the sort of demi-god that wouldn't just standby when a horrible injustice had happened, especially when it directly affected one of his friends.

As the judged pounded his sandals against the cobbled stones of one of the oldest streets in the Underworld, huffing and puffing his way into a hurried trot, the irony of the situation wasn't lost on Minos. He was the chief balancer of good and evil for the kingdom, yet now he seemed destined to watch wrongs unfold, powerless to do anything to stop them. With Cerebus out of the picture, the judge wasn't sure he was able to protect himself, let alone keep the demons he commanded.

Part of him wanted to scream, to cry. But he held it together – he just needed to find Cerebus. To find out if the dog was ok.

The hour was turning late and nymph-like monsters flitted around the street, lighting lanterns that created the illusion of dusk. The dull flames flicked this way and that, as demons, many giving Minos and his odd jog-come-walk a second, and then third, look, headed home, content with another day of hard tormenting.

With a small sigh, the tired demi-god pushed back an immense door, its surface knottier than the rope on a tent after a long summer of scouting, and slid into one of the Underworld's dankest drinking establishments. The judge attracted a series of unhappy looks from the motley collection of demonic drinkers inside. The glares weren't at the judge himself, it was much more a response to the small shaft of light he let into the dingy surroundings.

As Minos moved through the space, dodging wooden tables and chair, he passed some of the most depressive members of the Underworld's administrative team. Here and there, Accountants and their Clerks huddled together, exchanging grim words about whether the one really had been carried properly during the day. Without a departmental lead, there had always been little financial steer in the way the Underworld worked, something, Minos lamented, he and his colleagues appeared to be paying for now.

The problem with the finance team was that it was largely viewed as doing the work of mortals and, as such, no self-respecting demon (as well as many of those with no dignity whatsoever) was ever attracted to the department. It took the lowest of the low to actually want to crunch numbers all day. Alongside this, many of the workforce were put off a finance role due to the lack of progression. While many of the departments within the Underworld's operation offered interchangeable opportunities for an ambitious demon to carve out a great career (usually at the expense of his superior, who would get moved out of the way by being bonked on the head with something heavy and spikey), finance lacked this sort of structure. The roles were too specialist to lend themselves to moving demons in and out of the team, and when there was an opening it was usually filled by a freshly lobotomised demon (often following a particularly violent encounter with something heavy and spikey).

The accountants had become content with their lot, including the derision they had to live with, and had quietly withdrawn to the darker recesses of the Underworld. Some said that one day the bean counters would rise up and rule the land. Others quietly explained that the bean counters should go back to counting beans, lay off the mead and stop spreading rumours they could never live up to.

In the deepest, darkest corner of this particularly depressing accountant's haunt Minos found the ex-Head of Security, looking a little worse for wear.

Cerebus was perched at a table which was way too small for his massive frame. He didn't seem to care though, as he gentle swayed back and forth, his eyes slightly crossed. His snake head was resting on the table, content to simply blow bubbles through its fangs.

"How many did it take?" queried the judge as he perched himself onto of a three-legged stool. He waved to the barkeep, an oversized and very round demon with a tusk for a nose and seven eyes dotted across his face. The publican snorted slightly, and grimaced, having not yet accepted his lot as the drink server to the most wretched demons in the land. He did, however, start to prepare two drinks. This was as complicated as spitting in two goblets and then running his grimy hand around the rims, before attacking the old hand pumps, wrenching hard on the levers, in an attempt to pull more alcohol than dirt out of the rusted pipes.

"Three," gurgled Cerebus in answer to Minos' question.

"He's slipping."

It had become a tradition to track the number of pubs the pair had to slip from in order to lose Thantanos, the boring demi-god always popping up when he wasn't wanted. And that was the majority of the time. Half the reason the friends frequented the grimmer inns of the land was to try and give the Death deity the slip. He would follow them around for a time but after so long Thantanos would give in and set out for a kebab, ruining the night of whoever was unfortunate enough to be queueing at that time.

Neither Minos nor Cerebus said anything while the landlord delivered two frothy flagons of mead. He (although up close, Minos conceded it could have been a she) dumped the judge's goblet down on the table and upended the other into a plastic drinking bowl set out in front of Cerebus. The dog's head immediately lapped at the frothy liquid with his long tongue, splashing large globs over the wooden table and onto the hard, stone floor.

Cerebus finally came up for breath and a long moment passed where the only sound was the heavy rasping of the furry face.

Minos finally plucked up the courage to ask, "How are you doing?"

The hound's eyes glowed a brilliant red as he glared at his friend.

"How do you think? I've been with Hades' for as long as I, or anyone else, can remember. Now I'm out on my ear! I'm jobless and very soon I'll be evicted from my house too."

Minos started – he hadn't even considered the prospect that losing his job also meant he would be rendered homeless.

"Hades can't do that..." He wished he had something more reassuring to say, but even as he spoke the words, it occurred to him that the god most probably could.

"Yep. Turns out my flat was part of my employment package – whatever that means. It seems that it will go to whoever takes over my job."

A long silence hung between the two, Minos trying to think of something comforting to say but coming up with nothing. He sipped lightly at his mead, trying to put off the moment where it had been too long since anyone had spoken and he felt obliged to fill the void. Luckily, Cerebus caved first,

"What annoys me the most is that after all this time, everything I've done, Hades can't even face me with the bad news." He drank sadly from his bowl, his long tongue rolling in and out, beating at the liquid.

Minos sat upright in shock. He had assumed that their boss would be the one making the final cuts.

"Hades didn't tell you?"

"Nope! He sent his dirty mortals to do the firing. Apparently, he's too busy with the restructure to deal with redundancies. He has approved it and wishes me the best in my future endeavours! Can you believe that?"

Minos shook his head slowly, unable to believe it. This time he took a much deeper swig from his goblet, the sweet liquid cool and soothing as it ran down his throat.

So that was it then – wham, bam, thank you god's best friend?

Cerebus' gaze narrowed, as he continued, "I'm not even allowed to see my team to say goodbye. I'm to pack up my flat and move on. Oh, but I will be provided with a reference – the good that will do me!" The dog snorted loudly and went back to his bowl. The snake joined him and after a few sips lifted its head up, considerably woozier.

Minos leaned back, just catching himself before he toppled off his rickety stool, mulling over what a bad situation he was caught in the middle of. The tendrils of uncertainty, that had been clawing at the deeper recesses of his mind since everything had started, began to wrap tighter. He gulped deeply at his mead, reflecting that this turn of events really showed how much power the consultants wielded. Minos couldn't imagine what the dog would do now and could only assume that his friend was wondering the same thing.

With a long glug of his drink, Minos took a swift decision, choosing to toss his own concerns aside and take some action to cheer up his friend. Hades may not have done right by his loyal companion, but Minos would.

"Barkeep," he yelled loudly, rattling the other patrons out of their depressed stupors, "Two more meads here, and keep them coming!"

I may well regret this, he mused to himself, *but what's the worst that can happen?*

*

"And I'm telling you, they can't!"

"Alright, do we have to keep going on about it?" Cerebus grouched as he cocked his leg and marked his territory on one of the many lamp posts on the way towards the palace. His snake's head hung low to the ground, and seemed much too interested in the golden stream.

"I won't mention it again, provided you admit it," Minos swayed slightly, which surprised him considering he'd drunk more mead than he ever had, and he stared at where Cerebus should be (if he wasn't off having a tiddle).

"I can't," slurred the dog as he re-joined his friend and stared towards the rocky ceiling, way above their heads. "If I can look up, so can all dogs. It's as simple as that. You've been watching too many films!"

Minos responded by lightly shoving Cerebus, giggling as the hound drunkenly rocked back and forth on his heels.

"Just say it," the judge goaded. "Repeat after me – dogs can't look up!"

The pair took a few more staggered steps and then paused.

"What are we doing?" the hound asked. His snake had fallen asleep and its chin bumped over the cobbles as he gingerly took another few paces forward.

"Ssssshhhh," Minos held his finger up to his lips, missed and instead jabbed himself in the eyebrow. "It's important that we're quiet."

"Why?"

"I don't remember, but it's important, I think..."

"What is?"

"I'm not sure – what are we doing?"

"Beats me...owwww!" The dog yelped, more out of surprise than pain, as Minos playfully punched him. "What was that for?"

"You said beat me...owwwww!" Minos squeaked as Cerebus responded in kind. The old judge held up his hands, "Truce – this isn't getting us to the...errrr...what are we doing?"

The pair staggered on a little further, dragging their heels over the uneven stones, the dark silhouette of the palace looming up in front of them. Minos belched loudly, then turned a shade of green and gagged.

"Don't you dare!!" Cerebus scurried backwards, fearful his friend was about to spew up what had been a dubious-looking dinner. "I knew you shouldn't have ordered those deep-fried rats."

Minos sucked down a few deep breaths and then straightened slightly. He waved his hands to indicate he was ok (although still didn't trust himself to open his mouth), stepped forward and walked straight into the side of the palace. He groaned softly as his eyes started to close, weariness and alcohol taking over.

"I've got it!"

Minos stirred at the excited cry of the dog, this time finding his mouth with his finger, in an attempt to hush his companion. "We're going to the palace." With his head firmly resting on the wall of the building, Minos mumbled,

"No shit, Sherlock..." the judge mumbled as his eye lids became heavy once more. Cerebus, shock his friend's shoulder, as he continued,

"We're going to see Hades. To have it out,"

"Is that a good idea?" murmured Minos.

"You thought it was – it's your plan!"

The judge blinked a few times, as he rolled the concept around his head. His eyes widened as some level of recollection sparked inside him.

"It is! I mean – it was. No...wait...it is?" He scrabbled to make his words follow the flow of his mind, "Yes, that's right! We need to do this. We must see Hades. Convince him to right this wrong. And if not, he needs to tell himself that you've fired him." He slapped the wall enthusiastically, despite losing his way at the end of his rousing speech.

"Yes," agreed Cerebus, believing he had perfectly followed the confused words.

"But how do we get in? Isn't the palace locked up now?"

"Ah!" Cerebus grinned as he felt around in his ceremonial skirt and, from somewhere deep within the folds, pulled out a large rusty key. "Those mortals don't know about this!"

"You've got the front door key?" The dog's happy expression broadened as he shook his head and twirled the metal in Minos' face. "Back door?"

"Better! This is the master key! It opens almost every lock in the Underworld!"

"Excellent. In that case, we will go into the palace, and we will walk right up to Hades and tell him that he needs to sort this out."

Cerebus started nodding, then stopped and looked a bit sheepish. It was a strange look for a dog, and one that many foxes wished they could master.

"Well, it can't quite get us to Hades."

Minos drunkenly swayed, took the information in and then let his bottom jaw hang open. "Hades forged the key when he took over the kingdom. It was meant to take me everywhere, but once Melinda turned up, he revoked some of its power. Apparently, she wasn't happy about me sleeping on the bottom of their bed." A low growl emanated from Cerebus' furry throat as his disapproval for the god's wife shook his body.

Minos, whose head was starting to clear from the vaguely fresh air, looked the dog/man up and down.

"So, we can't see Hades?"

"Well we can get close – then we'll have to knock."

Minos, clearer but still not sober enough to really know quite what he was doing, drew himself up straight,

"Then we shall knock and knock until Hades fires you himself."

*

It had been 15 minutes of painful knocking and the pair were ready to give up. Minos shook his red knuckles, before blowing on them to ease the pain.

"So much for your all access pass," he complained, a dull haze having descended over his vision.

The friends had only made it to the outer door of Hades' sanctum. It had been a long time since Minos had been in the god's private chambers but he was certain that they were still quite a distance away from the bedroom, where no doubt Hades was tucking himself in for the night. Cerebus tried a few more rat-a-tat-tats before conceding defeat.

"The key does all the other doors," the dog whined. His face dropped, as he stared at the now useless piece of metal. "I can get into the offices, meeting rooms, even the stationery cupboard..." an odd look crossed his face as he trailed off. Minos tried to stick his whole fist in his mouth so he could soothe his throbbing knuckles, but failed. "Are you thinking what I am?"

"I doubt it..."

"We can go anywhere in the building. Anywhere!"

"Cerebus, I know you always speculated about what's up in some of the towers but now is not the time to go exploring." Minos could feel the early stages of a hangover threatening to crash over his cloudy mind.

"We can go to any room – any office!" Cerebus proudly turned the key over in his meaty hands.

"You're going to have to break it down for me?" groaned the judge.

"We could go in the consultants' office!"

"And do what?" Blankness was returned from the furry face,

"I don't know. We could find out what else they have in mind. What they are going to do to everyone else, including you." His dark furry face brightened even further, "and if nothing else, I think I could do with another pee..."

In spite of himself, Minos smiled.

He recognised that if he was sober, he might not think that it was a good plan, but as he wasn't, he decided he'd tag along. There was a part of the judge that was really tantalised by the idea that he could find out what had been written about him that afternoon.

Using the master key, the pair made their way back through the palace towards the office space. Despite noisily failing in their attempts to be stealthy, they did not see anyone else as they wandered the twisting corridors, passing a range of exotic items, most gifted to Hades in recognition of his work over the millenniums. Here, a plate stamped with the seal of the Guild of Sword Master Generals, there a statue with a detailed inscription hailing Hades' leadership of the Third

Battalion during the Great War. Not every surface was covered with memorabilia but there was more than enough to show how revered the god was across the land, and beyond.

Minos wondered how many of the groups might want these items back in the coming days. What impact would the silliness with the mortals have on Hades and his standing within the demonic community?

Instead of brooding the judge tried to focus on enjoying his time with his mate. Along the way they joked and told stories of the good times they had had together. As they moved through door after door, Minos continued to marvel to Cerebus about the key. He found it fascinating – whatever the lock, the piece of metal neatly adapted itself. The judge asked many questions and was pleased to keep the dog's attention on the item, rather than the lack of demons around. Minos had already been bored with a lecture about how there should be a full contingent of Kers on patrol at night, and was relieved that he didn't once more have to hear his friend talk about his old job. Deep down, he was well aware that when the sun came up and the pair sobered up, they were going to have to face some harsh realities. Minos definitely wasn't ready for that and even wished he had some more mead to keep the inevitable at bay just a little longer.

Despite a few wrong turns, the pair finally found themselves stood in what could only be described as the palace's blandest office. After the build-up, the reality was a bit of a let-down. The whole room was cleaner than a saint's soul. Neatly arranged filing cabinets rose up at the back of the room, while two desks sat completely empty, not even a pen on their smooth surfaces. The mortals were so picky about tidiness, the faded swivel chairs had been perfectly tucked away, exactly central, underneath the worktops.

"Well, that was a waste of time," Minos moaned at his companion, having expected plans to be strewn across the room, revealing everything he wanted to know.

"Speak for yourself," retorted the beast, who was in the process of lifting the flaps of his skirt. Minos groaned softly and moved away.

Averting his eyes from Cerebus' efforts (the huffing and puffing suggested the creature didn't have as full a bladder as he'd thought), the judge took a moment to study the filing cabinets at the end of the room. To his surprise (because he'd never done it in all the time he'd worked in the Underworld), Minos realised that the mortals had actually labelled the drawers of the cabinets. He took in the little stickers, ranging from 'Financial Analysis and Statistics' through to 'Data Protection Outlines and Proposals'. Most of the neatly written words were dull, or confusing, to the aged demi-god but one, towards the bottom of the stacks, caught his eye. In a rough scribble was the word 'ICE'.

Minos giggled slightly, his drunkenness still apparent,

"That's stupid," he mumbled. It was such a weird word to see in the Underworld, especially as the enclosed environment of the kingdom meant it wasn't subject to the weather patterns of the Earth. It was never snowing, cloudy, pouring down or a bit fresh (not that Minos had ever understood what the last one meant).

Despite the odd fascination mortals had with the weather, the judge couldn't understand why the consultants would keep some frozen water in their cabinets. He couldn't fathom it, but after all the banging on Hades' front door, the prospect of something cold was enticing. The judge suddenly wanted nothing more than to touch the frozen liquid, to feel it's cooling surface against the sore skin on his hand.

"I think I'll have to concede," stated Cerebus, as he trotted over to join his friend. "I should have had a few more meads before we left the pub. I'm not sure if there's anything more we can do here – damn mortals are so clean."

"Pass me your key," gestured Minos, his gaze locked on the three-letter word.

Cerebus obliged and handed over what was now a tiny piece of silver. The judge slid it into the cabinet's lock and enjoyed the quiet ppppfffftttt the cabinet made as the mechanism was released. To his great disappointment, the demi-god pulled open the drawer to find it filled with one paper file. He lifted it up, staring at its cover: 'Initial Consultation Engagement (ICE)'.

Minos' annoyance with the last few days finally got the better of him.

The stupid mortals.

Their ridiculous questions.

The unfair treatment of his friend.

The judge let out a loud yell, as he launched the file upwards, letting most of its contents fly into the air. Swinging the folder back down, he scrunched his fists in anger, tightening his grip around the few sheets which hadn't flapped over his head. "For Hades' sake — is nothing straightforward these days?"

As Minos stood puffing and wheezing, his body shaking with pure rage, a reassuring palm rested on his shoulder.

"It's ok — I'll be alright. You will be fine as well. All of this will pass."

Cerebus face registered acceptance, as he moved round to face Minos, clasping both of the demi-god's shoulders with his large hands. The judge felt a new level of respect for his comrade wash over him. He stepped away, dropping the file on the nearest desk, as he implored,

"You don't know that..." the judge stopped, unable to find the words to express the sense of despair he felt. Instead he absently let his gaze drift across the stupid sheets of paper in front of him. As he did so, he tried to put his jumbled brain back together.

He hated the situation. The affect it was having on him and everyone else. Minos despised having to say goodbye to Cerebus, and the bubbling fear that he was next on the chopping block was once more welling up within him. He rested his chin on his chest, "I think I'm just tired," he said softly.

Cerebus reassuringly patted him on the back.

"It is pretty late for a couple of demi-gods. Let's clear up and get out of here."

The dog stooped down and began to collect the papers that had fallen on the floor. Minos took a final look at the sheets in front of him as he prepared to help. For a second the judge's vision focused on the typed words and he noticed his name.

A few lines above it, he saw 'Cerebus'.

There were other words around each name and he immediately grabbed at the paper, steadying himself as he took a closer look:

- 'Once an agreement is reached and the firm is appointed, consultants are to attend the Underworld operations and work closely with Hades to gain his trust.
- While a thorough analysis is needed for recommendations, consultants should target specific individuals and ensure they are removed from the business.
- Cerebus, Head of Security, needs to be made redundant first. Discretion to his replacement is left with consultants.
- Following this, Minos, Final Judge of Souls, must be removed and Rhadamanthus appointed as his successor. Consultants will take the necessary actions to ensure a smooth transition.
- The next step of the plan is the most crucial...'

Minos immediately turned the page to find out more, unable to believe his eyes. To his sheer dismay there was nothing on the back of the sheet. He stared down at the other pieces of paper in front of him but found nothing that finished the sentence.

As the demi-god reeled, he turned and snatched at the pages in Cerebus' hand, eliciting a hiss from the dog's snake (which had been scooping up sheets in its mouth).

"Steady," cautioned the dog, looking put out. Minos wasn't listening as he flicked through the other sheets, trying to find the rest of the instructions.

"Here," he muttered, passing over his discovery. Cerebus took a moment to read the document and his eyes grew large, as his snake slinked up to join in.

"This...it's...but..." the dog stammered.

"Help me find the rest of it!"

For several minutes the pair poured over the remaining paperwork, finding nothing more than terms and conditions for engaging the consultancy the mortals worked for. They couldn't find the end of the text anywhere, even after rifling through all the other filing cabinets.

Eventually both sat down, defeated and depressed. Cerebus was the first to put a voice to their frustrations,

"So, me losing my job was a foregone conclusion? I never had a chance."

Minos glumly nodded, as he observed,

"It seems Hades had it in for both of us from the start."

"No," disagreed the dog, shaking his head in defiance as he stood. "This was clearly written ahead of those mortals arriving." Minos blinked a few times, "See – the words talk about gaining Hades trust. Someone else has given them these directions. They look like they are working for Hades but there's another person pulling the strings."

"That means someone else is out to get us. And," mused Minos, "Ruin the Underworld. But who?"

"That I don't know, but if those mortals aren't acting in the best interest of Hades, then we need to work it who they are and stop them!"

Chapter 7

Minos groaned as he creaked his eyes open. Daylight (well, the close approximation that the Underworld had) streamed through the window, boring into the demi-god's head, exacerbating his hangover.

"Never again," he moaned through lips that were so dry he felt like he'd eaten the Sahara Desert and followed it up with a course of gravel.

"Bllllaaarrrggghhh!!!"

Next to the judge on the threadbare sofa, in his small flat, Cerebus coughed up some form of communication.

Minos blinked a few times, wondering if he could go back to sleep or just give in and die. Of course, if he died, he'd just end up in the Underworld, which really wouldn't solve anything.

The judge finally decided to try and manoeuvre himself across to the tiny kitchen for a drink of water. It was a slow and extremely painful process. He just avoided stepping on Cerebus' muscled body, which sprawled off the sofa and onto the floor. In doing so, Minos managed to bash his shin on the nearby coffee table. The demi-god let out an agonising yell as his leg sent hideous messages of pain through his already delicate body. The noise jarred his consciousness further awake, only making his hangover worse.

With less grace than a baby deer on ice, Minos hobbled the final steps to the built-in kitchenette. Before the judge lay devastation: the sink filled with the dirty crockery he hadn't got around to washing (he had, after all, been busy with work during the last few days), the counter strewn with the remains of a takeaway. Soggy chips, wilted lettuce and splashes of red sauce ran amuck around a pile of battered polystyrene containers. The judge knew he and Cerebus must have brought the food back the night before, but had no recollection of it. It explained why Mr Mittens, his tabby cat, was nowhere to be seen. The animal hated mess as much as it despised dogs.

The judge decided not to extend his anguish by searching for a clean glass and instead threw his head under the sink's tap. When he finally emerged from the torrent of cold liquid his wispy beard was sodden. He slapped his moist lips together, feeling slightly less human and much more demi-god.

From the sofa Cerebus tried to speak again but managed nothing more than a string of unintelligible sounds. Taking pity on the dog, Minos poured some water into one of his cleaner saucepans and wobbled his way back to his friend. The judge plonked the pan down on the sofa and couldn't get his hand clear fast enough as both the dog and snake attacked the sobering fluid.

Minos landed heavily on the sofa and just listened to the soft lapping of dehydrated tongues on water. He closed his eyes and then instantly sat upright, visions of the night before invading his brain. His mind's eye saw a table covered in empty goblets. Then he vaguely recalled laughter and walking, stumbling and crashing into things. His knuckles suddenly sent an aching twinge through his fragile body and he peered down, noting the scuffed skin. Then his brain eased into recollections of the later part of the night. The desire to find out more about the mortals and then...then...

Did I really see that note?

Minos' memory felt as fuzzy as his tongue. Had he really uncovered a plot to deceive Hades and oust two of his most loyal team members? Words and thoughts drifted through the demi-god's brain and he turned to his side, seeking some level of confirmation from Cerebus. The stare that met Minos' shared an unspoken link between the pair.

Breaking eye contact, Cerebus glanced at the small wall clock, which was pushing its large hand dangerously close to the hour mark, while the other happily hung just below the nine.

"Shouldn't you be getting to work?"

"Stuff it. I think we both know how my day is going to go!"

As he spoke, Minos trembled, the fact that he had no control over his own destiny gnawing at him. Cerebus tried to grin, but it was a wonky offering that was as slanted as Minos felt,

"Come on mate – we need to tackle this head on.

"In that case, we need some breakfast and a plan!"

*

An hour later, Minos was liberating his second egg, from the mountain of fried food on his plate. He swirled the yellowy yolk, mixing it with bright orange bean juice and fatty deposits from his sausages. The judge, his feet uncomfortably crumpled under his fold-out dining room table, was already feeling so much better. As another mouthful of greasy food hit his stomach, he could sense the leftover effects the night before drifting away, leaving him clear and determined.

"Let's recap what we know," he stated, as he looked across at Cerebus and watched the hound attack his seventh sausage. The dog had focused on meat for his breakfast, ignoring the other goodies the judge had found lurking within the depths of his cupboards, old fridge and battered freezer. "Someone wants us fired."

"Well, it seems like it's much more than that," shot back Cerebus, between bites.

Minos paused, taking a moment to try and think about the whole picture, rather than just his own personal misery,

"Ok – stepping back further. Someone engaged those consultants before Hades, but on the basis that they had to be employed by him. They have been given instructions to do something here, but it isn't clear what." The demi-god scratched at his bearded chin, wiping yolk from it as he did.

Cerebus nodded, as his snake stole a piece of toast from Minos' still-bulging plate, clamping its jaws around the buttered bread before swallowing it whole. It left a triangle shaped lump half way down the creature.

"Whatever is going on includes getting rid of us. And there's nothing we can do to stop that."

"Can't we? Why shouldn't we just go and tell Hades?" asked Minos.

"With what evidence?"

The two of them had made certain to leave the room exactly as they had found it. It had seemed like a good idea at the time, but now the judge was starting to regret that decision. He conceded that wafting a piece of paper, with an incomplete amount of details, in front of Hades wasn't necessarily going to convince their beloved leader that it wasn't just sour-grapes. Voicing his concerns, the judge added,

"And, of course, we don't know how far those bastards have wormed their way into Hades' good graces. Right now, he could think we're the bad guys."

Cerebus' heads shook this way and that.

"Not Hades – no way!"

"You say that, but you've already been given your marching orders. Sorry mate," Minos added the last few words as the dog's wounded expression made him feel bad for being so blunt. He attempted a look of stoic support, as he continued, "For now, I think we assume we can't trust anyone, especially Hades, not until we can work out what's actually going on."

"But how?"

"We need to find the rest of that message. It's safe to say it's not down here – we looked everywhere last night. Unless those mortals have it safely tucked on their person. And, if that's the case, I still don't think we'll be able to get our hands on it."

Silence hung over the conversation, an impasse reached. The snake, spotting an opportunity, nicked another slice of toast. "How do we prove something when we don't have anything to back us up?" pondered Minos.

"We need the rest of that document," Cerebus reiterated the fact as he chewed a lump of bacon.

"Ok — but that's not here." Minos momentarily brightened, a thought hitting him, "But it was a print out which probably means that somewhere it's stored electronically."

"There were no computers in the office. It was all written notes, nothing electronic."

The pair shared a long stare between them, neither wishing to speak what was slowly becoming inevitable. Finally, Minos sucked up his nerve, swallowed a long swig of milky tea from a chipped blue and white striped mug, and pronounced,

"We have to go to the Earth and break into the mortal's office."

"No way — count me out!" fear flushed clearly across the dog's face.

"Come on — it's the only way we're going to get to the bottom of this. We need to access their office, so we can find out what is actually going on and who is behind this."

"Or," and Minos could tell Cerebus was doing his best to find a way to avoid a trip above ground, "We could do everything here to run interference and get those mortals to do something to incriminate themselves. I should still have a few Kers loyal enough to undertake some undercover work for me."

Minos could see the genuine desire the dog had not to return to the Earth. He couldn't blame his friend – the last time the animal had been there, even for a short period of time, he'd had such a serious allergic reaction everyone in the kingdom had worried for his health for days after. The judge didn't like the idea of travelling topside either but at this stage he didn't feel like there was any other option.

He screwed up his courage and committed himself,

"Alright, you stay here and do what you can to undermine the mortals. I'll go and find out more."

As he spoke, the judge threw down his cutlery, his appetite completely gone.

Chapter 8

Minos couldn't work out if it was the fear of returning to the Earth, or the strange swirling Exit Portal that stood before him, that made him feel cold to his bones. Either way, he shivered violently.

Set in the side of one of the many mountains that rose up around the Underworld, a by-product of roughly carving out a hole in the depths of the planet's core, the vortex whirled with a million colours. For what felt like an eternity, the judge stared into the frothing lights as they twisted this way and that. It felt like he was looking into all of time, everything rolling into one. Fearful that it would somehow warp his mind, the demi-god used all his mental might, to pull his gaze away from the Exit.

Still without any sign of Cerebus, Minos turned his focus on the counterpoint to where he stood. Down below him, on his left, was the island which housed the entrance to the Underworld. The magical gateway connected to a sandy beach, and was flanked by enormous doors which Hades had locked open when he'd first arrived in the kingdom.

Over the decades the entrance to the Underworld had varied in the amount of usage it received from the mortals. In the early days, souls would arrive in dribs and drabs, often the busiest nights being when emperors had held elaborate tournaments. During wars and major conflicts, the small island would fill with newly deceased figures quicker than the Arrivals Team could greet them. There had rarely had any period of quiet at the Underworld's entrance, though, mortals always finding some way to end the lives of their fellow Earth dwellers.

From his vantage point, Minos could observe two of his soon-to-be-former colleagues, going about their work welcoming souls into life after death.

Closest to the arrival point was Hermes, one of the trickiest characters within the kingdom. The Guide to the Underworld loved nothing more than the newness and gullibility of fresh meat after the slaughter. The disorientated souls played straight into the annoying pranks and general unpleasantness of the young demi-god.

If there was one member of the Underworld's operation Minos didn't want to sit next to at the Christmas party, it was Hermes. Even in the distance the judge could make out the spry figure, in full cowboy get up (Hermes had discovered a love for the Wild West when it had developed and hadn't changed his style since), flitting between souls, reigning confusion and misery on the recently deceased. His annoying high-pitched laugh floated on the breeze, making Minos scowl. As far as the judge was concerned the dead deserved more respect than Hermes ever afforded them.

For a second, Minos' mind niggled – why were he and Cerebus getting the chop, but not Hermes? Was the chirpy prankster also on the list? Is that what he would find when he tracked down the second half of the document?

He shivered once more and pushed the thoughts down, trying not to focus on the journey ahead of him, returning his attention to the scene below.

In contrast to the goading and tomfoolery of the Stetson wearing guide, Charon, the Underworld's Ferryman, went about his task with deference, and support, aplenty. As the souls boarded the long boat which would take them across the River Styx to await their fate at the hands of the demonic judges, Minos could see the scruffy sailor moving amongst them. A kindly touch here, a steadying hand there, demonstrated the kind-heartedness of the hunched Charon. Despite his shabby looks, the demi-god was one of the hardest workers in the Underworld.

When Thantanos' predecessor had retired, many had pushed Charon to apply to step up and take over the whole department. To every suggestion the wizened sailor had happily shook his head and assured them that he was happy with his lot. 'Content' was the word Minos would most easily associate with the experienced demi-god. Even when Hades had decided to stop charging souls for entry to the Underworld (in response to the number who were cluttering up the island because their loved ones had been too busy fighting over the good candlesticks to place two coins on the eyelids of the deceased before burial), and effectively changed Charon's role, as well as depriving him of his cut, the ferryman had simply rolled with the transition with nothing more than a shrug of his shoulders.

Minos suddenly found himself rubbing at his eyes, a pang of sadness catching him. He wished he could be as accepting as Charon. Part of the judge surprisingly yearned to be able to just accept his new place in life.

But, for Minos, it wasn't to be.

He scanned his eyes across the kingdom and dimly made out the shadow of the palace, off to his right. The demi-god pondered what was happening in there – were the consultants already sending out demons to find him so they could make him redundant? What would happen if he wasn't successful in his mission to the Earth? Could Hades do anything worse to him than take away his job? Minos didn't think so – his role meant that much to him.

Minos pushed his thoughts away from the palace, only to hone in on his office building, the tall marble rising up and leering over the small shops and restaurants which surrounded it. With sadness he wondered if the demons had noticed his absence? Was anyone missing him? Had his firing been made public, and if so, how was everyone reacting? Were they welcoming Rhadamanthus with open arms?

The demi-god pushed down questions he couldn't know the answer to without returning to his home. For Minos, that now wasn't an option. If he went back, his fate was sealed. While Minos yearned to be back amongst the demons and gods, he took some perverse relief in knowing that he hadn't been fired yet. In an odd way, having not been told he was redundant gave him the confidence and determination to continue to fight for what was right. He knew he had to take a leap and leave everything he held dear in order to save it.

Minos hung to the notion that once he found out who was behind all of this, he would be able to reverse what had happened. Once the scheming of the consultants, and their unknown partner, had been exposed, Hades would come to his senses. He would reinstate both

Cerebus and Minos, and life would go back to how it had been. All the silly nonsense about not having enough money, which Minos guessed was probably just a ploy to get the mortals into the Underworld, would go away and all would be well. The demi-god gripped onto this belief in the same way as a nervous trapeze artist, with a severe case of arthritis, clings to the high bar.

Minos' concentration was broken as, with a huff and a puff, Cerebus finally arrived. The exhausted look on the creature's face surprised the judge — he'd always assumed the creature was as fit as a fiddle. The hulking figure braced his hands on his knees as his tongue loll out and he sucked in deep gulps of air. Even the snake let its head sink down onto the dusty ground, looked dog-tired.

"How did you get on?" Minos enquired as Cerebus straightened his back. When they had split up, earlier that day, the pair had agreed a list of actions between them. Minos had had to focus on the practicalities of leaving his home for an undetermined period of time. He'd duly put the milk out and cancelled the cat. Some demon would no doubt enjoy the white liquid once it had sufficiently curdled, although the judge had to admit he would miss Mr Mittens, after having happily hired him for the last few years.

"I've spoken with a couple of the Kers and their devotion to me is firm." Cerebus reported, knocking off one of the major items on the 'to do' list Minos had given him, "They will monitor the situation across the land and report back. They have also agreed to provide me with sanctuary."

"Good — and you picked up the supplies we discussed." The pair had devised a list of items that would help the judge on his journey to the consultants' head office in London and Cerebus had volunteered to collect everything.

"Well, errr..." It was at this point Minos noticed the flimsy plastic bag draped around one of his friend's large wrists. It did not look like the rucksack they had discussed.

"It seems that, without a job, I may be suffering a bit of a cash and goodwill shortage. As in I don't have either right now."

"But you got me something?"

"Of course. I took the pick of the Kers' 'Lost and Found' box for you."

Cerebus presented the white carrier.

Minos groaned as he looked at the contents. He had asked for weatherproof clothes, tough walking boots, a range of equipment and any magical items the dog could lay his hands on. What the judge found in the cheap plastic was a selection of tired, torn and oddly smelling garments, alongside a gaggle of strange objects. As he plunged his hand into the items, Minos cringed,

"What's this?" he asked, holding up a hand blender.

"Well you said about a knife but there wasn't any of those. That's the only other kitchen utensil I could find."

Minos, having already given up on the whisk, was dismayed to also find a set of tacky fridge magnets; a cheap pair of plastic sunglasses; a broken key ring that was also a bottle opener; a battered pink travel mug (which Minos feared would leak the first time he used it);

and a selection of golden coins, all with different faces on them. It was a useless collection of items for keeping children entertained during a wet February half term and the judge was certain they would be next to useless for the quest he was about to embark on. Minos screwed his face up, appalled at Cerebus' lack of resourcefulness.

"Did you at least get the map we talked about?"

One of the many items Hercules had left behind during his trip to the Underworld to abduct Cerebus, all those centuries ago, had been a magical parchment which showed the user where they were and the easiest route to their destination. The map was so smart it even provided directions to ensure the traveller avoided anyone they didn't want to talk to, as well as those individuals who work for charities and insist on trying to stop everyone in the middle of the street.

The hound looked surprisingly pleased with himself as he passed across a plastic book to Minos,

"The Kers said it wasn't the original but this is just as good." The judge stared down at the cheap cover, entitled 'My First Atlas' in big bright letters. When the judge leafed through the lightweight volume, he found various depictions of the Earth outlined in black. Some of the pages had been attacked with wax crayons and, in every case, no attention had been paid to keeping the colour within the lines. Minos raised his eyebrows in complete despair,

"Thanks!"

Cerebus missed the fake appreciation in his friend's voice, his attention already fixed on the Exit Portal,

"You know, maybe I should have closed this," he mused, as if without the burden of his job he was suddenly gifted an extra insight into the holes in the system. "Although if I had, then we couldn't do this now, could we?"

"Don't you have to keep this open for Melinda and her trips to the surface?"

"Pppfff," Cerebus blew away the suggestion, "She uses the Executive Exit in the palace." Minos did a double take,

"Executive Exit?"

"Oh yeah – that one takes you wherever you want to go. This portal, and the few others we have, they have fixed destinations." Minos nodded slowly, already aware from their earlier planning that the portal they were stood at would bring him out in Naples, Italy. From there he would have to cross through the country and onwards towards England. That was why he'd ask Cerebus to collect the equipment for him – Minos knew that a long trek lay ahead of him.

"If there's an exit that can take me anywhere on the Earth – why aren't we using that one?"

"Well, it's in the palace. We can't access it."

"But we were in the building last night – why can't we just break in again this evening?" spluttered Minos.

"I...errr..." Cerebus stammered, the thought not seeming to have crossed his mind. "I thought you said you wanted to be on your way as quickly as possible. Using this portal means you're as close as possible to London, without having to wait until later. I don't know much..." Minos was getting to the stage where he wasn't going to argue with that point, "…but I'm sure it won't take you long to get there.

"You'll probably be thanking me in the long run."

The judge was starting to doubt if helping his friend get his job back really was the best thing for the Underworld. That said though, he wasn't going to let a few mistakes cloud his feelings for the loyal dog.

Before Minos could consider replanning his trip, something caught his attention overhead. He looked up to see a flock of Kers circling high above them. Cerebus followed Minos' gaze,

"That can't be good – none of those guys are the ones I was talking to earlier. I think we might be in trouble. We're not exactly meant to be using this Exit."

Minos watched as a few of the creatures disengaged from the group and started flapping towards the palace. The others closed ranks and began to descend, their talons twitching menacingly. "Quick," snapped Cerebus, "You better go – I can handle them, but I'm not sure if I can keep you safe."

Minos looked nervously from the grim darkness of the winged harpies to the vivid colours of his escape route. He briefly nodded at his friend,

"Very well," he murmured as he turned and threw himself out of the frying pan and into a very weird fire.

Chapter 9

As Minos suffered through the first few hours of his long journey across the continent, he decided he certainly wasn't going to thank Cerebus for sending him to Italy.

The demi-god's first view of modern Earth was through a series of long, watery blinks as he tried to acclimatise to the harsh sunlight. He was completely unprepared for the sight of the big gas ball (which suddenly made him miss Thantanos) in the sky.

Once the judge's vision had adjusted enough to allow him to move around without fear of hurting himself, it didn't take long for him to realise that Cerebus had ejected him into the middle of nowhere.

Minos' annoyance then changed to despair, as he quickly realised how useless the bag of goodies was. None of the clothes his friend had given him fitted, and there wasn't a single helpful item in the carrier bag. Even the sunglasses weren't large enough for his face and, despite his many attempts, their tiny frame couldn't be forced around the sides of the judge's head. They, therefore, became the first casualty of Minos' load lightening.

They were followed by the 'map'.

As the demi-god started walking, with no clear sense of location or direction, and in the process snagged his toga on the few sprigs of dry vegetation that poked up through the dirty land, he started really lamenting not having taken his chances with the Kers.

If not for the kindness of an elderly lady, who took pity on the dehydrated bundle of parched skin that flopped down near the entrance to her shack, the judge's quest may have ended before it even begun.

The woman helped the demi-god adjust to his new surroundings, showing him how to fix his travel mug so that it could store water, used her skills to let out some of the clothes to fit his ample frame, whilst also giving him a battered trilby hat to keep the rays off his head and out of his eyes. Had the old shrew not started demanding sexual favours in return for her assistance, Minos may have stayed with her a lot longer. While he was able to fight off her advances for so long, when the wrinkled woman appeared in nothing but a light splattering of honey and goat's milk, the judge finally decided to move on, at a very fast pace.

The next difficulty Minos faced was all down to a simple lack of planning.

He arrived on the Earth with no transportation, or directions. Through his lack of preparation (*well*, he often moaned to himself, *Cerebus' poor assistance with his preparation*), the judge seemed to spend quite a lot of his early days aimlessly wondering towards the edges of cliffs or dead ends. Had the Exit Portal been a two-way system, he would have been very tempted to try and retrace his steps so he could return to the Underworld, get properly prepared and then restart his journey. Sadly, this option wasn't open to him, so Minos had to turn his annoyance at Cerebus into pounding his feet forward until he finally managed to find a road to follow.

As Minos started progressing, passing from village to town then city, he was slowly able to learn more about the trek that faced him, picking up information from others. Quickly the demi-god learnt how to hitchhike (although where all the mortals got the cardboard and pens from, he would never know). Avoiding the fare collector on the trains was easy for someone who looked so old. All Minos had to do was close his eyes and pretend he was asleep (or simply just have a nap) and he was left alone by most. A few times he was ask to leave the train at the next stop, but a few pathetic coughs and unsteady steps seemed to melt even the most callous of guards. Sometimes, the demi-god wished he was kicked off the train, especially when he had to endure the ravings of the mortals into their small handheld devices. He found the insistence on continually talking into the flat rectangles, especially the general insistence of updating the box with where they were (why did it never know that it was on a train too?), annoying and distracting.

The most curious and difficult part of the long slog for the demi-god was trying to wrap his head around the world he now found himself in. Even though Minos was familiar with the changes the mortals had introduced over the years, and was aquatinted with concepts such as the internet (mortals had been using that for despicable sins for many years now), new religions (he attended a Jedi service at one point, merely out of interest, but found there to be way too many strange vicars on the large flat screen for him to understand what was really going on) and, of course, fast food (many of the establishments which he found on the street corners of the larger cities had successfully sold franchises to demons in the Underworld), it was really difficult for him to adapt to life in the modern world.

As a deity, Minos had the gift of tongues and therefore had the ability to understand any language spoken by the mortals. Yet often the words the judge heard made little sense to him. He often took rests in small (and therefore cheap) cafes, passing the time by listening to conversations, however confusing he found the content. He hadn't realised humans could now converse with birds, yet so many of them whiled away their days discussing what was being tweeted.

Minos was appalled at the continual displays of greed, a concept that had only been in its infancy when he had last walked the Earth. With a rumbling belly, the demi-god watched on frequent occasions as humans threw away perfectly good food, simply because they had ordered too much, often 'Super-sizing' just because it only cost a few cents more. The judge found the waste by children the worst, and it was all because parents were too engrossed in their handheld devices to stop their young ones launching food at each other.

And the price of everything was ridiculous! Despite the old coin dealer saying, with an odd gleam in his eye, that he took pity on Minos, the many little silver coins he received in exchange for his gold ones, didn't amount to much at other locations.

The nights were often the times when the most unacceptable examples of mortal behaviour were on display. On the occasions Minos had not had enough coins to afford a hostel (an amazingly strange concept to him, especially given the frequency in which everyone seemed to share beds, whether their partner wanted to or not), and had slept rough (a concept he had picked up from the other poorly dressed individuals he met – demi-gods, he could only assume, undertaking their own missions). The judge was, first, heartened by the acts of kindness from strangers before it was all taken away. Young men and women, dressed in what was considered to be the finery of these days (but looked like a weird selection of t-shirts, tops and smart shoes) would throw a few coins at him or deliver a warm beverage. Yet, a few hours later, he would be roused by the same individuals, to be taunted and abused. The girls were the worst. The young ladies, constantly pulling at clothes that were too small for them, would veer from offering kind words of comfort, before suddenly yelling at Minos, for no apparent reason. Then there would be tears before more screaming ensued. In other cases, the demi-god was forced to endure having kebab meat thrown at him, or vomit spewed next to where he had been trying to sleep. The demi-god wasn't familiar with this sort of behaviour that, based on the rules he worked too, wasn't classed as sins. Yet it all seemed so depraved and inappropriate to the judge. Each encounter left him more confused, and often soggier, than when he had started.

It was safe to say that the trials and tribulations during his trek across Europe, opened Minos' eyes to a new world of suffering, to acts that were wholly unacceptable, whether they broke the commandments or not. Minos was frequently appalled at the way the mortals were now behaving towards strangers, and even worse, towards their own friends.

Often the judge's mind would drift back to his home and the life he had left behind. Once he struggled through his feelings of homesickness, he couldn't help but reflect on the operation itself. How many souls had not been punished for some of the terrible actions the demi-god now witnessed? Which souls were serving sentences for the one time they had a small romantic indiscretion with their neighbour's cousin's dog walker, yet had spent their whole life barging people out of the way just because they felt they had somewhere more important to be? It was a thought that continued to roam around the back of Minos' mind, as he wandered his way through each challenge that life on Earth threw at him.

It was after eight long days of travelling, and with a great sigh of relief, that Minos finally found himself at the point of his trek that he thought was going to be familiar – the river crossing over to England.

In his mind's eye, the judge had pictured this leg as being similar to the welcome for mortals as they arrived at the Underworld. He wasn't expecting figures like Hermes and Charon (they were demi-gods, after all), but he pictured some form of processing and then a short river crossing.

If Minos thought he had seen the worst of humanity on his travels so far, he was in for a serious shock at the most northerly tip of Calais.

Chapter 10

Hades felt like he was going cross eyed as the brightly coloured squares floated in front of his vision.

"I'm really not sure how this is helping?" he moaned, for what felt to him like the hundredth time.

"It's simple," Sparkes tried to explain for what felt like the millionth time to her. She took a few more paces along the room, looking like a caged animal. "We need to ensure that your team all have clear job titles, which succinctly describe what they do. 'Final Judge of Souls' or 'Guide to the Underworld' won't really cut it when we start bringing business leaders down here."

Hades rubbed his hands lightly on the boardroom's granite table. The coolness of the rock felt reassuring to him as he continued to stare at the post-it notes that had been stuck on the wall.

The god once more gave into his confusion, and ventured,

"I still don't get it – why would people be coming here?"

Having moved out of the god's sight line, Sparkes rolled her eyes and ground perfectly white teeth together, once more going over details that Hades should have known from the update document that had been shared with him, via the newly installed cloud-based software. It had taken long enough to register the god for the system, and she was starting to think it was a real waste of time.

"Because we have potential investors coming down to talk about injecting funds into your business. Plus we have arranged a number of meetings for you with companies that are keen to engage you in outsourcing contracts."

Hades shook his head back and forth, his dark beard swishing with the movements,

"Nope – I tried a few bouts of sorcery before, but it never stuck. I'm sorry Miss Sparkes, I can't see that getting us out of this pickle. Unless you know one of those wizards that offers spells for cash, no strings attached."

"I think there may be a terminology issue," ventured Branaghan. The chubby consultant had been sat quietly scribbling away on more sticky notes at the far end of the table, "Outsourcing is the process of hiring a company to perform a function that you cannot, or which they can execute at a significantly lower cost."

Hades wondered at what point the young mortal had been fed the dictionary, and if it was done all in one go or a page at a time. Every other statement that fell out of the round man seemed to be a definition.

"So," the god tried to comprehend what was going on around him, "Someone is going to pay me to do something that they could do, but I can do it cheaper?"

"Exactly." Sparkes snapped her fingers right next in Hades' ear, pleased they were now getting somewhere.

She continued to clip clop behind the god, letting her red stilettos clack out her steps.

"Shouldn't I be outsourcing?" The god rolled the last word around his mouth, as if it was raw chicken a few days past it's sell-by date.

"Not at all," to the god's relief, the curvy figure moved from behind him and eased herself into one of the chairs, "You've got access to the perfect workforce to provide cheap services down here. With the right setup you'll find this a quick way of bringing in auxiliary revenue streams. Next week you'll be meeting with a host of organisations keen to reduce their call centre costs."

Hades bristled,

"Call centre? We're not setup for that. I don't think we've even got a phone..."

Sparkes pursed her mouth and hushed the great warrior, further getting on the god's nerves. He just about held his tongue.

"That's why my colleague here has already setup a set of subsequent meetings for you to negotiate usage of a host of the latest telephonic technology and hands-free sets. And..." she hurried on before Hades could get out the protest that was already forming on his lips, "...they will provide these at zero cost provided that you promote their business. It's as simple as picking up the phone and saying 'Ripped off company's call centre, enabled by suckers.'" She grinned broadly as she pretended to talk into her hand, waggling her little finger by her ruby red lips and listening to her thumb. Branaghan blew his nose loudly, as if, Hades thought, to underscore the brilliance of his manager's scheme.

The god scratched his head for a little too long,

"Let me get this straight – in return for mentioning them, someone gives me some of their equipment for free, so that I can do something cheaper than someone else." Both mortals nodded at different speeds, "That truly is sorcery."

Hades' dark brow knitted tighter together, wrinkles creasing across his forehead, "Yet how can we do the work? I don't think the demons have the patience for dealing with phone calls..."

Sparkes cut him off with a wave off her manicured hand,

"The demons won't be doing the work – the souls will be. All you have to do is add 'Yelling at customer care operative', or something like that, to your list of sins and we can sentence those poor saps to a lifetime doing exactly the same thing that annoyed them when they were alive.

"And the brilliance of the plan is that the very souls that are bleeding you dry will start generating revenue. Everyone ends up screaming down the phone at someone at some point. It will be the simplest judgement going. Bang – a lifetime dealing with the other end of those calls themselves. And, if the first bunch aren't that good at it, we'll end up with more souls getting sentenced, meaning we can expand the setup even further. You'll have a self-perpetuating operation!"

Hades' frown lines grew deeper than a set of potholes after a cold snap.

"Now Ms Sparkes – you may know about fixing businesses, but you are showing a distinct lack of understanding about the way the Underworld works. We can't just go adding sins willy-nilly. There are processes and procedures for that sort of thing. I mean we haven't introduced a new commandment in…well…a very long time."

Sparkes dismissed the god's concerns with a nonchalant shrug of her shoulders.

"Maybe that's how it worked in the past but let's be clear," her expression turned stern, "These are not normal times. You are in trouble and things need to change quickly. This is the best option – we'll have new kit installed within the week and then people will be flocking to have you undercut their current provider. And don't forget you've got Rhadamanthus overseeing all the judgement work now. He'll make things happen for you."

At the mention of the personnel change, Hades pushed down the concern that had been growing in the pit of his stomach for Minos. The judge had apparently gone AWOL (one of the few abbreviations the warrior hadn't needed Sparkes to explain) and hadn't reported for duty in days. The consultants had told Hades that this constituted gross misconduct (which they pointed out was very serious, and not at all icky, as the ruler had initially thought) and if he saw the judge, he should fire him on the spot. This didn't sit well with the god but the little voice in his head told him to ignore it. The tiny whisper also reminded the god that, as Sparkes had said, if Minos wasn't going to help save the Underworld, then he was better off without him.

"But these other companies," Hades raised another concern with the most recent solution to his troubles, "The ones I'm taking equipment from and the ones I'm providing a cheap service to – why couldn't they cut me out and do the whole thing between themselves?"

Sparkes' smiled in the way that a fox does when it corners a chicken.

"Because they will never meet. This is a large part of what my company does – we make sure that the right people get together and that others don't. There's layers you see, so that every business continues to flourish." She leaned forward, bringing the god into her confidence, "You haven't just engaged our services to change the now, Hades. Together we will make this operation great and you, in turn, will help our partners. It's all to the good of industries across the United Kingdom, and beyond."

If Hades hadn't spent millennia being cast as the devil, he might have stopped and wondered if he had actually made a deal with the dark lord himself. The god felt oddly comforted by Sparkes' words, even if, and he would never admit it out loud, the way the woman spoke sent a thunderous shiver down his spine.

The consultant flicked her blonde ponytail as she leaned back in her seat, "Give us some time and you'll have to convert a few rooms of this palace into a vault. You will be making that much money."

Hades didn't get a chance to respond, as Sparkes suddenly stood tall, laced her fingers together behind her back and started stalking the room again. "There is a lot of potential here Hades. I can see so many opportunities. Outsourcing is just the first step.

"Have you ever considered the number of businesses that would want a piece of the action down here? I mean you literally have a captive audience! And, you don't even exist as a recognised country so you've never featured in any international trade agreements. We could work out a whole new taxation system for the land and no one could stop us. You could set the percentage at any level you want, whilst keeping certain items – the ones we tell you – duty free. With the right contracts organised, you will be rolling in gold before you know it."

Sparkes leered at Hades, who, despite himself, and the fact he hadn't followed half of what the woman had just said, couldn't help but smile back.

While the main purpose of the Underworld was to bring in more souls, he had always enjoyed having money. He felt it was befitting of his stature. He could only imagine how jealous Zeus and Poseidon would be next Christmas if he turned up with a couple of Rolexes as presents for them.

The consultant wasn't finished in her convincing, "You have a great foundation here, just a few things have gone wrong along the way. I mean take your marketing – convincing people the 'devil' didn't exist – you shouldn't have been building up that message. People should know where they stand, and with a few sponsorship deals, and a little bit of creativity, we can turn all of that around. You'll be raking it in before you know it!

"Now – shall we get on with this brainstorm and get some more ideas up on the wall."

"And remember," Branaghan chipped in, his eyes unblinking from behind his thick glasses, "No idea, at this stage, is a bad one."

Hades, enthused with the thought of wealth, success, and finally getting one over on his older siblings, picked up a marker pen and started attacking the sticky notes.

As he scribbled away the god quietened the concerns he had.

He silenced the little murmur that again tried to point out how the Underworld operation was changing into something he might soon not recognise.

Hades also overlooked the disappointment he'd been feeling since Sparkes had told him that Cerebus had resigned. He refused to acknowledge the he had been missing the dog, concentrating on how hurt he felt that his loyal companion had not even spoken with him.

And, of course, as the mortal had reminded Hades, he shouldn't tolerate unhelpful behaviour.

Not even from his closest friends.

The god continued to scrawl on the post-it notes, focusing his efforts on those who were still there. He felt his determination to improve the Underworld's situation renew. He wanted to make the operation a success.

The god even allowed himself a moment of glee that, most importantly, he would show Melinda how serious he was about giving her everything she wanted. He would make sure he could provide for his wife, and any future off-spring. Hades may have managed to worm his way back into his own bedroom by apologising profusely, but it was time to get on the front foot.

He was going to show his wife who was in charge – no matter what it took.

Chapter 11

Minos was contemplating what it was going to take to continue his journey.

He was a long way from his home, and felt even further from what he had imagined he would find when he got to the English Channel. To the judge's dismay, there was no welcoming party or boats waiting to take him across what he had anticipated would be a short stretch of water. Instead, the demi-god looked out on a sad encampment of lost and dejected mortals, framed against the backdrop of an immense sea.

It was a grey day, the threat of rain hanging in the air, and the judge moved slowly through the latest horror of his trip. Flapping through thick mud in his sandals, Minos walked past sheets of plastics which had been turned, by some clever trickery, into tents. Here and there larger structures, created from mismatched materials rose up over the demi-god's head. The fabricated buildings seemed to offer more protection than their cloth cousins, yet they swayed worryingly against the light breeze that was blowing across the site, almost threatening to collapse the next time someone sneezed loudly.

As Minos tried to process the sounds and smells of the shanty town, he felt more confused and lost than at any point since he had arrived on the Earth. Here and there, women huddled around steaming pots, hung over barely visible fires, whilst men congregated in corners, talking in hushed, conspiratorial tones. Children played in the dirt, while barely-clothed toddlers strutted around, as unsure of themselves as the deity that walked amongst them.

As Minos moved forward, a scowl and a look of pure confusion fighting for dominance on his face, three men, all of very different nationalities, disgorged themselves from one of the nearby gatherings.

"Do you seek sanctuary, fellow traveller?" queried one, a short man with a pronounced side parting in his dark hair. He scratched at the short beard around his face as he gazed at the judge. The dark rings underneath the mortal's eyes added years to what Minos could see had once been a youthful face.

"I don't think so," replied the judge, still feeling unsure of himself, "I'm trying to get to England."

"Aren't we all," snorted a hulking figure, with a deep scar across his cheek. "This is as far as you can go, until they change the laws or the opportunity for passage presents itself."

"And those seem to becoming fewer" added the final group member, a wide man, whose skin was as dark as night.

"But I must make it to England and complete my journey," protested Minos. "I've lost everything and only by getting there will I be able to save it."

The first man took a break from rubbing bony fingers through his facial hair and put a thin arm around the judge's shoulders.

"We feel your pain, friend. Many of us are in the same predicament but this is the best we can do for now. We must sit tight and wait for our next chance to make the crossing, whether by boat, train or lorry." He squeezed the demi-god tightly to him. "Something will come along soon – you must have faith. Maybe offer a prayer to whichever god you believe in." Minos was about to point out that he didn't think any of the other gods would be keen on helping him, but then realised that his new companion was steering him towards one of the steaming pots. The rancid smell that wafted from the metal container was quite unlike anything Minos had experienced before, an odd smell of burnt socks clogging his throat. However, the stench still had the effect of making his empty stomach rumble loudly. Picking up on his belly's yearnings, the thin man grinned. "I sense you have come a long way..."

"You could say that," interrupted the judge, still feeling very out of place.

"Then come, join us. We will offer what we can until you too have your chance at passage across the great channel."

"But you have so little." Minos tried to untangle himself from his new comrade's embrace, very conscious of the sense of loss that enthused the camp.

"What we have, we are happy to share. That is the way of life here – we are all in this together. We support each other."

Minos was buoyed to finally find mortals who still demonstrated some level of decency. He was heartened to be greeted with genuine warmth, as he was introduced to others and presented with a steaming bowl of stew. Despite the smell, the brown sludge tasted wonderful and the demi-god tucked in. It was only on the basis of politeness, and recognition of the squalor around him, that Minos refused a second bowl. His ravenous stomach growled its protests but the judge stood by his morals.

Minos spent the rest of the day getting to know his new campmates, as, like them, he waited his chance to continue his journey onto England.

The judge was shocked and appalled to hear their tales. His mind was blown as he heard stories about dictatorships, persecution and terrorist regimes which had led many to flee their homes. The demi-god learned more about what it meant to be a refugee or an asylum seeker, while a deep scowl sunk into his weathered features as he was educated on the politics which prevented the individuals from settling in the countries they had already passed through. However hard his own trials had been, Minos reflected that they paled in comparison to the suffering inflicted on the mortals by their own kind.

As darkness drew in, and orange tongues of light from the fires licked the faces of each of Minos' new campmates, the judge couldn't help but be disturbed, both by the stories and how little the Underworld's operations reflected the chilling events. Sure – those who killed each other were punished, but did his judging team ever consider the ramifications of a soul's actions on their victims? How often did one person's behaviour result in a broken family fleeing from their home, or youngsters being orphaned? Minos was chilled to the core, as sadness clung to his heart and tears stung his eyes.

While he felt dragged down by the stories, he was equally renewed by the unbreakable spirit of the people who told them. Despite everything they had been through, each mortal the demi-god spoke with found some reason to be grateful, often filled with the hope of a brighter future, either now or in another life.

The judge didn't like to admit it to those around him, but there was little waiting for these individuals on the other side of death. Their fate would most likely be worse than what they had suffered already.

While Minos couldn't face dispelling the mortals' beliefs, he couldn't help but find the group's enthusiasm infectious. Against the harsh backdrop, the judge's very being was enthused with the collective hope of those around him.

For the first time since Minos had arrived on Earth, he found good company and genuine comfort. Little did he know that he wouldn't have long to enjoy it.

*

When the time came, it was a great strain for Minos to rip his eye lids open to confront the torchlight that was being waved at him.

A combination of the various hearty food he had sampled, warmth from the fires, as well as the comforting kindness of strangers had left Minos thoroughly satisfied when he had bedded down inside one of the tents. He had slipped into the first deep sleep he had had since leaving the Underworld and as the bright beam shone in his face, he only vaguely stirred, rasping out a few random words as his lips smacked together in confusion.

"Minos," hissed the voice of Imy, the bearded man who had welcomed him to the camp. "You are in luck." Minos again tried to speak and only managed an odd succession of vowels. "There is a truck driver who has offered passage across the channel."

The judge was instantly scrambling to his feet, the opportunity to keep moving towards his destination propelling him forward. As he scurried across the cold ground, stepping over, and around, guide ropes, Minos felt his heart flutter, surprisingly conflicted about the prospect of leaving this group behind.

When the demi-god had laid down a few hours earlier, he had continued to review the tribulations some of the mortals had been through and couldn't help but question the Underworld's reward and punishment system. He was certain that none of the camp's residents would make it to the Island of Elysium, given the strict and noble qualities that were required for that honour. Yet, during the evening, he had heard examples of true heroism, those doing the best for their families, despite the cruelty of Governments. Minos had been shocked by the way these mortals were viewed by officials. It all felt so wrong. As he had settled down, the judge had made a promise to himself that if he was successful in his quest and made it back to the Underworld, he would be putting forward a very strong case to Hades to review the criteria used for judgement.

As he concentrated on not stumbling along the dimly lit route, Minos couldn't help but feel pleased with how things had worked out. The short stop at the camp had given him a new purpose in his efforts. He must not only save Hades, and his home, but ensure that those who suffered in the mortal realm didn't have to do so in the afterlife. Ideas were already whizzing around his mind as he made it to the large white truck that would take him further on his quest.

The judge was glad to spot a number of faces from his dinner conversations gathered around the large truck. As individuals shook the hand of friends or shared a final embrace with a loved one, Imy presented Minos to the driver, a hefty man whose sweaty skin shone in the torches that flicked around the area.

In a gruff voice, the trucker confirmed he had space for the demi-god,

"What about payment?" the man enquired, wiping his forehead with the back of his flannel sleeve.

"Do you have anything you can offer?" Imy enquired, as Minos stared down at the sad bag of worthless items he had brought with him from the Underworld (he wasn't sure why he'd kept things like the fridge magnets and the knackered key ring). The demi-god's whole demeanour dimmed like the small hand torch his companion held.

The driver looked the judge up and down,

"Got any family on the other side? Anyone expecting you?"

Minos let his head despondently swish to show he didn't, fully expecting to be rejected. The big man gave a toothy smirk as his beady eyes surveyed the old demi-god.

"No one waiting for you, eh? Well, I'm sure we can sort out something when we get there." With that, meaty hands grabbed around the sides of Minos' waist, groping his back.

The judge looked to his companion for some level of reassurance. The young man slowly nodded his head up and down, matching the driver's enthusiasm.

"Yes, yes Minos – you go, and make arrangements on the other side."

Something in Imy's voice didn't feel quite right to the demi-god, but he shook it off. He'd been made to feel welcome since he arrived at the camp and was sure he should not start questioning his new friend how. "Please, got on board the back of the truck. I must have a few words with your driver before you leave us."

"Are you not coming?"

"Not this time – I give my place to others, like you, who are in greater need of making the crossing."

Something stirred low in the demi-god's gut, an odd feeling that just didn't quite sit right. However, he ignored this and made his way down the side of the lorry. He thought he caught snippets of conversation between the two mortals, including the words 'kidney', 'market', 'rate', 'usual' and 'fee' but these all seemed odd, so he assumed he must not have heard right.

Minos was quickly distracted from that as he discovered his travelling accommodation would be an eight by eight-foot section of the truck, with 14 refugees all packed together behind a stack of cardboard boxes. There was no light and the only area for ablutions was a simple metal bucket in the corner of the space.

To the other passengers' dismay, the odd feeling in Minos' stomach turned out to be a serious bout of indigestion, which kept him rooted over the make shift toilet for the first hour of the journey. Many would look back and suggest that it was the smell which gave them away when they reached England.

Chapter 12

Branden Roberts was an unhappy goth.

Of course, most people expect goths, with their dark clothes and appreciation for heavy metal music, to be depressed. Yet Branden was especially sad, even by the standards of his devil-worshipping colleagues.

The lanky, yet unathletic, youngster had always known he might struggle to fit in with his chosen past time – being of mixed Jamaican/British decent he was never going to master the pale skin aspect. Yet he'd tried so hard. He'd grown his hair long (although he couldn't get his curly Afro to flow down over his shoulders like the others), painted his nails and eyelashes, and invested in enough silver jewellery to ensure he was going to take more time than most through airport security. Despite all of this, he'd still struggled to find his place in the world of darkness.

Ever since his Mum had been asked to leave the local Mother and Toddler group, on account of a rusk related incident, Branden had had trouble fitting in.

When the youngster had tried out for the school's football team, he'd spent more time cutting halftime oranges than slicing passes to his teammates. His stint with the school's debating society had seen an unprecedented series of loss. He'd done so badly in that pastime his teacher had hatched a plan to start enrolling him in other schools just so that he could ruin their teams (and the grey-haired educator might have got away with it, if not for the fact Branden's parents started questioning why they needed so much new school kit, with so many different logos stitched on them).

Branden had even tried volunteering at an old people's home but he'd been plagued with similar bad luck. He'd always thought that the nickname 'Grim Reaper' was a little bit uncalled for, especially when it was the care home's staff who had coined it.

It had been his series of unfortunate losses amongst the seniors that had encouraged Branden to take up his newest hobby. After he had felt the chilly touch of death, something had stirred in him, and he had wondered if worshipping a dark lord might be the answer to his desire for a purpose in life.

A few online searches had revealed Branden's nearest group and he'd started attending evening and weekend classes. He'd already picked up tips on satanic rituals, the cheapest shops for black clothes and the most effective eye-liners.

Despite everything, Branden still just didn't feel like he fitted in.

Today had been a particularly brutal example of this, as Jenna, the group leader offering her wisdom to the newbies (for a mere £8.50 fee per session, which realistically turned out to be a tenner, because she never had any change) had singled out Branden for criticism and ridicule.

The computer nerd (not that anyone used that phrase to her face), seemed to take particular glee in the young man's awkwardness during their satanic chanting study session. She had picked on him from the outset, making fun of the fact he'd brought the exact fee for the class in a mix of silver coins. And she'd swiftly continued to ridicule his efforts – apparently all of his attempts lacked any form of rhythm.

The chubby, tattooed, woman seemed to find every reason she could to belittle Branden, before eventually kicking him out for his poor mood. Sadly, he knew that wouldn't be the end of it. Jenna had spent a lot of the workshop snapping pictures and posting them on various social media platforms. She had always been mean to Branden online and continued her attacks throughout the afternoon, with many of the group taking little coercion from their leader to join in.

And so, on a drizzly afternoon, Branden found himself trudging down a deserted street feeling low. The youth knew that if he continued heading in the direction he was, he was on course for being late home for dinner, running the risk of another of those 'Honestly, that boy!' moments from his Mum.

Head down, Branden kicked at a discarded drinks can, before guilt caught him and he scooped up the piece of rubbish. Not finding a bin anywhere, he stuffed the piece of aluminium in his coat pocket. It was a decision he instantly regretted as leftover liquid started to trickle down the inside of his jacket, quickly seeping through to his trousers.

After a few more pointless moments of fussing about the liquid, which just made his fingers sticky as well, Branden looked up to find himself staring at an odd-looking tramp. While the individual cut as dejected a figure as any of the vagrants found on the outskirts of the capital, there was something different about this one.

Despite himself, Branden couldn't help but stare at the scruffy character, taking in every detail.

From the faint wisps of hair around the man's temple, down to the scruffy pair of flip flops, there was something about the dejected figure that suggested that treading the streets was below him. Not in an arrogant way, Branden reflected, but there was just something about this particular individual that suggested he was meant for more. To the youngster it was almost as if the character was from a different time, another way of life.

"Excuse me, are you alright?" the words were out of his mouth before he could process what he was doing. As the question floated across the air, he didn't know who was more surprised – the tramp or himself. For a long moment, both stood still, just blinking at each other.

"No...not really," croaked the vagrant, swaying slightly as if it was the first time he'd stood still in a long while. The gaudy t-shirt around his frame fluttered slightly in the wind, as it declared how much he hated Mondays. Branden wasn't sure what to say next, but his lips had him covered again,

"You're not from around here are you?"

With a very deep sigh, the figure uttered,

"I am further from home than you could ever imagine."

He wasn't sure why, but Branden felt the right response was,

"Do you want to, like, get a coffee or something? On me, of course."

The figure shivered, his short shorts doing little to protect his wrinkled, almost hairless legs. For a second his face brightened and he opened his mouth, then a very deep frown crossed his features,

"You don't want to cut out any of my organs, do you?"

*

"...then I found myself on the ground and some guy with a very large gun is yelling something about cutting out my kidney..."

Branden was transfixed by Minos' story (the pair had dealt with introductions on their way to the nearest cafe). The youngster had never heard anything like it the tale in all of his life and was still struggling to get his head around the fact that he was speaking to someone from beyond the grave, "...Then there were all these blue flashing lights and more people, with even bigger guns, shouting. Well, I can tell you – I wasn't going to hang around any longer. I waited until everyone was waving their weapons at each other, and then I ran for it!"

Minos paused to slurp noisily at his hot chocolate, doing his best to suck the melted mound of marshmallows through his dry lips. Branden leaned back slightly against the plastic chair he was sat in, transfixed by the story, vaguely conscious the cheap seat was starting to separate from its metal frame.

Am I really speaking to a demi-god? He eased himself forward, *Can it be true?* Branden's brain screamed that the old man had probably just sniffed too much glue, yet something deep inside him, his very soul, was jangling with belief. Maybe it was the dark path he'd been following recently but the youngster was convinced that he really was having a drink with the Final Judge of Souls.

Imagine how jealous the rest of the goths would be if they could see me now!

As Branden rolled the excitement round his mind, he leaned back further, and suddenly he felt his chair giving way again. He dived forward and, to cover his embarrassment, grabbed at the first question he could,

"Was there like bullets and shit whizzing round you as you legged it?"

"No, no poo," Minos shook his head, "There was lots of loud gunfire but I don't think any of it was aimed at me…" he trailed off as he looked down and started patting his body, "…at least I don't think it was."

Branden watched with barely concealed reverence as the demi-god considered whether he had made it all the way from Dover to Croydon with a gunshot wound he hadn't noticed. As the judge's hands slowed, the youth tried to keep the conversation flowing,

"What happened next?"

"Well, I found myself running through all these fields. I had to just keep moving. I mean I literally had the clothes on my back. Everything I'd brought with me was still in the truck.

"I managed to hitchhike a bit and finally made it here. Although, I've got to say London's a lot bigger than I expected. I was sort of thinking it would be a few streets and it'd be quite easy to find where this company is."

Minos looked down, rather ashamed to have to admit this out loud, and to a mortal no less. He knew that it wasn't fully his fault – if anyone was to blame it was Cerebus (well, it made Minos feel much better to think of it that way). The judge's despair was eased slightly by the look on the young man's face.

The demi-god recognised that under normal circumstances (by which he meant doing his job in a nice judging chamber, without the threat of his whole way of existence about to crumble down around his ears), he wouldn't have taken any interest in Branden. Yet, right then and there, in a greasy cafe, something seemed right about sharing a hot drink (and, Minos hoped, eventually one of the tantalising bacon sandwiches being brought out for other customers) with the young man. The judge hadn't felt a connection with anyone else on his travel, but there was definitely something between the pair.

While there had been a sense of camaraderie in the camp in north France, Minos had sensed this was only formed through the necessity of a bad situation. It was simply acknowledgment of everyone being in the same boat (well, the same place waiting for a boat). By contrast, the youngster just seemed like a nice person, who was interested in the judge, and Minos welcomed this as a refreshing change especially after his most recent ordeal.

"It's ok," Branden spoke with reassurance, "I'm sure we can find the office you're looking for." He pulled out his phone, a beat-up version of the ones Minos had seen people tapping away at throughout his journey. The youngster's fingers flew across the screen and then he let out a long low whistle. "Jeez – their office is properly in the city." Minos' brow knit together, as Branden tried to explain further, "Like the city city. The important financial bit." There was no change in the demi-god's expression. "Basically, you've still got a way to go."

Minos' face fell – the difficulty of his journey so far and the latest setback pulling down his shoulders. Wearily he tugged at his beard, trying to rouse the energy within him to leave the warmth of the cafe and head back out into the cold (and the rain that was just starting to drip against the establishment's windows). The judge could almost sense the thunder storm that he knew was going to open above him as soon as he stepped outside.

"Thanks for the drink," he managed to heave out as he started standing.

Surprise rose up Branden's face, like a flag up a pole, and his hand shot out to grab at Minos' wrist.

"Wait!" The judge held steady, appreciating the few extra seconds in the dry.

Knowing that he didn't want to end the relationship before it had really started, Branden blurted out, "Where will you stay? What will you do when you get to the office? How are you going to sort out those bastards?"

Minos blinked a few slow strokes of his eyelids at the questions, realising once more that he was still one step behind where he needed to be. The demi-god tried to grasp hold of his next course of action, but nothing would creep into his fuzzy mind. Suddenly the judge felt the effects of the hundreds of miles he had walked and his legs wobbled. Tiredly, he slumped back into the chair,

"I really don't know," he whispered, defeated.

Despite his many flaws (which his Dad, in particular, was good at pointing out, whenever insult needed adding to injury) Branden had been brought up properly. His parents had tried to instil in him the difference between right and wrong, as well as the core teachings of the bible. Branden had never really grasped the tales about loving thy neighbour or the Good Samaritan, but today all of that stuff seemed to make a bit more sense.

Had Minos known that the Underworld's cheap marketing efforts were about to help him out, he may have regretted his previous criticism of the book's writer.

"Hang on," Branden told the demi-god, as he pulled out his phone and tapped a few keys. He knew he didn't have to wait long before the reply he had expected pinged up on his screen. "That's settled," he told Minos, "You're coming home with me."

The judge felt like he should protest, but any words he tried to summon up seemed pointless against the gleam in the young man's eye. "Come on. Mum's doing chicken so we better get going or Dad will have eaten the crispest skin before we get there." And with that Minos' new ally headed up to the counter to pay their bill.

The demi-god stood up, straightening himself and standing taller than he had in a long time, his spirit buoyed by the true kindness of a stranger. Despite his weariness, a grin to spread over his face. Minos finally felt like things were getting a bit easier.

"This is not going to be easy," whistled Branden as he stared up at the imposing building that housed the offices of Schneider, Schneider & Patterson.

The goth strained his neck muscles staring up the expanse of steel and glass as it disappeared into the gloomy cloud above, before focusing on the reception area at the structure's base. The area for arriving guests was bigger than his parent's house, several times over, and presented more challenges than Branden had expected.

Anyone arriving at the office had to first deal with the 'greeters.' The small, but efficient, group of employees, decked out in full weatherproof with the bright green insignia of the company emblazoned across it, spent their time checking, and rechecking, letters of invite for those daring to try and enter the building. From there, visitors were ushered inside to the patrolling security team, all gorillas with ear pieces, before proceeding through bag checks and metal detectors. It was only then that the army of immaculate receptionists could be approached.

Branden grabbed at Minos' sleeve, pulling the judge back across the large courtyard, past the mix of concrete and greenery, which was no doubt designed to promote peace and tranquillity away from the busy London streets.

"What's wrong?" the demi-god had clearly missed the reason they weren't executing their plan of presenting themselves at the office and requesting a meeting with whoever was in charge. This was probably because he had once more been tugging at the sides of the shirt Branden's Dad had lent him. Despite his days of trekking across Europe, there was still a substantial size difference between Minos and his host (made worse by Mrs Robert's insistence he had seconds of everything the night before), but the black trousers and retro shirt (a leftover from a fancy dress party) just about fit his large frame. After the downpour of the day before, the judge was also enjoying the brown brogues on his feet – it was the first time he'd ever covered his toes up – and he had to admit he rather liked the blue blazer his shoulders were squeezed into.

Branden steered the demi-god across the road, before leaning back against the wall of a coffee shop, surveying their target from, what he felt, was a safer distance. Inwardly he kicked himself, annoyed that he had not foreseen the fact that any company worthy of turning around an operation the size of the Underworld (Minos had given him an enthralling history lesson the previous evening) would be open to the pair just strutting in without an appointment. It had just seemed to make sense to pose as Hades' representative, with a young lad the operation was sponsoring on work experience. They had figured they could go straight to the top of the company and be told whatever they wanted to know.

The reality of this misjudgement was now biting harshly with Branden.

The youngster sucked a deep lungful of air – trying to shake off the sense of self-recrimination he often experienced when he'd got something wrong. The feeling welled up inside him, reminding him of his past failures, and the teasing from others that had gone with it. Branden tried to push it down, to focus on a new plan. He scratched at his arm, taking comfort from the way the many loose lengths of material that hung from the faux leather, twitched in response. It something he always found comforting, even if his Mum hated the jacket, feeling certain it was an accident waiting to happen when he travelled on the tube, a lift, or anything else with moving parts.

By focusing on his jacket, the young man was able to calm his mind, and he reminded himself that he hadn't used one of his best excuses to skip college and accompany the judge on his quest, only to fail at the first step. He wracked his depressed brain to think of something that he could do to help the demi-god. He'd felt an instant connection with Minos and wanted to make a difference for him (plus, which adolescent didn't want an adventure to save life-after-death?).

While Branden mulled over their next course of action, Minos had to back up as an elderly gentleman, bedecked in a very fine suit and bow tie, ploughed past, screaming into his phone,

"I know I need some more pocket money, but I can't believe that you seriously thought I was going to take a nine to five pushing papers in some corporate office! And certainly not with that bunch of crooks! I'm a thespian for goodness sakes! And you, supposedly, are my agent – so pull yourself together man and find me some acting work."

With his free hand, the man screwed up a piece of paper and dropped it with a theatrical twist of his wrist. A gentle breeze caught the ball letting it teeter its way across the ground towards the odd duo, while the actor continued his string of beratements.

As Minos recovered from almost being barged, he started to form the words he needed to tell off his attacker. For the demi-god, life in the mortal world was really starting to wear thin. Everyone was so self-obsessed, and it was really starting to grate on him. Even the craziest Underworld demons had some level of respect and manners, especially towards their immortal superiors. Before Minos could express himself, he felt a calming hand on his shoulder.

"Don't draw attention," Branden hissed, "Just be cool for a moment." The judge followed the directions (as best as he could – he had never really grasped looking anything other than old, and a little wise, over his many years), watching as the youth dropped down to adjust his shoe lace, squirrelling the scrunched-up paper into his hand as he did. With a deft move, Branden was upright, with his back to the office block. He tugged at the document revealing a familiar green logo. Scanning down, the youngster grinned with glee at their 'golden ticket'. "Look," he could barely contain his excitement as he spread the paper out flat. "They're having interviews today and this letter would get someone called Marvin Griggs inside."

"Good – now I know that man's name I shall make sure that there is an unhappy judgement waiting him when he makes it down to the Underworld," Minos' face was like thunder.

"No," gestured Branden, trying his best not to look suspicious to anyone who was passing them. "Marvin Griggs can get in that building in 15 minutes using this letter!"

"But that man is not going to help us."

Branden choose not to yell out in frustration. It was not an easy decision. He thrust the letter forward as he explained the new plan. "But how do we get you in with me?" queried the judge, as he once more tried to close the gaping holes between his shirt buttons.

"I think you'll have to do this bit by yourself."

Branden sized Minos up, ignoring the slightly pale shade the demi-god had suddenly taken on. The judge wasn't going to make a great first impression when he went in, but there wasn't much they could do about that now. The pair could only rely on one of the few things Branden had learnt from the careers people at school – nothing starts an interview better than being early.

As Branden ushered Minos towards the building, a spark of inspiration hit him. With a rough tug he ripped off one of the longer strips of material from his jacket. With a few swift movements he knotted the cloth before slipping it over Minos' head, creating a makeshift tie.

Studying his efforts, Branden was heartened by his ingenuity. It wasn't perfect but it would do – just like the judge himself.

*

Minos was certain he'd sprung a leak.

Sweat seemed to be pouring out of every part of the demi-god. His arm pits, hands and forehead were getting soggier with every step he took through the plush reception area. Everywhere the judge looked, visitors milled around, all waiting to be met.

Outside, beyond the two checkpoints which had been surprisingly easy to navigate with the letter in his hand, Minos could still make out Branden's shape. Far off to the side of the building, the youngster was tucking down to wait for the judge while Minos did…well, he wasn't quite sure how he progressed next.

In the background someone shouted,

"Mr Griggs?"

Although he was there for a job interview, that he didn't want, the most important thing to the demi-god was that he was in the building. He felt a slight tingle of excitement, slightly giddy from the thought that his long trip had culminated in the last few steps across smooth tiles.

Branden's plan now centred around the judge slipping off and being able to bluff his way further into the building, until he found what he was looking for. As his companion had explained, Minos was going to have to 'wing it'. Somehow, the demi-god didn't think this was a plan that played to his strengths, especially as he lacked any ability to take flight.

"Mr Griggs!?"

Minos took a moment to ogle the wall behind the receptionists, taking in the various awards and accolades hung there. It seemed that the company really knew what it was doing – shame that there appeared to be something fundamentally wrong with those who worked there.

Who takes two contracts to work on the same job, and inflicts misery on those who have been in their job for centuries? It was all…

"Mr Griggs?!?"

Minos lost his train of thought as he really wished that someone would put the blonde out of her misery. The girl, dressed in a smart navy-blue suit, with a pink carnation tucked in her lapel, had been pacing back and forth, alternating her gaze between her notes and the sea of faces, before shouting the name with increased panic.

Minos glanced down again at the bit of paper that had let him in and almost jumped out of his skin when he realised the name born on the document was the one being hollered across the vast reception.

"Mr Griggs?!?!?" the tone had reached near fever pitch volumes.

"Yes, that's me." Minos looked flustered as he tried to think of a way to explain away his forgetfulness. Luckily the petite woman got there before him.

"I am so sorry if I missed you. I'm having a hell of a day. Like you wouldn't believe. Please come this way." She didn't even take a breath as she started heading towards a door just beyond the vast desk where the receptionists were chattering into headsets. Minos, taking her cue, followed, still feeling uncertain about what was going on. "I'm Lucy Young, one of the HR Assistants – you know Human Resources, hiring, firing, that type of stuff. Not that I think we do much firing. It's all good stuff really. Anyway, I'm so glad you can join us. It's wonderful to have had such a great response to the advert we put out. I mean it's just fab. To be honest with you, it's my first week in the job and there's so much going on. And, of course, so many different recruitment campaigns. Have you come far today?"

The vacuum left when the woman finally stopped talking felt all consuming. Minos took a heartbeat to shake the ringing of her voice out his ears,

"You...errr...could say that, yes," he got out, before another tirade of sentences fell from the pretty girl's head.

"Oh my goodness and here I am keeping you hanging round. That was rude of me. I do hope you won't let my unprofessionalism reflect badly on this company. It is a wonderful organisation and I do love working here. It's only my first week – wait, did I say that already?" Minos opened his mouth to answer but never got the chance, "Either way, I can't recommend it enough. Everyone is so lovely. I've been places where the people are nice but this is another level."

By this stage of the conversation (if it could be called that, because Minos wasn't sure), the pair had made it into a long corridor and had arrived outside a door with fogged glass in its centre. Minos looked beyond the young woman, taking in more doors, and even stairs at the end of the passage, but couldn't see a way he could squeeze past the blonde and continue into the rest of the building by himself.

"Can I get you anything? Tea, water, juice..." Minos vigorously shook his head at the question for fear of having to wait a decade while the girl rattled through every possible beverage. "No problems," she responded, in a lot fewer words than the demi-god had expected, and she pushed the door open, letting the demi-god into his own personal version of a punishment.

What Minos had ever done to deserve this experience, he would never work out.

Chapter 13

As Minos was facing his first formal interview, Hades was finishing the latest in a string of complicated and face-achingly long meetings.

Over the last few days, Sparkes had wheeled the god out in front of a host of important mortals, representing a variety of industries. Hades had had to painstakingly sell the benefits the Underworld offered, trying not to rely too much on the notes the consultants had given him.

In each case, the outcome of the meetings seemed to come down to how Hades handled questions, observations and, most troubling for him, good-hearted joviality. It was the latter that was causing the god the most displeasure as he had to unnaturally smile his way through an infuriating pretence of understanding and enjoyment. The god was not used to having to please mortals and the act was wearing thin, and making his cheeks sore.

The once-mighty warrior eased himself into his chair at the head of the boardroom table, feeling drained after so much time spent with the living. He took a second to frown deeply, feeling relief at being able to do this without being told off by Sparkes (apparently it wasn't the acceptable response to a joke about the German Chancellor's current domestic policy).

To the god's immense delight, he loosened the psychedelically coloured 'power' tie that he had been forced to wear with his new pinstripe suit (both items niggled him, especially given the fact that, despite them being for work, he'd been told he couldn't claim them on expenses). With the unpinning of the stiff shirt collar button (also new, and attached to a very pricey shirt), he felt like he could finally breath again. He took some time to just scratch at the chest hair which peeked up from the itchy white fabric.

Hades' joy at slowly starting to peel himself out of the monkey suit, and the relaxing feeling that came with it, was all short lived, as Sparkes sauntered into the room. She was definitely enjoying the trials she had been putting the god through. Hades had also noticed that his performance in the meetings directly affected how much of her cleavage the woman revealed. In the early meetings, where the god had fluffed and mumbled his lines, the mortal's bosoms had been barely contained in her outfits. Now, with his confidence growing, the dapper black dress the woman wore seemed to be winning at least the battle, even if the war remained out of reach.

Sparkes stood proudly at the end of the massive table, dropping a large folder down, before hunching herself over the dark surface. Hades was careful to maintain eye contact, well aware that at the angle the woman stood her dress had almost fully surrendered its attempt at maintaining her modesty. The god definitely didn't need anyone thinking he was spending his evenings staring at the particulars of his mortal assistant.

"Really nice job with Mr Takagi," Sparkes cooed, coolly. "He was eating out of your hand there." She winked and started to pace across the room (while Hades got annoyed with the constant striding around, he was glad he could finally break eye contact with the woman). As she moved, Sparkes' back was ram rod straight and she intertwined her fingers in that particularly smug way she had. Before Hades could acknowledge her praise, the woman swung her finger up to point at the once-domineering ruler. "You really are good at this. And you know what – with your talk and my contacts, I think we are actually going to pull this off." The mortal took a few more steps with the spring of a tiger before it ruins a gazelle's day. "I was worried when we started this, but you really have brought you're A-game.

"I must say – the rumours are definitely wrong. I'm starting to think you are better than Zeus..."

Sparkes paused, as if mentioning Hades' older brother (which was always a sensitive topic for the god), hadn't been intended. The woman's features contorted, as if a wicked thought had crossed her mind, her eyes momentarily darting up and down the god's chest. She appeared to dismiss whatever she was thinking, as she returned to the table and her delicate fingers slid the huge folder down to Hades. The binder moved with a grating sound that irked the god to his core. "This is your reading ahead of tomorrow's meetings. Make sure you are prepared – you've been sloppy with the return on investment figures and the guys tomorrow will want to see you've got a handle on them, especially Osborne. He's recently been made a Lord and he will want to be reassured that you offer good value for money."

Hades groaned as he peeled back the top of the folder and took in his schedule for the next day: he was kicking off with a breakfast meeting (which was a misrepresentation, as there was always more talking than eating) at eight o'clock, before being in non-stop appointments until the early evening. A quick flick through the rest of the binder's contents presented another Herculean night of reading for the god, including stats and figures that had been updated since the day before. *I'm going to have to memorise these all over again*, he groaned inwardly.

By the time Hades looked up, Sparkes was gone. No doubt, he told himself, to send more emails, dictate more diabolical plans into her handheld voice recorder or perhaps just polish her broom (*ok*, the god conceded, *I've only seen the woman do the first two but I'm sure that she must, in some way, be descended from a witch*). The ruler wondered if he could squeeze in an afternoon of annual leave, all in the name of finding out if Sparkes would float or not. Or maybe he could just burn her at the stake for the fun of it.

After a small chuckle to himself, the god collected up his homework and switched off the boardroom's lights (every little helps when you're trying to financially save a business). As he stepped out into the corridor, Gronix, the Executive Assistant to the new Head of Arbitration Experts (the role that had been Minos' before all this had started – *sigh*, thought the god) appeared.

"Ah, Hades, I'm glad I found you." The diminutive, scaly demon hefted up several reams of paperwork, which Hades accepted without thinking about it (had he stopped to mull this over, he would have realised he was developing a very bad habit for taking paper off anyone who offered it to him). The ruler let his jaw drop open as he flicked through the pages,

"Gronix, it's late. I already have things to deal with this evening, and I do want to spend some time with my wife tonight. What is all this?"

The creature's big yellow eyes blinked a few times as a set of misshapen claws clicked together.

"Rhadamanthus said he'd emailed you about it already but wanted me to personally deliver the hard copies. Everything needs your review and approval."

Hades groaned, it really was the last thing he needed on top of his busy schedule – a new member of his team who was brimming with enthusiasm, yet didn't have the backbone to just get on with the job. Every time Hades turned around, the newly promoted demi-god had sent him something else to review, comment on, or sign off. It would have been tiresome when he wasn't spending all his days hobnobbing with mortals.

Both the loss of Minos and Cerebus continued to bother the god.

Gone was the straightforward understanding he had with his direct reports, replaced by uncertainty about what was actually happening in each part of organisation. Without a natural replacement for the Chief of Security (by which Hades now meant, Head of Contingency Planning and Well-being) Branaghan had taken on the responsibility in a temporary capacity. Hades hadn't seen the four-eyed mortal in a few days but got the distinct impressions that the Kers were not happy. *Perhaps*, the god tried to irk a smile out of himself, *the creatures had eaten the boring mortal and were all suffering from a serious bout of indigestion*. He could only hope...

"And don't tell me, Gronix," he felt very weary, as he returned to the matter in his hands, "Rhadamanthus needs this all back as soon as possible."

"Sooner, was his actual phrasing, my lord."

Hades growled slightly. *Trust Gronix to remember who is in charge, even if he could have pointed this out to his own manager before waddling over with more work.*

The god flicked through the stack of whiteness, noting budgets, forecasts, 'scorecards' (didn't the nuisance know that Hades had no interest in sport) and updated policy documents (no doubt with the changes the ruler had told Rhadamanthus to make a few days ago, but he couldn't be certain they had all been made, so he would need to read everything again).

Hades' whole body seemed to start folding in on itself as he let out a very deep sigh.

"I'll do what I can, when I can."

Gronix almost bent double as he snivelled,

"Of course, great one. I shall let my master know." And with that, the half-pint wretch was gone.

Hades stood for a moment and wondered if actually keeping the Underworld afloat, and making the vast quantities of money Sparkes had promised him, was really worth it. He was starting to feel like he was spending almost every waking hour at work. He hadn't even seen any of his friends in god knows how long (and given he was a god, he still didn't have a clue).

At a slow pace, Hades (who had once been a mighty solider) trudged home. More than ever he felt the crushing weight of the whole Underworld on his shoulders.

As Hades lumbered along, he longed for the good old days. When getting home at a reasonable hour was the norm, and he didn't have to take paperwork with him. When finding his dinner in the dog wasn't a problem because it meant his best friend was there, ready to spend some time with his much-loved master.

Hades finally admitted to himself that he really wasn't very happy.

*

Minos was finding Marvin Grigg's interview very tiresome.

Truth be told, the process was something the demi-god had never been involved in as part of his responsibilities in the Underworld. Hades had appointed Minos based on his reputation as the fairest of them all, and at that time they'd just had a chat about the job and what it entailed. As the Underworld grew, and reached the point that the god felt the judge needed deputies, Hades had also dealt with the recruitment for the posts. That was just the way he was back in those days. By contrast, Minos had always been happy leaving his deputies to get on with making their own appointments.

Now, inside a bland, grey room, sat on one side of a short desk, the demi-god could confirm he was definitely not a fan of the back and forth. The whole thing seemed unnatural and forced, although, Minos conceded, it didn't help that he was posing as someone else.

Sally Kitchener, the overweight HR Manager, had started by reciting Marvin Grigg's CV at Minos. The woman's ample girth had bobbed up and down inside the frumpy spotty blouse, as she had enunciated every point and detail. The judge had initially panicked, thinking that his cover was blown, until the dour faced woman had started underlining key points and dates with a black biro. Lucy had sat completely silent throughout all this, much to Minos' surprise. The young girl had diligently made notes with a large pink pen, although the few glimpses Minos caught of her writing pad suggested she was also doodling flowers and hearts.

After remarking on a couple of Marvin's acting roles (it seemed he'd made minor appearances in some of the HR Manager's favourite soaps – words that further confused Minos, as he tried to imagine what washing and acting had to do with each other), Kitchener had launched into a set of questions about his experiences and what made him suitable for the role of Administrative Assistant (which the real Marvin had deemed below him):

When had he hit a deadline?

He didn't think he had, he wasn't very good at throwing things.

What role did he normally play in a team?

He didn't – usually he was in charge so he left the team to get on with it.

How computer literate was he?

He could definitely read and write the word computer.

If he was a biscuit, what type would he be?

One that didn't get eaten.

Despite his best efforts, Minos seemed unable to evoke any positivity from the stern, purse lips of the woman, who was clearly deepening her disapproval of him with every answer he offered up.

"Why exactly did you apply for this job, Mr Griggs?" the woman queried, her brows knitting more than a WI's convention on a wet afternoon during wool season. Minos felt like he could blag this one with a little bit more confidence.

"Well, I'm really interested in the work you do. Specifically helping businesses with cash problems. You know, the consultancy stuff."

Kitchener waited patiently then decided that her interviewee wasn't going to add anything more,

"Hhhhhhmmmmm," was all she could manage as she scribbled away, switching between black and, the increasingly popular, red pens. Whatever the colour, the biro dipped and dived like an overambitious figure skater. "And what preparation did you do for this interview?"

"Oh, practically none. I mean I've never had one of these before..." Minos was silenced as Kitchener's eyes shot up from her writing.

Very slowly, and deliberately, the woman's head turned to scowl at Lucy.

"Have we possibly crossed our wires again, Miss Young?"

Lucy was already sifting through a selection of paperwork that had been tucked at the back of her pad. For a second, Minos thought he was back in the Underworld sentencing a soul – the look of sheer terror on the girl's face reminded him of the expressions ex-mortals pulled when they found out that the punishment for worshipping false gods (this included the Scientology followers and anyone who believed a word that any of the Kardashians said) was spending an eternity scrubbing the real gods' toilets. Lucy leafed this way and that through a collection of printed documents.

"No, no, no – it can't be. I'm sure..." she chattered to herself as she dumped the whole lot on the desk so she could tear through all the personal information, notes and schedules. "I'm fairly certain I didn't confuse the two..." Lucy's face went redder as she continued her manic search.

"Mr Griggs," Kitchener drawled as she appeared to lose patience with her junior colleague. "Am I correct that you have not had an interview before?" Minos slowly nodded, trying not to look at the panic etching its way across Lucy's face, "And would I be right in thinking you are over sixty years of age?" Minos confirmed this, choosing not to explain how old he actually was.

Kitchener barely held back her anger as she glared at Lucy. "I think it's safe to say we have confused ourselves here. You shouldn't be in this interview," Inwardly, Minos conceded that he definitely knew that, "but you should have joined us yesterday for the return to work programme.

"I can only apologise for any distress this experience has caused you, by us asking you questions meant for a higher-level role than that which you applied for. I can assure you that this should never have happened, and definitely will not again." Despite speaking to Minos, the woman's steely gaze was fixed on Lucy, who had given up on the paperwork and was now sat very still, stiffly staring ahead. All the colour had drained out of the young woman's face.

Kitchener finally returned her eyes to take in Minos. "Miss Young will take you up now, and get you enrolled in our scheme for those seeking their first office-based role."

Lucy was up and beckoning the judge out of his chair before her boss could even finish the sentence. Minos willingly followed, not sure quite what had happened but feeling like it was working in his favour. Surely, he reasoned, if the company was in his debt then he would have a better chance at finding out what he wanted to know. He did feel guilty that his opportunity was coming at the expense of the chatty Lucy.

As soon as they were out of the room (and sight of the unpleasant HR Manager), Lucy launched into a string of heartfelt apologies. She carried on during the short walk to the lift which took them up several floors.

"Once again – I am so so sorry. I'm not sure what happened. I could have sworn you put in for this role but of course you didn't. You couldn't have – I mean look at your paperwork. All your past work is on screen or stage. There's no office experience. And I'm sure someone like you is finding it harder to come by work these days..." she squeaked, clasping her hand to her mouth before trying to backtrack. "By which I don't mean that you are old. Of course, you're old. Well, in comparison to me, but then again not to someone who's a hundred. Although I imagine not many people are old in comparison to someone that age."

The string of seemingly never-ending words continued as they arrived in a vast office, filled with desks occupied by heads that seemed to float behind wall dividers. Most of the young faces seated across the room had their eyes turned down giving full focus to their computers. The rhythmic thud of typing kept a steady pace to the environment, as other figures in suits and plush outfits drifted up and down the aisleways, clutching folders and fancy mugs.

As they slowed by one of the banks of desks, Lucy grabbed a spare chair for Minos and slipped into a seat herself, swivelling to reveal a workspace where a great war was being fought. On the flat surface a white army of paperwork crashed messily across the desk, while photos, pink fluffy stationery and random postcards struck back from the far edges and up the dividers between Lucy and her co-workers. "Thank goodness you're seeing me on one of my tidier desk days," explained Lucy as she delved into the first warring party. As he watched her, Minos suddenly really missed Gronix. The little pointy demon would have had a fit if he'd seen this sort of chaotic approach to paperwork.

"I should say – I am sorry if Sally scared or upset you at all. She's a bit...well...you know. Sort of a bad egg," explained Lucy, as she continued to sift through all manner of documents, post-its and screwed up pieces of paper. In response to the curious look on Minos' face, she continued. "You get me – she's just rather unpleasant. A bit of a nasty piece of work. Especially when she's in one of her moods. And, trust me, that's more often than not. I sometimes wish I worked for someone else. But then I suppose she did give me a chance in this role. And I am thankful. It's just..." she let her voice trail off, as her face saddened for the briefest of moments. Then, as suddenly as it had appeared, the unhappiness was gone and the sunny disposition was back. "Now, look, I know I've cocked up here, so let's just sign you straight up for the programme. Just put a signature there for me, Marvin" Lucy disgorged a crumpled form from the mess on her desk and passed Minos a pink flamingo that, to his complete surprise, was also a pen. Thankfully the girl had reminded him in time that he was pretending to be someone else and he was able to scribble something that looked like his fake name on the paper that was entitled 'Work Training Volunteer Placement Scheme'. While he did this, Lucy extracted a laptop from the sea of chaos and flicked up the top. Minos watched with intrigue at the speed of the computer, whilst marvelling at the size of the dinky device.

"And to make up, I'll put you on the best placement we have. This way you get to do a lot more with the consultants. I remember you saying that interested you, so we'll just make a few tweaks, switch that person there, and viola you are all sorted. Please don't worry at all. You'll love working here – I know it's not for long but our programme is sooooo amazing. Afterwards, you'll be able to find a job no problems. And we'll get you involved in all the good cases while you are here. We've got some really special ones – real hush hush stuff. You'll love it."

Minos was definitely happy. He didn't quite understand what he had committed himself to but it sounded like it was going to allow him exactly the access he had been seeking. The demi-god could sense the end of his journey. If all it took now was to prance around and pretend to be a mortal for a little bit, then he was sure he could cope.

Chapter 14

The irony of reporting for a programme that was designed to help him back into employment was not lost on Minos.

The following day, in another outfit that Mr Roberts helped him to squeeze into, the demi-god was escorted up to a large training room within the Schneider, Schneider & Patterson building. The whole space had a magnificent view of the zig zagging London skyline, but Minos wasn't able to appreciate it as he quickly discovered he was lumped in with a variety of mortals, all from very different and, in many cases, trying backgrounds. From ex-druggies to single parents, everyone had a tale to tell.

And, boy, did they.

Minos counted off almost 140 minutes of story sharing during their mandatory company induction. This, coupled with the team building exercises and corporate information about why the organisation was committed to helping them return to work, made for a long and tiring experience for the demi-god. By clocking off time, Minos was both physically exhausted and frustrated that he hadn't got anywhere further in his quest to find the document that he needed.

The judge's mood was made worse by the journey he had to endure back to the Roberts.

Travelling with Branden during the afternoon of the previous day, the trains and tube system had fascinated Minos. He had welcomed disappearing into deep dark tunnels (it made him feel just that little bit closer to home), enjoyed the soft beep as doors opened and closed, as well as the gentle announcements of the woman who seemed to travel on every carriage that the pair did.

However, during evening rush hour the demi-god's enthusiasm for the transport system was wiped out. He was constantly shoved and barged by his fellow commuters, especially when he got confused about which platform he needed. Despite being the oldest traveller on the network, the judge couldn't get anyone to offer him a seat. He drew the conclusion that the vaguely padded cushions were offered on a first come, first served basis and once a backside had landed it wasn't moving. This left Minos standing on tired feet, and no matter which way he turned or positioned himself, he always ended up staring into someone's sweaty armpit. The judge's joy at the magic of the Oyster (which was a lot flatter and less edible than the ones in the Underworld) was quickly overtaken with blind confusion as he lost all sense of when he was meant to be using it.

In an attempt to overcome the sheer horror of public transport, the demi-god decided to leave the Roberts' house at a quite ungodly hour the next morning. Sadly, the demi-god discovered, to his disadvantage, that the earlier the trip, the sleepier the other travellers were, many a pair of half-closed eyes, ignoring his pleas for help.

To add insult to a tube-door-related-injury, the judge arrived at his new place of work before anyone associated with the programme did. As he wasn't allowed past reception without a member of staff to escort him, and none of the flashy receptionists could (or would) take him in, Minos ended up sitting on one of the hard benches, patiently waiting. So exhausted was he from his first day, and early start, he eventually dozed off, and missed the start of his training.

When he did join the others, the judge wished he hadn't. During the morning, overseen by the ditsy Lucy, they had to fill in paperwork that contained a variety of bizarre questions (why a company like Schneider, Schneider & Patterson needed to worry about what happened after death in service, Minos didn't know – that was the Underworld's task). This was followed by a lunch with department heads and senior managers, who all seemed more bothered with tapping away on their phones and loudly high fiving each other.

The day concluded with each of the new arrivals meeting their 'work place mentor'. This, Minos learnt, was someone who could provide an ear and a kind word to make sure the trainees got the most out of their experience, whilst helping each of the recruits not to fall back into old patterns of crime, drug misuse or just generally sleeping until midday.

To the judge's slight horror, he was paired with Lucy. As they walked along long corridors, trying to find a quiet place to sit, Minos was very aware that this meant that he had to remember everything he'd said so far about his cover story. The judge understood that a mistake could be costly and end his opportunity in the company before it really started. The small silver lining was that they finally settled in the vast staff canteen and therefore Minos could enjoy another hot chocolate, complete with whipped cream and a flake this time. And Lucy kindly paid for it.

Thankfully, the HR Assistant spent most of the session in complete disarray, as she pushed question pages and prepared notes this way and that. She also talked non-stop about herself which, while being a real strain on the demi-god's ears, did take the speaking burden away from him.

During their time, Minos learnt about how Lucy was settling into her new role and getting used to the workload (although she confessed, she seemed to be permanently entrenched in Kitchener's bad books). It then became apparent to the demi-god that there were no holds barred when it came to what the happy blonde would share.

The judge learnt about the nasty split the girl had had from her boyfriend after she discovered him involved in loud, and very passionate, love-making with the lady who delivered the milk (Minos resisted the temptation to ask the names of those involved, for future judgement purposes). Lucy explained that this had prompted her to change everything about her life. She'd moved out of the flat the pair had shared (she wasn't sleeping in the bed that the skank had rolled around in, apparently), switched jobs (she used to work in advertising but didn't have the passion to sell tat to people who didn't really need it anymore) and, she confided, had even decided to start getting her hair colour from a bottle (Minos wasn't sure he followed this bit, but nodded just to keep from saying anything about himself).

Lucy also told the demi-god about her hopes and plans for the future. Truthfully, she explained, she wanted to give up the whole nine to five thing (having done the commute already, the demi-god shared her view), and have her own little cafe. Somewhere nice, and out of town, she told Minos, like Crawley. The woman's enthusiasm dimmed momentarily as it was just a dream – she could barely make ends meet, let alone save up enough to start a business. She wistfully prayed to any god that would listen (Minos almost spluttered hot chocolate everywhere at that moment) that one day she might have the opportunity to do what she really loved.

Before the pair knew it, the time scheduled for their one to one (including setting of a personal development plan, which Minos had particularly disliked the sound of) was up, and to the demi-god's relief he had dodged talking about Marvin Griggs. Lucy sprouted sincere apologies, as she scrambled to pull her now organised paperwork together into a sparkly folder, returning it back to its original chaotic state as she did. The blonde promised that next time they had a catch up she would be better prepared.

Despite himself Minos actually smiled.

So often in the Underworld, life was regimented. Meetings started on time, deadlines were met and desks left tidy at the end of the day (and if this wasn't done by the worker then one or more of their colleagues would feast on any leftover paperwork or stationery). The judge had to concede that he was actually enjoying being with Lucy, and the light hearted, if not somewhat scatter-brained, approach she had was refreshing to him. The sweet girl may be by far the craziest person Minos had ever had to deal with (in the context of general disorganisation and babbling, not crazy like psychopaths – in his days Minos had judged many of those), but he was actually starting to enjoy his time with her. The fact that she tried her hardest warmed the demi-god's heart.

Something stirred deep within Minos, an uncertainty over his lies about his employment. It made his mind itch and, for a brief moment, he considered confiding in the girl. As quickly as the thought arrived though, he dismissed it. The demi-god refocused on his purpose, reminding himself he couldn't jeopardise that, especially not because he'd developed a soft spot for a mortal.

Had Minos known that within twenty-four hours he was going to be exposed as a fraud anyway, he may have reconsidered this stance.

Chapter 15

The realisation that something was very wrong caught Minos by complete surprise. And at exactly the point of the third day when he was enjoying himself.

Having once more fought his way across the densely packed transport network (this time the trials included a middle-aged man barking into his phone right next to the judge's ear; his head being rocked back and forth into a woman's shockingly hairy armpit; and getting kicked in the shin multiple times by a child who looked way too big for his pushchair), Minos had been filled with a sense of dread as he had arrived at the office. He hadn't been sure he could take much more enforced learning with the sad-sacks and dubious characters in his training group.

Happily though, Lucy had greeted the demi-god and set out the agenda for the day: work.

Minos' heart had jumped for joy, as he was finally able to start doing something at the company. It had felt invigorating to have the chance to be productive (even if it was at an organisation that had been plotting against him). He had been sure it would not be long before the opportunity to find the horrible document that had ruined his life would present itself.

Lucy had escorted Minos up to the Finance and Policy team, explaining that all of the consultants were required to complete a placement in the team, as it ensured they had a basic understanding of the company's recommended monetary matters before being let loose on clients. During his tour of the vast section of the building, the judge was introduced to an almost endless collection of faces before being given an overview of the department's tasks. While the demi-god held financial matters in low regard, he had accepted that he should really play the part for the day. He had cooed and nodded as one of the surprisingly interesting chaps, with a cool hair style and bright red braces to hold up his trousers (Minos wondered if Mr Roberts had any of those – he liked the look), had explained how the team processed the funds, planned budgets and dealt with the general transactions of the oversized company.

Against the judge's better instincts, he had actually found himself following the outline and, more surprisingly, asking questions. The way the dude (as the team referred to each other) had went over the information actually engaged the judge and before long he had been seeing the numbers in a completely new light. It hadn't taken much for him to grasp the concept of balance sheets, debits versus credits, and accruals. For Minos it all felt astoundingly good.

That morning, Minos' eyes had been opened to a brand new world and before he knew it he had been revelling in processing expense forms (a necessary part of his development – he had been told). Part of the excitement related to the tiny thrill the demi-god got filling in the 'For Office Use Only' boxes on the bottom of the pages, but after all of his tribulations in the mortal realm, he had learnt to get his wins where he could.

Minos had been gleefully half way down the huge stack of forms he had to process, and almost on the verge of whistling a jaunty tune, when the substantial shadow of Sally Kitchener had fallen across the desk. The scowl slapped across the heavily made up face, coupled with the way she had quivered with barely contained rage, had told Minos that she had not been there to ask when she was going to get her £6.78 (for an espresso and a chi tea latte) paid to her.

*

The mood was very different from the last time the trio had sat in the small interview room. The demi-god's confusion was plastered across his face, as clearly as the annoyance on Kitchener's. Lucy was barely present, her delicate head was slumped against her chest, her view remaining on the floor.

The HR Manager consulted her notes and ran her tongue over lipstick stained teeth. She then looked up and only when her head had delicately nodded to itself ten times, she locked eyes with the demi-god, and demanded,

"And how long did you think you could get away with this?"

Before Minos could attempt a response, she continued, her tone harsh. "Do you think we are idiots? That you could fool us indefinitely?" She waved her hand at Lucy, the girl flinching as the chubby digits veered towards her head. "I mean you obviously pulled the wool over the eyes of the more naïve of us. But, did you seriously think we wouldn't find out? Did you assume we are all that stupid?"

Minos opened his mouth but got no further. "Who actually are you? No, wait – don't answer that…"

Fat chance of that, thought the demi-god who still hadn't got a word in edgeways, sideways or from any other direction,

"…I don't want to know. If something more serious comes of this I want deniability. Unlike others," she shot a withering glare at her assistant, who seemed to shrink even more into herself. "You may wonder how we worked it out?"

Minos concluded that the business of the day was rhetorical questions, as the woman pushed on, now turning her full-bore stare at the judge. "We had a call from Mr Griggs in response to the Employment Pack we sent him from the address on his CV. He queried how we could have given him a job when he hadn't sat an interview. Well, you can imagine everyone's surprise when I told him he'd been working for us for two days!"

The woman's eyes seemed to be trying to send Minos back to the Underworld (without knowing that was where he really wanted to be right at that moment). The stare was deadly and unblinking – making the demi-god think of the Kers. Not that any demon would ever have dared speak to the demi-god in the way that Kitchener was at that moment.

Despite his annoyance at the way he was being address, an unusual feeling of guilt was coursing through Minos and he held his tongue.

He recognised that he had done wrong, and worse still, got Lucy in trouble. The blonde was desperately trying to blink back tears, no doubt because she was too petrified to move a hand to wipe them away. Her eyelashes flashed so fast she looked like she was trying to send a Morse code message. Minos desperately wanted to reach out to her. To apologise and explain why it had all been necessary.

Before he could do anything, Kitchener slapped down an extremely important looking document in the middle of the desk. The company logo topped the tiny rows of minute detail and legal jargon. A highly polished silver pen followed, meticulously centred in the middle of the text.

"This has been put together by our lawyers. It admits your faults and deception, whilst exonerating all Schneider, Schneider & Patterson employees of any wrongdoing. It also acknowledges that you will not speak of this, and certainly take no action against the corporation or any individual. Not that some of them don't deserve it." The woman's gruff displeasure once more found Lucy, who was at risk of disappearing under the desk if her diminutive frame contracted any further. "You will sign it and then leave the building, post-haste."

Minos tried to speak, to say something. Even if he didn't appeal to the overbearing manager, at least he could apologise to Lucy.

And yet, he choked.

He just couldn't find the words.

Ultimately, the demi-god who spent his career punishing the sins of mortals, had borne false witness against his neighbours. The mortals had passed judgment on his actions, exactly as he would have done in the Underworld.

A punishment to fit the crime – acceptance of his wrong doing and banishment – had been served.

With a heavy heart, Minos scooped up the pen. The ink shrieked against the crisp parchment as he scrawled his own signature. The second he lifted the nib up the document was gone, Kitchener tucking it under her enormous armpit. "Now get out!"

It was the clearest, crispest order Minos had ever heard and despite his desire to apologise to Lucy, he was on his feet. He couldn't even catch the blonde's eye as he exited the room.

And before he knew it, the demi-god was outside the building. His chance of finding out who was responsible for ruining his life, and his home, had gone.

Chapter 16

Branden, so used to being sad himself, could not have expected the crumpled mess of a demi-god he found in the front room of the mid-terrace, when he returned from college.

All day, the boy had been hoping and praying (although he wasn't sure that was the right thing to do as a goth who had now met an actual deity) that Minos was able to uncover the people behind the plan against Hades.

In the same way as he had the previous two evenings, Branden burst through the front door in a haste to see his friend. He dumped his devilishly dark bag, containing books for classes that he hadn't paid any attention in, and pushed forward into the compact front room. The goth's excited features quickly jackhammered back to their usual downcast appearance as he took in the depressed demi-god that was parked on one side of the sofa. The judge's face didn't even twitch to acknowledge the youngster's presence – his eyes fixed on the blaring television as some muscled man screamed across a table at a stick-thin redhead about how his scallops were better than hers.

"What happened?" groaned Branden, unsure what could have left the demi-god so crestfallen. As he dropped down next to the judge, he quickly started to try and fill in the blanks himself. Had Hades actually hired the consultants? Did that mean there was no conspiracy? Perhaps it was Cerebus behind the whole takeover? If so, what did that mean for Minos?

When the truth was uttered from the judge's mouth, the boy couldn't believe it. "I don't believe it! But how did they even work it out?"

A soft moan was all the youngster could offer up when the details were shared, the demi-god's gaze staying on the taxi travelling mortals as they held up large score cards relating to their dinner (not that Branden was paying any attention, but Minos was intrigued by the fact that the host was being marked down for the fact they had let the dog come to the table. Minos did that all the time when he had Cerebus round for dinner).

"So, what now?" Branden asked, trying to recapture some of his earlier enthusiasm. He considered his own question for a moment, before adding, "Do you think they have a work experience scheme I could apply for? Or maybe they've got an admin job going and I could try and get myself recruited. Take a few weeks off college…"

"You will not," boomed the judge, coming to life as he met the youngster's shocked stare. Sensing the disservice he'd done to someone who was only trying to help, Minos softened. "By which I mean, you can't go missing your studies and throwing your life away for me. For the Underworld." His vision blurred, as his mind's eye saw the dishevelled Lucy again, all meek as Kitchener had cut her down with a withering glare. "I've already cost one person their happiness, I can't keep dragging you mortals into this battle."

It was Branden's turn to bark,

"Hello! Look around you Minos – I'm already in this. You're sat on my Mum's sofa, wearing my Dad's clothes. I'm involved and there's no going back on that. I've already had to keep quite a few lies going to get my parents to help you."

This was true, Minos had to concede. Ever since that first text message, the boy had been maintaining a convoluted web of dishonesty to get his parents to support the demi-god. Mr and Mrs Roberts had absolutely no clue that the deity known as the Final Judge of Souls, who was on a mission to save the whole of life-after-death, was currently unmoulding the delicate backside imprints that they had happily woven into their sofa over the years.

As far as the adults of the house were concerned, Minos was Branden's favourite lecturer, who had helped the boy pass the challenging subject of French the previous year, and had now fallen on hard times following confusion with a marking scheme that had left him disavowed from the profession and in need of a new career (something which was essential as he'd lost his own home to a fire, for which the insurance company wouldn't pay out, due – Branden had ironically convinced them – to an act of god). As such, the judge had been afforded full hospitality by the Roberts, as he tried to find a job, so he could save enough for the deposit on a flat (there was also a story as to why Minos didn't have any cash at the moment but that had been the straw which broke the camel's back in terms of the demi-god keeping up with Branden's stories).

The youngster continued his objections, the exasperation clear in his voice "I mean, there's got to be something more we can do. The answer has got to be in that building."

Minos suddenly felt very claustrophobic and pushed himself to his feet. As he shuffled this way and that, he struggled to focus his mind. In one thought the burning defeat of his failure made him question how colossally awful he was that he had pretty much been sacked from two jobs in less than three weeks. In the next moment, he was plagued by his memory of the broken Lucy. The normally cheery girl's spirit had appeared whole-heartedly ruined by the judge's actions.

What's was becoming of her? he wondered.

As misery coursed through the judge, his attention turned to his demons and the Underworld. Mortals were still dying so the organisation hadn't folded yet.

Are they, Minos sadly mused, *actually better off without me?*

The demi-god turned to what felt like his only friend in the whole world, and sighed wearily,

"It's all over Braden. I've failed, and I don't have any other options up here or back home."

The demi-god hadn't realised, until it was snatched away from him, but he had actually been finding the work experience programme interesting. He had taken some reassurance from the knowledge that if he had failed in his efforts and couldn't return to the Underworld, he at least had a chance to find some sort of a new life on Earth. He hadn't expected to ever find himself judging souls on the surface, but a little retirement plan where he processed finance forms, or just did something mundane and mind-numbing, like working in a cinema or being a politician, would have kept him happy. Without knowing it, the demi-god had taken comfort in the idea that he had a future purpose.

And what did he have now?

Nothing.

Greedily, the judge eyed up the drinks cabinet in the corner, where he could see a ruby red bottle of wine. Wearily, he eased himself towards the alcohol container, which glinted in the stray sunshine streaming through the front room's window.

As he shuffled onto his second step, Minos ground to a halt, his mind reminded him that stealing was a sin. The Roberts had opened their home to him and he wasn't going to repay them (well, he couldn't actually do that anyway, but he wasn't going to make matters worse) by taking their alcohol.

As he stood, swaying slightly, Minos committed to himself that he was not about to give up his beliefs. He knew, better than anyone, the difference between right and wrong. Whatever his shortcomings, savagely exposed as many of them had been over recent weeks, he had his principles and he would cling to them, whatever came next.

Desperate to help his friend, Branden suddenly bounced up on the sofa, grasping at straws with the only idea he could think off,

"Can't you bring up an army of demons to bust their way into the office? There must be someone else who can get into the building."

Minos shook his head sadly, wishing the boy would just accept the inevitable.

"It doesn't work like that. No demon worth is going to volunteer to come up here. It just isn't the done thing. You wouldn't find any of them on Earth, no more than you'd find a mortal in the Underworld."

"But," blustered Branden, shaking his head to show how unwilling he was to concede to the demi-god's depression, "There are mortals down there right now! That's your problem. Isn't there someone else we can call on?"

Minos waved outstretched hands at the youngster, his defeat only missing the white flag to complete the look.

"There isn't. Gods live in the Underworld or on Mount Olympus. And I'm not welcome up there, before you go suggesting anything." He chose not to add the fact that there would be a lot of fun poked at Hades' expense if the tale of mortals saving the faltering business got up to the clouds. "All the demons are below ground, with all the souls. Well, not all the souls, but that's another story..."

Minos trailed off as he suddenly realised that there was one source of help that he hadn't considered. It was a small group, and a long shot, but just maybe it was worth a try.

Chapter 17

There was a common misconception in the Underworld: that the soul of every mortal who died arrived at the kingdom's gates.

There was only a few in the top team who were aware of the very small percentage (and in this case we are talking 0.0 – more zeros than a sophisticated binary programme whose creator has only one functional button on their keyboard – 01) of the deceased that hadn't.

The few souls that never made it into the Underworld were barred on a matter of policy. Although, a lot of this came down to simple political muscle-flexing.

Around the time that mortals would refer to as 800 AD, Thantanos took over as the Chief of Death from his mother, Erebus. The goddess had lasted just a few centuries in the role (which only just got her through her mandatory probation period), before deciding it wasn't really for her. There were many theories as to why she gave up, but that is neither here nor there for the purpose of this story.

Needless to say, Erebus retired and after a well fought competition between a range of applicants, including Rhadamanthus, Hermes and even the Tooth Fairy (which was a very odd interview, by all accounts), Thantanos was appointed to the role. This came as something of a surprise to many of the Underworld inhabitants, given the fact that very few people could actually bear being in the same room as the dull deity.

Many gave the new member of the Underworld's senior management team the benefit of the doubt, but there was a few who took the opportunity to try and impose their own will on the demi-god. Poor Thantanos had to cope with demons in his team trying to sneak in their own working practices (many of them attempted to convince him that Wednesday was actually the last official working day of the week), as well as his own deputies seeing how far they could push their new boss.

And there was no one who applied themselves to this practice with more vigour or deviousness than Hermes. The sly guide soon had Thantanos wrapped in knots, as he tried to first confuse, then trick his new boss, before acting honestly, but in the manner of someone who was trying to pull a fast one.

Within all of this mayhem, Hermes delicately pointed out to Thantanos how wonderful it was that every soul was welcomed into the Underworld, even those who had had their heart removed and buried somewhere else, away from the body. The smooth-talking deity explained to his new manager that there was something wholly unnatural about this method of burial, yet, he added, so good to see the organisation being fair to all. Why Hermes picked this particular custom, no one could ever work out, but he did.

By that stage, Thantanos was so wound up, he decided to disagree with the point that had been made by his subordinate. As one of his first official acts in the department he updated the appropriate policy, banning any soul which had had their body mutilated in that particular way from entering the kingdom.

The demi-god had no idea that any change to working procedures of that scale needed to be approved by Hades personally.

It was only in 1918, during the long-running 'should there be an event to mark the end of the world war' debate that the ruler stumbled across the adjustment Thantanos had made. While it was not funny at the time, many of the senior team would look back and smile on that afternoon, as the god's epic meltdown caused more than a fair share of souls to scurry for cover, many in the fear that a new conflict had started. Hades had fumed for days as he dragged the demi-god, quite literally, over the coals.

It didn't take long to remind the pale character that the second rule of Underworld management was to let every soul in (the first, of course, being to make sure no one got out). Thantanos learnt his lesson the hard way, much, many conjectured, to Hermes' delight.

The other rule Thantanos became familiar with during that period, was the inability for even Hades to reverse the results of a policy change once they had been enacted. No matter the ideas the Chief of Death came up with, there was no way that the excluded souls could ever be allowed into the Underworld. The rule had been in place at their time of death, and there was nothing more that could be done about it.

Hades, recognising that it was down to the mistake of his team member that these few had been left in limbo, had done what he could to make amends. He had ensured Thantanos paid to create clubs, bars, and (in the case of

England and Ireland) pubs, to accommodate the souls left behind. These refuges offered the wandering souls somewhere to lay their head, for as long as they wanted. Little expense was spared by Hades – but then it's always much easier to spend someone else's money than your own.

It was outside one of those establishments that Minos and Branden now found themselves.

"Explain to me again how this helps?" queried the youngster, still not quite following the explanation Minos had given him.

"I don't know but you said there must be someone we can turn to. This is the only group I can think to ask."

Branden took in the imposing wooden door, covered in dark metallic studs and deep hinges. It was set in the side of Charing Cross station, on the sloped path which led down towards the Thames.

"Why here?"

"This is the nearest spot for souls. Hades tried to put a place of shelter in the easiest place for the souls to access. It is the dead centre of town after all."

Branden blinked a couple of times, unsure how he should respond. Finally, he decided to just voice his main concern,

"So, you're going to rely on a bunch of souls who weren't allowed into the Underworld, and still won't be, even if you succeed in saving the kingdom?"

"Huuussssshhhhh," Minos glared at his friend, starting to wonder if it was a mistake bringing the lad on this part of the quest. The demi-god may have given in and accepted that he needed assistance but maybe this was taking it too far. At least, he conceded, it was Friday evening, so Branden wasn't missing college and the youngster helped him blend into the sea of mortals moving from attractions, shopping trips or drinking establishments to their next destination. As he pushed the door forward, Minos added, "Fair warning – I may not be very welcome in here..."

*

Bad music assaulted Branden's ears as they entered the old-fashioned pub. Not 'bad' in the way that it wasn't to his taste, it was more awful in the way a tone-deaf elephant would be if it tried to play a very small keyboard.

A strong Russian voice chimed out as the din ended,

"No, no – it is D, D, E! Not, as you insist, D, C, F!".

"Please don't shout at me. You know I can't concentrate when you are standing over my shoulder picking apart every mistake I make."

"I would not keep doing it if you applied what I have taught you. Look at the positioning of your wrists, for goodness sakes!"

"Boys, boys – will you quit squabbling. We have company."

Three pairs of dead eyes fell on Minos and Branden. The youngster tried to take in everything in front of him. He failed, but on his second attempt had a little more success.

The first thing the youngster processed was the long, slender room. Booths, with low fitted bench seating, lined the walls on either side, while a bar, complete with an array of hand pumps and spirits (hard alcohol, not souls), sat at the far end. Everything was made of wood, including the strange items that hung off the walls, ranging from medieval xylophones to mountings for various sets of antlers. Branden could have believed he had stepped back in time, if not for the familiar drink brands he could see dotted around the tables.

Branden hadn't known what to expect a soul to look like. He'd half imagined flowing white shadows, reminiscent of the cartoons he'd watched when he was a kid. The other part of him, the goth-infused part, had anticipated the devastated remains of human beings, all bloodied and disfigured. Instead, the figures before him looked like washed out versions of humans. Branden found if he concentrated hard enough, he could actually see past the bodies as if they weren't there. This sort of appearance, he assumed, must really suck when you're left to roam the Earth.

There was a number of souls around the drinking establishment, all in various outfits that reminded Branden of pictures he'd seen of the Pope. They huddled in the booths, gathered around chess sets and draught boards, talking in hushed whispers.

Slap bang in the middle of the room was an upright piano – the type you'd usually associate with a good-old-knees-up down a 1950s boozer. It was around this item that the gaggle of voices was congregated.

Seated at the ivories was a knight, dressed in chain mail with a faded white tunic bearing a red lion's head. On top of the soul's short curly hair was a small crown, the type a king would wear into battle, as opposed to, say, the opening of Parliament. Towering over the armoured figure was a rather erect gentleman, dressed in a long black suit, his tie an elaborate succession of loops and stray ends. The soul clasped his hands behind his back, the tutting at his colleague's poor performance dying on his lips.

To the side, a thin woman stood tall and proud. She wore an exquisite dress, which cut tightly to her bust before pluming out. Her dark brown hair was tightly arranged into elaborate curls above a delicate, fragile face, which was tucked between her side and right arm. The daintiness of her appearance contrasted with the large leg of meat that she held in her left hand and appeared to have been gnawing at. From beneath the woman's armpit, she cleared her throat (a difficult proposition when it's a good foot above your mouth) and continued in a rough tone, "It seems Hades has deemed to send us a messenger. What now – you're taking away the sorry set of records in our jukebox?"

Minos inched forward, gingerly. The look on his face suggested he was about to negotiate with a mad woman who had way too many hostages and bullets.

"Anne Boleyn, I presume?"

"Your right there, slugger – and if you have any other bright observations you can share them with your mortal lapdog out on the street." A nasty tone dripped around the words, clear displeasure plastered over the face.

"Hang on a minute!" spat back Minos, stepping forward. In response the knight leapt up,

"Please let's not get off on the wrong foot, shall we?" his gaze nervously twitched between soul, mortal and demigod. "We shouldn't be getting into all that before we've at least extended some hospitality. I mean, his boss does pay for all this." As if to make his point he picked up a cocktail glass from the top of the piano, a tooth-picked olive bobbing happily as the liquid swished back and forth. "I am Richard the First, and my colleague here is the renowned pianist Frederic Chopin. If you have the time, I can introduce you to the various religious leaders who join us today. Publican," he looked around in confusion, finding no one behind the bar, "Where did the landlord go?"

Although no response was immediate, a loud Scottish voice suddenly echoed from the back of the room.

"Darn! I canna believe I've dropped another one!"

"Honestly," it was Chopin's turn to raise his voice, his thick accent contrasting against his near flawless English, as he directed his annoyance at the booth tucked to the far right of the bar. "Can we watch our language please? There has been more 'darns' today than the time you took up sewing."

"It's no' my fault, laddie" returned the voice, "You'd be havin' the same trouble tryin' to knit with only the leftover chopsticks!"

"One who uses his fingers to create beautiful music does not ever consider putting them to use with such trivialities." As the words escaped Chopin's mouth they were followed with a thick cough, bending the soul over as he spluttered into a fancy handkerchief. Seemingly unconcerned by the choking noises, a further yell came forward,

"Och aye, that's as maybe, but if someone hadna broken the Ker Plunk set, I wouldna be resortin' to findin' a new hobby!"

Richard the First now stirred into life (or a close approximation, as he was, technically, dead), yelping,

"That really is unfair! I have explained until I am blue in the face, that I did not know that those straws were going to melt. I just wanted to make some nice nibbles and finger food for everyone. I mean we can't live off takeaways forever."

"Aye, you can say it until you go purple for all I care, laddie. It's time like this that I wish we still had the stocks! Bend someone over and stick them in between two bits of wood. Get the crowd in a nice stir as they chuck rotten fruit and veg – that taught any scallywag a good lesson in my day. You can bet there wasna no more mistakes after that," the heavy voice chimed, disgust radiating from it like warmth from a heater. After a moment of thought, it added, "Besides, what's wrong with livin' off takeaways?"

Cutting in between the chatter, Boleyn moved towards Minos, a grave look on the face she still held against her side,

"I think the key word there was 'live'! Lads, we are neither alive, nor dead. And one of the main reasons why we aren't afforded eternal relief from this horrid land is stood right in front of us!"

As she advanced a few steps a wild face poked up from where the Scottish voice had been emanating. Shaggy hair, an unkempt beard and crazy eyes gave Branden real cause for concern. The strange soul caught sight of the arrivals and was instantly out of the booth, heading for them at a brisk pace.

"Is that one of them-there Underworld busybodies?!? The ones that says we're no' good enough to enjoy our sweet rewards." The soul was dressed in a smock, with a chequered kilt, which flapped as he moved. At the bottom of very hairy legs, his feet were bare, revealing stubby feet with only three toes between them. The soul, who wobbled as he walked, thrust a two fingered hand at a small scabbard on his belt but found nothing there. "Och! For my weapon! Quick someone break open the Cluedo set and give me the dagger. I'll cut that damn god into wee pieces."

Chopin, having recovered from his coughing fit, rolled his eyes, as he calmly stated,

"We lost that game piece years ago – remember we only have the revolver and the candlestick left. And, once again, Robbie, please mind your language."

"Then brin' me one of those – I'll club him back to the death world he came from."

The look on the Scot's face was pure hatred as he continued to advance, hands twitching aggressively at his side. The other souls remained routed to the spot – unwilling to get between the wild soul and his prey. Minos started to step backwards, raising his hands in protest and defence. As the short figure got closer, the demi-god sped up and suddenly was falling backwards, his feet tripping other themselves. He crunched to the ground, a jarring pain shooting up his back and arm. Howling in agony, he cradled his sore limb whilst cowering from the fearsome Scot.

"STOP!"

The shout surprised everyone, especially Branden as it was him hollering. In the seconds of silence he bought himself, the young man moved across to Minos' side. At the same time, he tried to make eye contact with the rest of the room, explaining as he did. "Look, I'm not sure I get this issue between you and the Underworld. But I really don't think Minos had anything to do with you not being allowed in." He looked to the judge, who, between his grimacing, nodded solemnly. "The point is, this guy has come to you as a last resort. Things have happened, and he's at real risk of losing his home and everything he holds dear.

"I think on some level you all sort of understand that situation better than I do. You might not be able to help him, or want to, but please would you at least hear him out. I think you were all been great people in life and I would ask you to at least take a few minutes to listen to what he has to say."

The souls exchanged solemn glances between themselves, their heads dropping (with the exception of Boleyn's, as this would have meant hers ended up on the floor). Eventually the well-dressed woman settled the matter,

"Rob, help the god up. Richard, sort out a drink for him and his friend. We might as well listen to what's going on. It's that or break out the scrabble board again, and I don't think I can stand another argument about what year our dictionary was published."

*

Branden had to admit that once you took the confrontation out of the group of souls, they were actually quite civil.

Sat in one of the booths, with a selection of drinks, nuts and crisps (which Richard had fussed over), the whole gathering had become rather amicable. For their part, the souls seemed to have reached an unspoken understanding that they had behaved poorly in their initial dealings with the visitors, and to make amends they had been more than cordial, sitting and listening with rapt attention to Minos' story. As the demi-god brought the group up to speed they nodded (including Boleyn, who sat at the end of the table – her dress too large to squeeze into the booth – holding her head between both hands, hovering it just above the table surface) and even asked the occasional thoughtful question. Frowns appeared on their faces as the judge concluded the story with details of how he'd been fired and the way Lucy had been treated.

Robbie (who Branden had now learnt was Robert the Bruce, proud Scottish hero), curled his few fingers into fists and brought them down on the table with such force it made chess pieces on a nearby board topple over. The pair of Popes who been playing the game (and had refused to acknowledge Minos' presence as they clung to their belief of the one true god, despite the clear, and very present, evidence to the contrary), simply reset the pieces and mumbled between themselves.

"They truly have nay honour, the mortals of this time. It's no' the way of life I fought for," grouched the Scot.

Richard the First (apparently also known as Richard the Lionheart, although Branden hadn't seen anything resembling a brave warrior so far) took a long sip of a freshly prepared strawberry daiquiri, as he added,

"I'm afraid we do see this sort of behaviour all the time. The way mortals are today – honestly, it's all wrong. Think of the delivery drivers that turn up here. They get more and more sullen as the days go by. And how often do they get the order wrong? I mean, when was the last time they actually delivered the seaweed without the powered scallop on top for Frederic, as we keep requesting?"

"Pigs," observed Chopin, as he downed the remains of an expensive looking glass of red wine and followed this with another bout of spluttering. After composing himself, which involved none of his musical talents, the well-presented soul added, "Those ingrates sometimes do not deserve the life they possess." There was a wistful tone in his voice as he finished.

Boleyn indicated Branden with a slightly over-energetic tilt of her head which left her momentarily looking down at the table, before her hands recovered, and addressed Minos,

"Matey boy, here, said you were looking for help – what makes you think any of us can assist you?"

"Well," started the demi-god, as the woman sucked a long chug from a stein of beer, using a long red and white straw that poked precariously over the edge of the glass, "I'm not sure, if I'm honest.

"I didn't know who would be here or if any of you would even listen to me. You have heard me out and I guess I just want to ask if you would consider lending me some support?"

"And what do you want us to do exactly, fella?" Boleyn's cheeks shrank inwards as she sucked hard at the straw, and Branden wondered why the liquid didn't splosh out of the bottom of her head.

"Well, I think attempts at overtly getting into the building are now behind me." Minos paused, appearing to consider the options available to him and a bunch of translucent helpers, "So, I guess I need to go covert now."

"Speak English laddie!" yelled Robbie, the irony of the words not at all lost on Branden.

"Would you help me break into the consultant's office and find the document I need?" offered up Minos, his eyebrows expectantly hitched high up his forehead.

The statement hung in the air like a fart in an elevator. Everyone avoided eye contact and all that could be heard in the background was the deep pppsss of the beer tap as the landlord, a tall non-descript character, poured another drink for one of the holy souls, who definitely would not be offering his services to the deity.

"I must confess that it is an intriguing proposition," put out Chopin, waving his large handkerchief around as he spoke. "But, where is the incentive? Your colleagues have made it quite clear that we will never get into the Underworld. So, what is in it for us?"

"Seriously?" Branden found his voice for the first time since he'd saved Minos from the angry mob. "I thought you were the good guys! I know I don't know much about history, but haven't at least two of you faced down armies in battle? Aren't you some kind of knights – don't you have to help out because of some sort of moral obligation?"

Chopin blew out his cheeks,

"Well, young man, that's not really how it works. In truth while Robbie may be a fierce foe – he is rather out of practice these days..."

"I'm as spry as a spaniel!" shot back the Scot, looking like he might punch something other than the table this time.

"And, if truth be told and we put all our cards on the table, I was a lot more focused on military strategy than actual fighting," interrupted Richard. "Funny story really – everyone thinks the 'Lionheart' nickname comes from my bravery in battle, when really it was my signature dish. Fried with a little parsley and onions – delightful!"

"Och aye, we all know the tale. We canna remember a time we didna know it!" grumbled Robbie, as he rolled his eyes and pulled at his thick beard, getting the couple of fingers he did have matted in it. Chopin took this as his cue to resume his point,

"And, of course, others of us are not fighters. Although we all know Anne has a mean right hook on her."

"I told you chaps getting a punching bag was a bad idea." The woman followed this matter-of-fact-statement with a loud belch. The composer lifted his nose slightly, as he continued,

"Anyway – the point I am trying to make is that while we are a talented bunch, we have spent decades cooped up in places like this. The only entertainment we get is sharing stories – and those are very tired now – alongside the small selection of boardgames that we have not lost pieces for, melted or destroyed in a furious rage…" He glanced at Robbie, who swigged from his mug of beer and looked the other way. "Truthfully, we were put in this situation through no fault of our own. We have suffered and the only way we are going to consider lifting a finger is if we get something in return."

Minos cut in, concern ringing through his words,

"And it's been made very clear to you that the policy was the policy and there is no changing that. It just can't be done. If Hades could, he would – simple as. My boss has always wanted more souls in the Underworld – he is definitely pi…" he was about to use a very bad word and caught himself, as he recalled Chopin's delicate ears, "…unhappy that you were excluded from the kingdom. But he can't change that."

No one spoke and the silence finally pushed Branden into asking,

"Is there anything else we can offer?"

The group exchanged looks,

"Would you give us but the briefest of moments?" queried Chopin, as he fought down another wheeze. Minos and Branden nodded and slipped out of the booth, the youngster bringing the rest of his fizzy drink with him as they went. The pair stood at a polite distance, as the souls drew close, hectic whispering and low-toned mumbling running through the tight knit gang.

Branden turned momentarily to his friend, overtaken by the question he felt he had to ask,

"Minos, are all souls...well...errr...a little weird?"

Minos looked a bit confused and glanced at the quartet, as Branden added, "You know – missing heads, fingers, toes..."

"Oh – that! No – a soul initially looks like it did at the moment of death but that is fixed as they enter the Underworld. Each of those souls still bear the scars of their fate – be it something unseen like a heart attack, or more serious like tuberculous, leprosy or beheading."

As Branden slurped at his drink, Minos' words registered on him. He stopped, looked at his glass and decided to deposit it back on the bar. A silence settled in on the pair, as the young man chose not to ask anything else.

The souls continued to mutter between themselves, and suddenly the young man realised he was about ready to give up. When he'd seen the dead characters, he'd expected them to leap at the chance to come to the rescue. To ride into battle (metaphorically speaking) one more time. Sadly, the band of misfits they'd found seemed more worried about their own interest than doing something productive.

The young man tried to rouse himself as he wondered if he'd made a mistake offering to help Minos. He'd wanted to be useful, to achieve something worthwhile but was now concerned that this was just another bad choice, like all of his short-lived hobbies. He hoped not – he liked the demi-god and really did want to help the judge get his life back.

Finally, the souls lent away from each other and signalled the pair to return.

Minos and Branden slipped back into the high-backed seats of the booth, holding their breaths. Branden sensed that for the judge this was literally the last resort. He knew how Minos had struggled with the fact he had failed individually. Branden was certain they wouldn't be in the pub if there was any other option.

A negative response from the souls would leave Minos with nowhere to go and nothing to do.

Chopin cleared his throat with a very delicate noise. Then, obviously annoyed by the stalling, Boleyn leapt in, lifting her head up to look Minos in the eyes.

"We've considered what you want and, as a one-off fella, we are willing to help you. This is, of course, all subject to you agreeing to our demands."

Minos wearily went over old ground,

"Now, I have already said that I can't get you into the Underworld. It's just not possible. And neither Hades, nor anyone else, can change that."

Boleyn's body swayed as she shook her head from side to side.

"We understand that score – although still feel that there should be something that could be done – but what we're looking for is something to make our stay here much more palatable."

Minos looked confused as the group now chipped in,

"A keyboard, including a synthesizer," stated Chopin.

"A vegetable spiraliser, plus one of those dinky rice steamers, would be divine. Also, a wok and a subscription to one of those fresh vegetable delivery services," chimed in Richard, as Robbie stirred to life,

"A whole new set of games – we want the classics, plus all the new ones, laddie. I hear talk about a game where you recognise logos. That would be bonnie!"

Richard picked up the thread again, "If it's not too much trouble, we would also like a plasma tv and unlimited tv channels. One of those on-demand boxes type jobbies…"

"…But dinna you think of stiffin' us with Freeview!" growled the Scot, as he drummed his few fingers on the table.

"Plus reading material, including plenty of detective novels, and a few bibles for the religious types," concluded Chopin, as he held up his hand to cover his mouth, sniffed a bit and then shook off the false alarm.

Branden watched with concern as Minos weighed up how much his job and home was worth to him. He pulled at the judge's sleeve, moving closer.

"You can't really be thinking about agreeing to all that can you?" he hissed urgently.

"What choice do I have?" sighed Minos. "If I'm serious about saving my job, I guess I've got to give this four what they want." His words made him stop and the judge glanced at Boleyn, who hadn't expressed any demands yet. The woman merely shrugged, her shoulders rising far above her dismembered head,

"I'm just happy to have the chance to get out and kick some butt," she stated. "Although, I can't help but feel I'd make a more valued contribution with some new threads. After all mate – everyone knows you have to dress for success."

Minos looked from the soul to Branden, thought for a moment and then steeled himself,

"Alright – write down everything you want, within reason," the last words were added as if the judge thought that might rein the group in. "You can have half whatever the result of our efforts, and the rest if we get what I need."

Branden could see clearly that the demi-god knew he was taking a gamble. If they failed the judge would have a hefty debt he'd have to pay off. The demi-god closed his eyes for just a second, and the youngster could almost sense imaginary dice striking the table.

In the end, he knew it didn't matter – Minos had to try.

Oblivious to the inner concerns of the mortal and demi-god, grins were exchanged between the souls and a wave of excitement washed over everyone. Minos tried to force a smile, "Now, whose up for robbing an office block?"

Despite the requests being made of the demi-god, one slightly see-through hand stayed sheepishly down, with nothing more than an apologetic shrug and an excuse.

Chapter 18

It was an extremely odd sight.

Under the gaze of the tall building, three souls (only two of which had heads on their shoulders), one demi-god and a young lad tried to keep to the shadows as they crossed the empty plaza. Although it was the middle of the night a lot of the concrete ground was lit by free standing lamps. Against the light sources, the harsh grey of the pavement contrasted with the green foliage that had been added in tubs and soiled areas, creating the impression of wilderness soothingly sprouting up from the ground.

The group moved in ways which matched the level of effort they had put into their outfits. Minos, kitted out in actual green patterned material (another of Mr Richard's fancy dress leftovers) with a heavy black rucksack thrown over his shoulder, hugged the foliage and moved cautiously between the shadows. He was followed, to a lesser extent, by Branden, dressed in his usual black minus any metal adornments, and Chopin who had pulled his dark jacket around him. Behind the trio, Boleyn was less bothered by her movement but had opted to ditch her bulging dress in favour of tight black leather trousers and a navy-blue tank top (no one should been seen dead in matching colours, she had advised the others), her head tucked securely under her arm. At the rear came Robbie, who had made no effort to change his clothes and crashed this way and that on his toe-light feet.

If there had been anyone around to see the odd collection, and their attempts at being stealthy as they trampled across the concrete jungle, they may well have sworn of alcohol for the rest of their lives.

One by one each of the group reached the edge of the cover and looked out on the ten-metre expanse of flat, open ground leading to the brilliantly bright reception. Minos, still in a crouch that was starting to make his aged knees ache, pulled out reams of paper from his backpack and consulted the fat collection.

Scribbled across the sheets were instructions, suggestions and crude building plans, compiled by Richard the Lionheart. It turned out that the soul's statement about not being a fighter was more accurate than anyone had believed. Whilst he had been content to pull together a dossier of useful information using Branden's phone, he had been set in his refusal to join the raid. In the end the soul had thrown such a hissy fit, even threatening not to make them mugs of hot chocolate when they returned, that Minos had given in and accepted they were a party of five.

"Although only four of us are going in," the judge stated out loud, receiving odd looks from the others. Minos shook his head quickly, refocusing on what he needed to say, and gestured for everyone to gather around him. "Look, I appreciate everything you're all doing – there is great risk here and I'm sure no one wants to be caught by some over enthusiastic security guard. There is no telling what they would do to any of us..." he took a breath, knowing he was about to become very unpopular, "...especially to Branden. This mission could end in this fine young companion going to jail, ruining the next few years of his life. It's for that reason I've decided he's going to be the look out."

"No way!" protested the goth, with such a crushed look on his face Minos wondered if he'd inadvertently just bumped off the boy's first pet. "I'm coming in with you. You can't leave me behind."

Minos looked deeply into the youngster's eyes, as he said with sincerity,

"Not this time. I'm sure you've got great adventures in your future and I'm not going to see you pay any price if we fail. I've got to go in and this lot have quite literally sold their souls," The corners of Branden's mouth tugged slightly upwards at the words, but the rest of him was more crest fallen than a peacock suffering from a serve bout of impotence. "I know it's hard, and I do appreciate everything you've done so far, but I'm doing this in your best interests. Besides, I want to make sure these three earn their rewards."

To Minos' relief the souls chose not to protest this point on Branden's behalf. Collectively they appeared to understand what the demi-god was doing and were doing their best not to watch the scene unfold.

The matter settled, the judge leant down and fished in his rucksack before pulling out a plastic packet he had found when he was rifling through Mr Robert's wardrobes. The demi-god ripped apart the wrapper and handed a cheap walkie talkie to the mortal. "If you see or hear anything out of the ordinary, call us and then get out of here. Understand me?"

Branden, looking like he didn't trust his voice in front of the others, took the radio and nodded solemnly. Minos clapped him reassuringly on the shoulder, trying not to let his own emotions show too much. He really liked the kid and understood how rough his decision was. But he also knew it was for the best.

Pulling himself together, the demi-god turned to the souls, and commanded, "Come on you lot – we've got a document to steal!"

*

With the forlorn silhouette of Branden disappearing into the darkness, Minos and his team scampered (and wobbled, in Robbie's case) up to the front of the building. The light from the immense welcome area was almost blinding.

Peering in, his eyes watering from what Minos tried to convince himself was the dazzling scene before him, the demi-god took reassurance from being unable to spot any of the security guards Richard's intel suggested would be on patrol. The judge pressed his hand against the cool glass, trying to work out how they could break through it without making too much racket. He conceded that he maybe should have considered this before they gave up their cover, but the judge knew he couldn't have looked at Branden's depressed expression any longer.

As the phrase 'breaking and entering' tracked its way across Minos' mind, a wild war cry emanated from Robbie and the stout soul launched himself against the nearest window. The warrior bounced off the toughened glass with a thud and landed on his backside.

"Bugger," was all the Scot could manage as he rubbed a finger along the bridge of his nose. While Minos helped the soul back onto his feet, Chopin wheezed slightly before he ran his hand over the metal frame which fixed each window pane in place.

"Perhaps, Minos, you have brought some form of tool which would allow us to more delicately gain entry?" he mused.

"Alternatively, we could just use the normal way in, guys" called Boleyn's voice as her body pushed its way through the revolving door. The circular entrance clanked a few times behind the woman as the men followed, shared embarrassment apparent on their faces.

Inside the building the lighting felt even brighter and somewhere in the distance a radio was playing a pop song, that seemed vaguely familiar to Minos. The judge blinked a few times as he tried to identify where the noise was coming from.

Another great shout suddenly rang out from Robbie as a uniformed mortal, who looked like he'd just woken up, poked his head up from behind the reception desk. The man's perplexed expression turned to panic as Boleyn sprinted and leapt across the sleek counter, using one arm to vault the surface, while the other gripped tightly around her face. She crashed body first into the mortal and they collapsed out of sight with a loud pair of grunts.

The next few seconds felt like hours before the woman's head was hoisted high by one of her slender hands. "One down," she stated at a slight angle.

"Quite literally," beamed Chopin as he helped Boleyn tuck the man underneath the desk.

Minos once more consulted Richard's comprehensive bible taking in the outlined suggestions for the best routes to follow. *Shame*, the demi-god thought, *that it didn't include the helpful tip that the front door was unlocked*. The sound of plastic wheels clanging on metal made the demi-god turn.

Robbie was beaming to himself as he roughly wedged the guard's swivel chair into the revolving door, fixing it into position. In response to the strange looks from his companions, the Scot proudly stated,

"There's nay chance of reinforcements gettin' in now."

"I really do think that you have watched one too many films, my dear friend," drooled Chopin, choking back a slight splutter.

"That's as maybe laddie, but I'm no' takin' any chances."

Minos wistfully looked out on the black expanse beyond the glass walls. He couldn't spot Branden and felt oddly disconnected now that the entrance was blocked. He hefted the rucksack higher on his shoulder and considered using the walkie talkie. With a shake of his head, the judge reminded himself that the young man was in the safest place.

With that the demi-god turned his attention to their next move,

"According to the plans that Richard drew up, the senior managers are stationed on the upper three floors. Let's head up and see what we can find. And everyone please try to keep quiet – just in case. We don't want to attract attention to ourselves." He glanced towards the desk, "Well, any more than we have to."

Outside, hidden in one of the large soiled areas with plants rustling up around him, Branden's awe at the way Boleyn had taken down the security guard was now being replaced with envy as the foursome disappeared into the depths of Schneider, Schneider & Patterson.

It isn't fair.

I should have been allowed to see this through with all of them.

The youngster's frustration at being left behind got the better of him and he kicked at the decorative gravel around his feet. The small pebbles shot out, flying through the air and leaving a small cloud of dust behind. "Caution be damned," he muttered to himself.

He screwed up his face and mocked the judge, "'I'm doing this in your best interests' – stupid old god."

Branden still couldn't believe he'd been left out of the best part of the whole adventure. He had desperately wanted to be involved in breaking into the building – it was so cool (despite the fact the group had tamely just walked through the door)!

And more than anything else Branden wanted the deity to remember exactly who had got him through the final part of his journey. "But, no," he whined, "I'm stuck out here on the sidelines."

Annoyance got the better of him and he struck the gravel much harder. More pebbles flew out and away.

"Owwww – hey! Watch what you're doing."

The expletive that dropped out of Branden's mouth was quite rude and very loud as he stared into the face that was suddenly only inches from his own. The features that confronted the youngster belonged to a figure that he didn't recognise but was known to Minos.

*

The lift that Minos had once ridden with Lucy, when he'd been offered his short-lived work experience, pinged as it arrived on the ground floor. To everyone's relief no one stepped out of it.

Despite the late hour, and lack of apparent activity in the building, the lift's doors still took an eternity before they decided to close. And that was even with the ferocity of one of Robbie's digits jabbing repeatedly at the little button set into the control panel.

When the two pieces of metal finally did grind together, the lift rocked and began its slow ascent. The group all fell quiet, uncomfortably waiting as the box slowly dragged itself up the inside of the building. Chopin, who, just for a change, seemed to have a clear throat, looked down at his shoes, while Boleyn chewed at the nails on the hand that wasn't holding her head, and Robbie let his eyes dart this way and that. They all listened to the delicate trickle of music that drifted out of the speakers secreted somewhere in the ceiling. With nothing better to do, and without making eye contact, Minos queried out loud,

"Any plans for the weekend?"

It was with great relief that they finally disgorged themselves on the forty eighth floor. Fluorescent lighting blinked on over their heads, as it sensed their arrival, and revealed no mortals in the long space. Collectively the foursome spread out through rows of desks, finding no evidence of anything that would support them in their hunt.

"Guys, it appears there's something of a very strict attitude about having tidy desks before you go home." Boleyn did not seem amused as she held her face overhead (well, over her shoulders) to scan the worktops.

"Tidy desks?" grunted Robbie as he delicately lifted up a white fluffy unicorn from one of the desks. Sheer disgust was plastered across the soul's face as the couple of fingers he did have squeezed the creature's leg and he held it out at arm's length, "These mortals waste a lot of time and money on pointless knick-knacks."

"I have to disagree profusely" said Chopin, appearing from a point over by the windows with an oversized pencil in one hand and a multi-coloured stress ball in the other, "I quite like a lot of these items. Is it too late to re-negotiate the terms of our agreement?" He squeezed the ball tightly, grinning as the plastic let out a soft puff.

"Do you lot think we could focus on the matter at hand?" Minos was becoming increasingly concerned that the souls were of little help now that they were inside the building.

The group continued forward, checking through the banks of workspaces, still finding no hint of what they sought. They moved up the stairs at the end of the room and were presented with more desks to scour.

As they drew close to the end of that floor, Minos had to wonder if once more he had bitten off more than he could chew. "One piece of paper, that's all we need," he grumbled, feeling his hope fading.

"Startin' to look impossible to find it, if you ask me." Robbie did not look happy, but a smile pulled at the edges of his mouth as he added, "Unless, of course, you want me to start pullin' filin' cabinets apart?" Minos could only begin to imagine the carnage that would ensue if he agreed to that request. Before anyone could say 'angry Scot' he was sure the office would be white with strewn paper.

"That will take too long to clear up," he muttered, as he referred back to Richard's pile of notes and found little to help him. "We just need to track down where they keep the specific files relating to the Underworld."

"Maybe, fellas..." called Boleyn, "...if we knew who was working on which project, we could narrow it down." She was holding her face in front of a large whiteboard with words scribbled across it.

Minos shrugged at her, despair starting to overtake him,

"I can't see us working that out. I can't even remember the names of the mortals I met when I was down there."

"Sparkes and Branaghan?" ventured Boleyn.

The familiarity of the names hit Minos smack between the eyes. "I'll take your silence as confirmation I've read this right, matey." Boleyn started running her head down the board, reading as she went. "So, they are being assisted in the office by Adams and Chadwell. And, it seems, keeping documents in Records File Purple."

"What's that meant to mean?" queried the demi-god, looking around him as if the answer would magically present itself.

"I could not possibly imagine I know, but I have found Chadwell's desk. She – I am assuming here – has some lovely glittery letters spelling out her surname...oh my word – look at this." Chopin reappeared a few rows away, shaking a cheap bauble and watching with glee as white powder whirled around the insides. He was so fascinated with the trinket that when another cough welled up inside him, he didn't even bother covering his mouth.

"That doesna help us," grouched Robbie, as they all scurried to join the composer.

A wide range of items that must have held some sort of sentimental value to the mortal were scattered across the surface of the desk and the team poured over everything, looking for any clue that pointed towards their goal. They even let Robbie launch himself below the desk to see what he could find in the darker recesses.

The whirlwind that surrounded Chadwell's place of work quickly dissipated, with nothing helpful forthcoming. Wearily, Minos and Chopin slumped into nearby swivel chairs, while Boleyn perched on the desk's flat top, letting her legs bend up against Chadwell's seat, her head balanced across her knees.

"This is truly useless," moaned the demi-god, his hope of having any level of success that night fading to nothing. For a moment he once more wondered if he should have left Branden outside. Maybe the youngster would have spotted something they hadn't. Perhaps the young man could have deciphered 'Records File Purple'. Had Minos blown their chance of succeeding, this time by being too cautious?

"Dinna go givin' up just yet…" Robbie's head reappeared from underneath the desk. His eyes glinted, as he looked in both directions and then crawled along the floor, nose to the ground, with a fancy stiletto gripped between his fingers.

"I think it is safe to say that he has finally lost it. Did we have a pool on when it would happen? I am certain I said sometime around now, if we did," Chopin quipped as they watched the Scot wriggle off on all fours. He reached the end of the bank of desks, glanced one way then the other, before thrusting the shoe aloft.

"Although it only leaves a wee indentation in the floor it's quite a distinct mark, this heel," was all the soul added as he scuttled down the office, looking like a dog seeking a treat. Shrugging between themselves, and otherwise out of options, the others followed.

The tracks brought the Scot to repeated dead ends, stopping at the kitchen, stationary cupboard and ladies' toilets. Despite the groans of his colleagues, the soul continued to scour the floor until he eventually followed the trail away from the main work space, down corridors created between meeting rooms, and ended up in front of a closed door, blandly marked 'Purple' in tiny black letters (rather missing a trick, Minos felt).

"I canna help but think I've just earned those boardgames," smirked Robbie, as he got to his odd feet.

"Not yet," observed Minos pointing at the locking mechanism on the door. To everyone' dismay a numbered keypad kept the door in place, the red bulb on top of the mechanism glaring as fiercely as a cyclops trying to pick a pair of glasses at the opticians.

"Well that's us screwed, boys. There must be thousands of combinations! And it looks like that lock is a bit too sturdy for us to smash our way through."

"Unless we use Robbie as a battering ram," the non-existent enthusiasm in Minos' deadpan comment demonstrated how close, but truly far away, he felt as he sized up the imposing barrier. He threw his hands up in sheer desperation. "It's a one in a million guess. We'd be here for days trying to go through all the possible options. We don't even know how many numbers we need."

Knuckles cracked behind the demi-god, reminiscent of the sound the trolls made when they accidentally stepped on a soul's neck.

"Stand back dear fellows, I think I have this one." Chopin stepped past the others, wiggling long fingers. He stared down at the inert adversary, ignoring the slight wheeze that pushed up from his chest. "Most mortals can only successfully recall three or four digits with ease, therefore we shall assume the latter. Now, there will be a few obvious options, so let us start with those." He bashed at the button numbered 'one' four times in quick succession. He elicited no response from the door and its red protector, so tried a quartet of taps on the 'zero'. Then the soul punched the numbers from 'one' to 'four'. "Hmmm – tricky chap here."

"Since when do you know how to crack codes, piano man?" asked Boleyn, eyeing up the composer with surprise, as she shifted her head from one side of her body to the other. Chopin looked genuinely hurt, clutching his hand to his chest,

"My dear. You and the others may enjoy frittering away all of your after-lives in the pursuit of working out who 'did it' in which room, but some of us like to occasionally develop our minds. I have spent an inordinate amount of time over the years familiarising myself with any volume or publication which helps to expand my understanding of the world around us. I am, after all, not just a pretty face." He continued as Robbie stuck out his tongue at the last comment. "I recall an extremely interesting article in one such magazine which outlined the different approaches and techniques towards this exact type of scenario. Now that we have exhausted the most obvious options, we can move onto some of the more straight forward choices. Minos, does our friend's fact file include a demographic break down of the security guards, or perhaps the birthday of the most senior member of their team? We can try four digit combinations of dates and work from there."

"Or just type in 8068."

The whole group spun and Minos started as he stared into the eyes of someone he had never expected to see again, especially not on the forty ninth floor of the office, and at this time on a Friday night.

Chapter 19

Hades desperately wished that he had turned around and gone home, rather than joining the late evening Turnaround Meeting.

How, he wondered, *have I allowed this to be organised for such an ungodly hour, and on a Friday night, no less?* The Underworld's ruler stared around at his team and couldn't help but notice his own exhaustion reflected in the faces of each and every one of them.

The only person in the boardroom who was bounding with energy was Sparkes. The freshly appointed Improvement and Strategy Director (how Hades had agreed to that, he still wasn't sure) was continuing to enthuse about the many graphs she was showing on the brand new 'smart-screen' (the god had given up trying to understand what made it so clever – as far as he could tell the damn thing couldn't make a cup of coffee, which is what any vaguely intelligent person would have known to offer Hades at that moment). All the meeting rooms had been fitted out with new gadgets and gizmos as part of a package of deals done with the stream of suppliers that had trotted in and out of the kingdom during the recent weeks. How it all worked, and whether a demon could actually operate any of the devices, was still to be seen.

Hades adjusted his tie slightly and then stifled a yawn behind his massive palm, as he turned his attention away from another set of RAG updates (standing for Red, Amber, Green – although if he had to sit through many more briefings like this one, he had a feeling he might lose his own). The god looked over at his beautiful wife, who was barely visible amidst the humongous volumes of operational specifications and instruction manuals that had become constant companions to her. Hades once more felt saddened at the crow's feet and worry lines that had appeared, and deepened, since he'd had to expand the demi-goddess' role to include IT.

Hades zoned back into the meeting, as Sparkes angrily rounded on Thantanos for not having completed all the workforce reviews. The complexion of the pale figure had faded further than Hades ever thought possible, making the slashes of red that zig zagged his face stand out like lipstick on an iceberg. Hades could only assume that 'negotiations' about the new work rota for the Kers, part of Thantanos' expanded responsibilities, had not gone well.

"It's not my fault," moaned the insipid figure, reciting what was quickly becoming his new catchphrase, "We're talking about thousands of demons having to coral their team into structured evaluations. It takes time..."

"Enough excuses," growled Sparkes. "This needs to be sorted. You have had more than sufficient resources to get this work done."

"If I could just remind you that when we started this process, I clearly referred to section 203, paragraph 14 of the..." the demi-god didn't get any further as Sparkes smashed her hand down hard on the granite table,

"I swear to god, Thantanos," no one stirred at the poor choice of terminology (they were all well past the point of making the joke about the pun being intended), "If you keep quoting the rule book at me, I will not be responsible for my actions. There is a whole host of work that needs to follow those reviews and right now you're being a blocker, aren't you?"

The demi-god practically whimpered in response, whilst Sparkes shifted her position to stand that little bit closer to Hades. "Just sort it!" The 'or else' radiated from the mortal's posture and Thantanos pathetically nodded his consent.

Without any further comment, Sparkes returned to her new toy and moved on to the next slide, which covered operational capability, prompting her to turn her ire on Rhadamanthus. The usually immaculate demi-god looked like he had slept rough for the last few decades. Hades, though mildly disturbed by his underlining's appearance, was understanding, given the number of policies that had been rewritten recently. By the god's reckoning, Rhadamanthus was currently dealing with more changes in the average day than had been enacted across the whole of the Underworld's long history.

As a repeat of the scene with Thantanos played out (only Rhadamanthus was much more apologetic than his colleague), Hades could feel the tendrils of sleep trying to wrap around his mind. He wasn't surprised – he'd been doing so many extra hours himself recently he was quite literally burning the candle at both ends (mainly to give him enough light to keep working by). The god allowed himself a few heavy blinks, knowing that he could have gladly let each one last for the rest of the night. Knowing he wasn't setting a good example, he tried to refocus on

Sparkes' enthusiastic summing up (her chewing out of Rhadamanthus had concluded without the need for the mortal to stand by Hades).

"All in all, the numbers are continuing on an upwards trajectory. Turnover is up by over 12% already, while costs are 7% lower. I can safely predict that the first set of quarterly bonuses for the senior team will be significant." Hades thought he detected Thantanos mumble something like 'shame, we won't have any time to spend it' but it could have just been a nasty tinkle in the back of the demi-god's throat and the projections of the god's own feelings.

As Rhadamanthus started his update on the latest new rules and punishments, ineffectively using the smart-screen, to the amusement of Sparkes, Hades let his mind drift back to earlier in the day, when the god had taken a short stroll through the palace grounds.

At the time, he hadn't been proud of the fact he'd had to trick Gronix, his newly appointed Executive Assistant, into thinking he was having a catch up with Melinda, but he'd started to learn that was the only way to guarantee himself the ability to slip away from the spikey pain-in-the-backside.

During the god's stroll the mist, which was particularly conducive to hiding from assistants but much less for surveying a kingdom, had thickened. The former warrior had strained at his senses, trying to figure out what was bugging him about his realm. Moments had ticked by as he attempted to cut through the gloom, whilst enjoying the feeling of the moist blades of grass tickling the top of his ankles. Just as the god was about to give up, his thoughts had finally clicked together to reveal the answer.

Hades had finally realised that the noise of his operation was off.

When the god had strained his ears, he had suddenly found the ambient noise was different, almost disturbing. The background hustle and bustle, that all of the gods, demons and souls had become so familiar with, had gone. The ruler could barely detect any screams of agony or pain. There was no longer grief or retribution hanging around the palace. Instead a bland rustle of chatter permeated the fog. Hades sensed unsettled souls, sad with their lot, but not in the way that punished them for the consequences of their misdeeds on Earth. All the god picked up on was the disquiet that came from facing an eternity of trying to help people deal with their software issues or how to fill in document EF42 to apply for a tax refund (a commonly misrepresented item of paperwork, Hades had learnt, as no one ever got money back from the Inland Revenue).

The god couldn't have comprehended that what he was hearing was efficient monotony. Instead his senses reported sadness and general futility, making him wonder if his once great kingdom was now going to waste.

Hades hadn't got into the business of death by choice (and if he'd had the option, he really would have liked to have ruled the oceans) but, once he'd got the swing of things, the god had had a new lease of life. Sadly, it didn't feel like he was in the punishment business anymore. The organisation had already become something that felt alien to him.

Standing on the damp ground, the god had recognised in himself a sense of defeat that he had never experienced before. It had been that sense of apathy that he had brought into the boardroom and which he still could not shake.

Rubbing at his brow, the god once again found his brain churning over the question, *Is this really all worth it*?

The ruler knew that it was important to keep the business going, or order to ensure death existed for the mortals, but was all this really worth it?

While Hades had been reflecting, Sparkes had once more been grilling Rhadamanthus. Finally satisfied that she was going to get the results she needed, the mortal was wrapping up the meeting. With a clap of her hands she dismissed the team, who responded filing out like naughty school children, heads down, insults muttered under their breaths.

Much to Hades' irritation, Sparkes moved forward, intercepting him before he could consider escaping. He slumped heavily back into his chair, trying to imagine what issue the mortal had now or which member of his team she had taken offence with. The god tried to shoot a pleading expression at Melinda, but she had already made her escape, as best as she could while weighed down with the enormous weight of manuals.

To Hades' surprise, as soon as the room was empty, the mortal grinned warmly at him. The god found it very disconcerting – reminiscent of the way a casino croupier shows their teeth to a gambler when they've spread their life savings across all the red and black numbers before the roulette ball lands in the little green section.

"That went very well," Sparkes reported. Hades wondered if she'd been in the same meeting as him. His team appeared broken by the woman's iron fist. Not even the god was sure he could stand up to her now. "I think it's time you and I took this to the next level."

Hades sat up in horror, suddenly revived from his sleepy stupor,

"Miss Sparkes, I can assure you I am a married man and have no interest in you."

Sparkes looked the mighty god up and down before shaking her head sadly,

"Hades, I want you to focus on work and understand what I'm saying." He couldn't put his finger on it, but somehow her response made him feel like he'd just suggested an affair. "Everything is going so well with the business, it's time to move us to the next stage of my plan. Floating the company on the stock market."

Hades could only blink, unsure what any of those words meant when put together in that manner.

"Is that good?"

"Very! We'll help you become a limited company and bring in even more external investment. That will provide us with the platform to take this operation further than your wildest dreams."

"But don't those people who put money in want something in return?"

"Yes – dividends. And we will be able to pay them handsomely. Of course, there's a few extra bits and pieces to do. We'd have to hold annual general meetings, report on our progress publicly, change your title into more of a Chief Executive type of wording, appoint a Managing Director, add in some non-executive board members. Simple bits and pieces. Nothing major. You've got my assistance for the coming weeks and it will be child's play."

Hades felt uncertainty once more rising up inside him.

More change? Is she crazy? his tired brain protested. He wasn't sure he'd got used to the differences already in place, let alone having the energy to start thinking about more. Out loud he tried to be more diplomatic,

"It's just, I'm not sure. We've always been quite an isolated bunch here. I know customers and suppliers coming in is one thing but I don't think having others involved in the day to day running of the place is wise. Perhaps I should sleep on it." His attempt to duck the suggestion was immediately rebuffed.

"Hades, come on. You've adapted with ease to having us here. It's both right, and timely, for a god of your stature to have an organisation which really reflects his status. You'll be the figurehead of one of the most profitable empires in history. We'll continue to focus your efforts on meeting with other business leaders, convincing them of the good you can do for their companies."

"I'm just not sure I have it in me..." Hades practically pleaded his point, and tried to ignore the tiny voice that quietly whispered,

What have you become?

"I get that you're run down – it's not easy going through restructures like this, but trust me, you've done much better than you think. What's wearing you down is the difficulty of trying to balance the stakeholder meetings with your duties managing everything else. With a properly setup board and some new expertise injected in, you'll have a support team that can take more of the burden on while we set you out as a pioneer of industry. Imagine it – you'll be on the front of magazines, speaking at corporate events! That's big money – and it's paid directly to you. And then there's the fancy lunches, dinners and ceremonies you'll get invited to. They will be truly amazing and so befitting of you."

As he took in the words, Hades brightened, surprisingly reenergised by the chance to show off what he and the Underworld were really made off.

That will show Zeus and Poseidon! the god smirked.

The pair would be so jealous when they heard about how successful he had become. And less work would mean he could finally spend more time with Melinda. Plus, some extra cash would come in very handy when they did have a little one.

Things might not be the same as they used to be, Hades told himself, *but maybe what I heard in the garden earlier is success. Perhaps, this is what it really feels like!*

Without giving it too much more thought, the god nodded his ascent.

Sparkes' eyes gleamed,

"I'll get the paperwork drawn up for the stock market and as soon as you sign it, we can move everything forward."

Little did Hades realise he'd just consented to let Sparkes start the final phase of the instructions she'd been provided with before she had arrived in the Underworld.

Chapter 20

The last time Minos had seen the blue eyes that he was now staring into, they had been fighting back tears. He spluttered out the name of the mortal he'd let down,

"Lucy..."

The demi-god couldn't manage any more than that. Guilt and confusion whirled around his brain. Questions rattled this way and that, but he couldn't grasp onto them.

For her part, the HR Assistant just sent a large smile straight at the judge. Her blonde hair was loosely pulled back, and in the bright light of the office small strands shone around her face, making her look angelic. Her professional work outfit was gone, replaced by a set of exercise trousers, and a loose-fitting top. As Minos took in the vision of loveliness, Branden's head suddenly appeared from behind her.

"Hi Minos! Hey souls!" he waved cheerily. "Look who I bumped into!" Confusion reigned on the semi-transparent faces and it was Robbie who first expressed what was on all their minds,

"Are you no' goin' to introduce us to this bonnie lass?"

Around the buzz of his emotions, Minos still couldn't find any words. As the demi-god's mouth flapped, Branden stepped forward to explain who everyone was. Lucy shook hands and let out a long, low whistle.

"They really are just a bit see-through, exactly like you said Branden." Her comment was followed by a small yelp, as both Robbie and Boleyn glared at her, jaws tightening as they readied retorts to this untactful remark. "Oh my word! I shouldn't have said that, should I? That was so rude. I am soooo sorry. And can I just say thank you for everything you did in life. Well, not that I know much about you in great detail, but I did study your music at school. It's great, not that I can play much." She nodded towards Chopin, who looked giddy with delight, and bowed stiffly,

"Thank you, madam. It is a true honour to meet a fan, especially as most of mine only came out of the woodwork after my death!" he coughed faintly, as if to underline his point, "Can you imagine how hard it is to only be appreciated after you have passed on? Especially worse when you are in my situation and have to watch all the acclaim from afar."

"That must have been terrible. For all of you. Not having the chance to truly rest. Stuck in some type of limbo. Like the Bermuda Triangle. I think. I mean, I've never been there myself but you hear of all these ships and planes disappearing and you think they must be stuck somewhere between our world and the next. That must be just awful."

Minos finally broke out of his mental funk and grinned broadly. He hadn't realised quite how much he'd missed Lucy until his ears were once again ringing with her particular brand of waffle. The demi-god could have stood there and listened to the mortal's ramblings all night, but he was conscious that he still didn't know where she had come from, and why Branden was with her.

"How did you two meet?" he cut in.

"Well, that's a story," chimed Lucy. "I'd been at the gym when I remembered a few things I hadn't done. My workload has been non-stop ever since Sally set about trying to get me to quit. She decided I wasn't up to the job but wanted me to leave of my own accord. Apparently that's better for her..." the girl trailed off, her cheeks suddenly flushing red. Sensing the woman's discomfort, Branden picked up the thread.

"Lucy spotted me as she was arriving and thought I was stalking her or something. Pfffttt!" The noise wasn't meant to be rude but the look on Lucy's face would have broken a small puppy's heart. Branden, realising his accidental rudeness, tried to backpedal. "Not to say that you're not attractive and that I...err...wouldn't stalk you. I mean I would, but it's kind of against the law, so I wouldn't..."

"If someone doesna tell me what's goin' on soon, I'm a goin' start breakin' thin's!" Robbie practically hollered as he gnashed his teeth together. Branden shook himself out of his awkwardness and resumed,

"Well, when Lucy got close, she saw me watching you all and, of course, recognised Minos."

"I just had a feeling you'd be back in my life one day Marvin, I mean Minos. Although I hadn't imagined it would be in the 'breaking into my office' type of way. But when I saw you sneaking around reception, I said to myself that I had to find out what you were up too. I pounced on Branden and he was so surprised to find out I knew you, he told me everything. He tried to radio you but that toy you gave him has no range on it whatsoever," Branden shook the plastic walkie-talkie at Minos, his eyebrows hiked high, as the hint of a smile pulled at his lips, "So we used my pass to get in the back door of the office – some idiot had blocked the main one – and we took the service lift up here." No one choose to admit that the person responsible for obstructing the entrance was stood just a few feet away from Lucy. "And the rest is history." It was at this point the woman's voice changed as she spoke directly to the demi-god. "Why didn't you say something when we talked? I would have understood. I could have helped."

Minos, conscious that he couldn't really recall having the opportunity to say much when he'd been with the mortal, shrugged slightly,

"I guess I just didn't think you would understand. It all sounds a bit extreme."

Lucy reached out and gripped the demi-god's arm, squeezing a lot tighter than he thought she could have.

"I would have listened, if nothing else." The look they shared felt like it defied the age gap and distance between their lives. Minos felt a bit gooey-eyed as he met the warm expression on the woman's face. Behind them, Boleyn loudly cleared the throat that was a distance away from her mouth.

"While this might all be great for you folks, but can we get on? I don't mind a bit of backside kicking, if it's needed, but I think the sooner we're sorted and out of here the better."

Lucy nodded at Minos, before confidently moving past him and keying in the door's four-digit code. She pushed through the entrance to reveal stacks of filing cabinets. The others followed, watching in awe as the girl consulted a list on the wall and then manoeuvred over to a specific metal guardian. She let her finger pass down the drawers before selecting one. A quick rifle through folders and she pulled out one single piece of paper.

"Is this it?" she asked as she passed over the sheet to Minos.

The demi-god's hands shook as he gazed down on the exact words that had launched him on his thoroughly miserable quest.

Suddenly, Minos was back in the Underworld, on that wretched night, when his life had taken a turn for the worse. It had been the point he'd realised that his own fate was no longer in his hands. The demi-god's body wobbled recalling the unsteadiness caused by the raw emotions of that moment. He steadied his body, reminding himself that he was a whole world away from the revelation.

The printed words before the judge peered up from the page, confirming the sinister actions of an unknown somebody. Once more the deception against Hades turned Minos' stomach and curled his toes.

"It is real!" Chopin's voice broke through the judge's recollections. The soul simply shrugged at the accusing look he attracted for his words. "Come on – you cannot blame a man for doubting."

"But what's on the back?" Branden's curiosity was getting the better of him as he bobbed around behind the demi-god, like an excited kid on Christmas morning.

With shaking hands, Minos started to turn the paper. He was very conscious that his whole journey had been heading towards this point.

Without warning, an alarm sounded.

The high-pitched din both screeched from the corridor and right on top of the group. Fear crossed Lucy's face and she snatched at the sheet.

"Oh jeez – we are in so much trouble."

Minos panicked and grasped tighter at the sheet. He hadn't come this far to miss out now. At the same moment, Branden lunged forward grabbing out as he yelled over the racket of the alarm,

"There'll be more trouble if we don't find out what's going on."

The flimsy document strained this way and that as a three-way tug of war started. Robbie and Chopin looked at each other unsure quite what to do, while Boleyn moved to the door, sticking her head out into the corridor to check on their escape route.

"We've got to put it back. I can't be caught. Please!" Lucy started to blub as she stared at Minos. Her eyes implored the judge, fear and panic welling up in the deep blue pools. The demi-god's heart melted, and he relinquished his grip. He calmly moved Branden's hands away and let the girl take control of the page.

"I'm sorry," Lucy stammered at Minos, as she smoothed the sheet with care. "This is just...I mean I shouldn't have...it's, well..."

"It's ok," conceded the judge. He smiled meekly, "I don't want to cause you any more trouble." He draped his arm over her shoulder, feeling that his decision was for the best. He'd caused issues for Lucy already and he wasn't going to make it any worse. They moved towards the door, the pair squeezing tighter together as the others followed. As they crossed the threshold, Lucy shook herself and looked down.

"Oh my goodness – wait! I need to put this back!" she waved the paper at Minos.

A small twinge of disappointment ran up the demi-god's spine as he realised how close he had come. Yet he forced the feeling down. He was going to make amends to Lucy. Even if it meant living out the rest of his days amongst the mortals, with nowhere to go and nothing to do. Maybe the souls might need a new bartender – he'd always enjoyed the film Cocktail and had often imagined he'd do a good job of throwing alcohol bottles around. And, he reflected miserably, he had a debt to pay off.

"It's alright," said Branden as he made it through the room's doorway. "I'll drop it back. Honest." He added the final word as he caught the stare Lucy was shooting him. "I get it," he added, "No trouble." He dipped into the room and then reappeared. "All done – you wouldn't know we'd been anywhere near it." The young man grinned to himself as they moved off down the corridor.

Boleyn began to lead them back towards the office, raising her head up as if it was an umbrella and she was a tour guide. Lucy reached forward and grabbed the soul's shoulder.

"This way," she indicated the opposite direction with a twitch of her head. "We can take the same route Branden and I used to get up here. It's a quieter part of the building so we might stand more chance of escaping without being detected."

The group trotted through a series of corridors, the walls becoming starker as they progressed. The siren continued to blare, keeping them on edge, each looking over their shoulders, hoping that they wouldn't spot anyone else. Finally, they found themselves at a small lift door, a soft light glowing through the slits that looked inside.

Moving at speed, the six bundled inside, squeezing themselves against each other and the walls. Elbows and hair got everywhere and each person tried to budge around to make themselves more comfortable. Chopin tried to stifle a cough, failed and spluttered over Robbie. Branden, last in and therefore closest to the door, jabbed at the big 'G' on the control panel and the doors slid shut before the tiny carriage lurched downwards.

As the lift wobbly and picked up its pace, the alarm seemed to raise itself up a notch. Sweat ran down Minos' forehead and while he wanted to shake it off his brow, he feared getting a face full of Lucy's ponytail if he tried. The demi-god couldn't see the HR Assistant's face but her body quivered with fear. His own worry deepened – what would happen to the girl if they got stopped? What about Branden? This was exactly why Minos had left the lad behind. Now both mortals were in danger of suffering serious repercussions, all because of the judge's actions.

An idea struck the demi-god, and he called over the top of the blond hair.

"Lucy – is there a set of stairs near to this lift?"

"Yes," breathed the woman, struggling between the demi-god and the wall. "They wind around it. Why?"

"Branden can you push the button for the first floor, please."

The goth twisted slightly and managed to jam part of himself against the relevant button. The carriage's downward descent slowed, before it lurched to a sickening stop. The door peeled back, letting a puff of fresh air in, and Minos hurriedly pushed forward. "Come on, all of you, out." Puzzled looks crossed everyone's face (not that any of them could really see the other) as the judge urged them on.

Once Minos and Lucy had eased themselves through the tiny exit, the lift's door began to slide shut and it resumed its journey to the ground floor. "Quickly," the demi-god herded his five companions towards the stairs, "We haven't got much time. And get organised – souls at the front, mortals behind me." Despite the odd expressions they gave Minos – at least one of the group was inwardly starting to question the judge's sanity – they followed his instructions.

As they reached the ground it immediately became obvious to Robbie and Boleyn, who led the descent, the thinking behind Minos' plan.

Ahead of them, two security guards stood in front of the lift, nasty looking batons raised above the head of each as they stared into the empty carriage in front of them.

One lowered his weapon and used his free hand to quizzically scratch at his head.

Without instruction, Boleyn and Robbie charged forward. The Scot crashed his formidable weight into one of the mortals, who lost his footing and smacked down hard onto the floor, his baton skimming into the empty lift.

Just a split second behind the Scottish warrior, Boleyn swung her arms and brought her head down on top of the other guard's skull. He grunted loudly and crumpled into a pile at the woman's feet.

"Minos, what a clever old bean you are!" Chopin bounced up and down near the unconscious guards, as if he had taken them out himself. Minos ignored the soul, who had now got overexcited and was suffering a coughing fit, and looked into Lucy's wide eyes.

"Which way out?"

Torn by loyalty to colleagues she didn't know, and her newfound association with the small band of otherworldly individuals, Lucy couldn't process speech. Timidly she raised her arm and pointed at a small grey door that almost blended in against the surrounding wall. Following her finger, the souls pushed forward, escaping out into the night.

Lucy slowly followed at the rear of the group, pausing for a moment to look back at the still humans, taking stock of the results of her misadventure.

"What have I done?" she whispered softly.

Chapter 21

Tiny trails of red were cutting across the night sky as the group returned to the bar at Charing Cross. The sun was slowly rising over the sea of office buildings, kissing the Thames with the first rays of a new day.

Lucy dumbly followed the souls inside the wooden tavern. She failed to spot much of the decor that had attracted Branden's attention when he had first arrived at the drinking establishment. The woman was numb after witnessing the way Robbie and Boleyn had attacked the guards at her office.

She had helped Branden, and Minos, on the basis of the youngster's passion and belief they were doing something noble together. She'd been convinced she was with the good guys. Yet the way the souls had behaved towards her colleagues made her wonder if she was right. Had she just been aiding and abetting criminals?

After all, she mused, the group had broken into a secure office and tried to steal confidential information. Yes, she got that someone was trying to screw over a business but wasn't that just life? Corporate takeovers, dodgy dealings – didn't it just all come down to the pursuit of profits?

Without being aware of what she was doing, Lucy accepted a glass of champagne. Chopin began an elegant speech about their great triumph, only interrupted by a mild bout of croaking and spluttering, which he ignored with a flick of his long-stemmed flute. The roar of the crowd (a handful of Popes and a knight) echoed in Lucy's ears, as she failed to take in the little ditty of might conquering evil the composer was ad-libbing. It compounded the woman's sense of confusion and she detached herself from the celebrations, dropping despondently onto one of the benches circling around a nearby table. Her mind ached as she tried to process her feelings.

"Penny for your thoughts?" queried Minos as he sat opposite the woman. Lucy noted that the demi-god's face wasn't right – it looked happy but the hint of sadness across his eyes resonated with her. The crowd around them continued their merriment, ignoring the pair, as Robbie told the tale of his battle with a 'dozen or so' security guards, his few fingers dancing this way and that to illustrate his mighty struggles.

"It's nothing." Lucy tried to brush off the demi-god's conversation opener, for once not wishing to say anything more. Minos maintained eye contact with her,

"Come on, now," he stated calmly, "I can tell there is something bothering you – I just want to know if you feel able to say it to me yourself or if I need to drag it out of you."

Despite herself and the situation, Lucy stifled a sniff and smiled. She tried to express her feelings but struggled to know where to begin. Minos took a lungful of air and let it escape him, before he filled the space between them. "You're starting to wonder if you did the right thing helping me, and by extension, them." He nodded over his shoulder where Boleyn's body was pouring champagne over Robbie. This was all done much to the great delight of the religious figures who found the soggy Scot's slurring and staggering particularly hilarious. As the bearded soul teetered back and forth, Boleyn's body turned to her head, happily perched on the bar, and emptied the remaining alcohol into her own mouth.

"It just doesn't seem…" as Lucy struggled to finish the sentence, she met Minos' gaze and recognised a kindred spirit.

"I have to concede, that I agree with what you are thinking." Minos wheezed, the exertion of the night appearing to catch up with his body. "Can I confide a secret?"

The woman nodded positively at the demi-god and her confirmation seemed to ease a weight on the judge's shoulders. After thoughtfully stroking at his little beard, he stretched and then leaned forward. In a low tone, he spoke softly, "I came up to this land to save my way of life. I wasn't bothered what I did, or how – my goal was all that mattered. I had to find that bit of paper. Whatever it took." He shifted, trying to find a more comfortable position to air his inner feelings.

"I've always prided myself on knowing right from wrong. Murder is a big no no. Sleeping with your husband's uncle's friend – definitely a sin. Stealing is a crime against another and humanity.

"But I've come to see that life on Earth exists in shades of grey. Many of them in fact, perhaps 40 or 50…" Minos paused as he regrouped his thoughts, "My point is the mortal existence isn't as regimented as I'd thought it was. Stealing is a bad thing to do, but what if it's to feed your starving family? Maybe infidelity is because your partner spends their life ignoring you, or worse. What if someone was provoked into hitting another person? Shouldn't that be considered?

"I've spent my life judging others by categorising their worst actions and consigning them to a fate based on that. But the human experience isn't that simple. Sometimes you help a homeless person by buying them a meal. Other times, you pee on them," to Lucy's shocked expression, he added, "Trust me – it happens.

"What I'm trying to say is that I think my beliefs have been wrong. I hate to admit it, especially after all this, but maybe there is something to those consultants in the Underworld. Maybe I've been a fool trying to hang onto my old way of life, because, now that I think about it, it's actually broken. I'm ashamed to admit it, but it's taken seeing what you lot go through day in and day out to open my eyes and convince me I need to rethink my job...well, should have rethought my job."

Lucy reached out and wrapped her fingers around the demi-god's hand. She beamed broadly at the tired old judge in front of her.

"I'm glad you said all that," she told him. "I was worried that you viewed everything we did tonight as ok."

Minos leant back and let his head slowly drift from side to side, his neck cracking loudly as he moved.

"No – I see that now. We hurt people, all for my selfish needs. That's not right. Those security guards were only doing their job. They didn't deserve what we did to them for the sake of a bit of information.

"I'm sorry to you as well. I should never have deceived you."

The final statement hung between the pair, as Branden came to join them. He nudged Minos up the bench and squeezed himself next to the demi-god.

"Isn't this great!" he enthused. Minos grinned slightly, trying to avoid eye contact with the lad, as he added,

"I think I've taken a lot from this experience, but sadly this is where it all ends. Thank you both. For everything.

"Now, it's time we thought about getting you both home. I have a lot to consider, including what I'm going to do with the rest of my life on Earth."

Branden blinked a few times,

"What do you mean? Aren't you going back for your job? To save the Underworld?"

"Well, I was just saying to Lucy that I don't think I'm up to my old role anymore. Too much water under the bridge and that sort of thing. I think the Underworld is probably better off without me. Besides," he added, with a small hint of brightness, "We failed – I still have no idea who was behind all of this or what they were really up to."

"Oh, I forgot." Branden jumped up and starting patting down his pockets. With a flourish he pulled his phone from one of the many pockets in his outfit. "When I went to put the document back, I took a picture of it for you. Seemed pointless to go all that way and fall at the final hurdle. I still don't get why you didn't look."

Minos started as the youth dropped the device in front of him. The demi-god's instincts, built up over so many days of focused effort, was to grab at the mobile and read the words captured there. But his newfound revelations held him back. He hesitated and looked at Lucy.

"What are you thinking?" she asked.

"That I just said that this was all behind me, and that was for the best. But I am still damn curious…" he trailed off as his eyes fell on the phone. He didn't move as he added, "It's wrong I know, but so tempting to just find out once and for all."

To his amazement the woman leant over, picked up the phone and passed it to him.

"You know Minos, you said a lot of things that made a lot of sense. I get the impression you've changed and you didn't expect that when you left the Underworld. I don't know much about your job but it sounds to me like if you took your learnings – the ways your eyes have been opened – back to where you came from, it could only be a positive. You've gone through a lot for the information on that mobile. So have others. I think you should find out what's going on. Everything we've been through tonight has to be for something."

Minos found he couldn't argue with the logic (or his yearning to finally have some answers). With bated breath, he asked Branden to show him the picture.

Chapter 22

Minos read, reread, and then once more went over the words on the document he had been chasing. He was in a state of shock – the revelations were far worse than he ever could have expected.

Lucy, who had watched the judge's mouth hang open until his jaw looked ready to swallow the table between them, gently took the phone from his grip. With an expert touch she moved between the photos of the two pages, seeing for the first time the plan to oust Minos and then what came after. Branden sat awkwardly next to the demi-god, clearly having already read the information.

When she was satisfied that she had understood what her firm had been instructed to do, Lucy placed the phone down. In complete sync with her movements, Minos reached forward and again hoisted up the lightweight device. He let his eyes go across the photos and then, failing to get any further in his comprehension, he read aloud, starting at the final sentence of the first page:

- "The next step of the plan is the most crucial – quick success. Consultants must ensure that changes are implemented so that the Underworld starts generating additional cash from external sources. It is important that Hades sees there is a direct link between positively promoting the organisation to others and its success.

- Throughout this phase, Hades must be kept very busy, almost overloaded, pushing him to believe he needs more help.
- From there, consultants are to ensure that he signs the necessary paperwork to offer shares of the business to the general public. As soon as this is complete, Schneider, Schneider & Patterson will make arrangements for all shares to be purchased using the following bank information: account number 010000027, sort code 010201.
- When this is completed, consultants will ensure Hades is moved into the non-operational role of corporate figurehead. His duties will be light and his involvement in the business non-existent. Consultants are given full responsibility, and freedom, to appoint whoever they see fit to run the company going forward, however the individual must ensure the delivery of a healthy year-on-year profit. From there Hades' involvement in the Underworld is to be minimised and slowly reduced until it practically ceases."

Minos was still dumbfounded as he finished reciting the words he found terrifying. He stared up for a moment and then complained loudly, "This is so much worse – these bastards aren't just getting rid of the established team. They are taking over the whole operation and removing Hades."

"They can't do that, can they?" Branden threw in.

"If someone buys the Underworld as an organisation, then they can do whatever they want," clarified Lucy. "It happens all the time with other companies, but this, this is so much bigger."

"It can't be done," protested Minos, "They can't just take away one of the kingdoms that is ruled by a god. Can they?"

"If Hades puts it up on the stock market, then absolutely. It's a bit like selling a family business. It might have started in the back room of your house, but when you sell it to strangers, it's all belongs to someone else. Lock, stock and barrel."

Minos didn't want to think about how many barrels and locks there were in the Underworld to be bought up. He was devastated at the thought that someone was tricking his boss – his old friend – out of the whole kingdom,

"They can't do it – Hades won't let them."

"You've seen the instructions," insisted Branden, "He's got no clue – they are making him think it's the right thing to do."

"They probably won't even explain what it means to sell shares," added Lucy. "They'll just convince him that it will make him more money."

"It's a really underhanded takeover, but why?" asked Branden, looking between the two.

Minos scratched at his hairless scalp, uncertain,

"I don't get it – no mortal should want to run the afterlife. Unless they know something that I don't?"

"This whole plan seems to work on the basis that there is money to be made by changing the Underworld's operation," Lucy observed. "Do you think it's all just about profits?"

Minos felt more tormented than a soul sentenced to an eternity of cutting the Kers' claws. He held his hands up in depressing surrender,

"I give up! I really don't know! I thought this document was going to answer all my questions. It doesn't even tell me who wrote it! There's no clue at all. I have nothing else to go on." He crumpled, his mouth pointed downwards, as his eyes drifted into space. "Hades is going to be tricked out of the Underworld, for who knows what reason. And there is nothing I can do about it."

"There is one way we could find out what's going on," pointed out Lucy, drawing an incredulous stare from the demi-god. "The bank details – if we could trace them, then we'd have the name of the person who hired my firm. I get the impression that there aren't honourable intentions behind all this, especially given how much effort has gone into duping Hades. Isn't it on us to try and find out what's going on?"

Minos nodded slowly, taking on board Lucy's point. It wasn't exactly what he'd thought he'd be committing to after his big revelation. But Minos felt he owed it to the god he'd worked with for so long to find out what the mysterious person's true reason for wanting to get their hands on the kingdom was. It was only then he would stand a chance at stopping them.

"But how are we going to do find out the name on this account? Even if we did know which bank to ask, I don't imagine they are going to give out that sort of information to someone who just wonders in from the street. And I bet they don't have their own 'return to work' programme I could infiltrate. Not..." he added as he met Lucy's gaze, "...that I think I want to do that sort of thing anymore."

"Is there some way we hack it or something like that?" it was the woman's turn to look lost, as she had the over-arching idea but no clue how to implement it. "I mean it's not exactly legal but maybe this is what you were talking about Minos – shades of grey. No one gets hurt – other than the person who is out to get you, Hades and the others?"

"I can't see one of that lot having the skills to do that," snorted Minos as he indicated the souls, who had calmed their merriment and were now curling up, preparing themselves for the land of nod.

"We could ask?" Lucy suggested vaguely.

"I might know someone..." Branden's voice was very quiet, only just above a whisper. With his eyes down, unable to meet the stares of the other two, he added. "But she isn't very nice and it's going to cost..."

Chapter 23

After Minos had heard Branden talk about the girl who had 'trolled' him, he'd expected something much more imposing (scaly and one eyed), than the plump girl who opened the door to the trio.

The goth leader stood in the doorway of the quaint semi-detached house, looking as thoroughly grumpy as the Underworld's trolls, but that was where the similarities ended. An indifferent scowl was plastered on the pale face, which was framed by large black and purple pigtails. The girl's strappy top revealed way too much flesh, and tattoos, for Minos' liking.

"Dickweed!" was the lukewarm welcome that came out of the purple lips, around a large chunk of chewing gum. "Haven't heard from you in a while – figured you'd finally taken my advice, curled up and died!" She paused, using a fat finger to stretch out the gum before chomping it back into her mouth, past a dull metal piercing. "Or, like everything else, did you try and fail that?"

"I've just been busy, Jenna." Branden didn't bring his eyes up as he mumbled his response. Minos' cheeks glowed as red as the hats of the twee gnomes that surrounded the doorstep. The demi-god disliked seeing the affect Jenna had on his friend.

The girl, barely registering the meek words, shifted her gaze, finally recognising that Lucy and Minos, still dressed in their outfits from the night before, were present.

"You didn't bring me some new recruits, did you Branden? Because if they are anything like you — by which I mean useless — I'm not really that desperate for the extra numbers." She cast a probing look at the group, before adding. "Besides your grandad looks like he's got one foot in the afterlife already, even if he is in the army — which I doubt! And it would take a lot of dye to wash the blonde out of that."

Minos whipped out his arm to halt Lucy as she moved forward, annoyance plastered over her features. In response to the restraint, the HR Assistant let whatever she had been about to say die on her lips.

Jenna, clearly pleased she'd touched a nerve so easily, goaded,

"Come on Barbie! I'll show you that blondes don't always have more fun!" She cackled noisily as Lucy bristled.

Minos moved forward, imposing himself in front of the horrible girl.

"I can ensure you that neither of us are here to join your deluded group of false god worshippers."

"Oooooohhhhhhh..." the sarcasm dripped from the fat lips, "...I suppose you know that because you were around when the god's walked the Earth!"

Minos leaned forward, his nose almost coming into contact with Jenna's chubby snout as he breathed,

"I was, as it happens." Grabbing hold of the brief window of silence provoked by his honesty, the demi-god got to the point of their visit. "I understand from Branden that you can do things with computers. You have skills that may allow you to undertake tasks that others cannot, or will not, do. Is that correct?"

The goth leader let her head pump up and down in time with her rhythmic chewing,

"You better come in."

Jenna led them through a well-presented hallway, complete with decorative plates hanging on the wall. They trudged upstairs, past a variety of school pictures that charted the change of a sweet young girl to the grumpy lump that now screamed at her unseen mother that she had guests and wasn't to be disturbed. Halfway up the ascent, the pictures switched to a shorter series focusing on a plump boy, who went the opposite way to the girl as he aged, becoming slimmer and increasingly smiley. Along the way the yelling continued, as a voice asked whether they wanted tea and biscuits. They did not, screamed Jenna, using a number of expletives which would have made Chopin's head swivel. "She's so fucking rude," the girl told Minos, as they reached the landing.

The new phrase the demi-god had learnt from Lucy – bad egg – resonated within him as he weighed up the youngster. From his years in the Underworld, Minos knew this was just another angry teenager lashing out at society by being mean. Jenna hadn't committed a sin yet, but if she didn't change her attitude then she was on a course for an unpleasant punishment in the afterlife. It would be even worse if Minos got his job back and had the chance to make some of the changes he'd already discussed with Lucy.

As they crossed the short stretch of fluffy carpet on the landing, Minos thought he detected the tinny sound of music behind a closed door. There was something that tingled within the demi-god, but he was certain he'd never heard a song about a winner bee before.

The foursome settled themselves uncomfortably into Jenna's room. The space was like something out of a bad psycho movie, complete with black walls that had had red slashes gouged into their surfaces. Fake spiders and crystal skulls adorned dressers and bedside tables, while framed photos paid tribute to evil looking bands or scenes from depraved movies. Minos sensed Lucy baulking next to him but, before he could offer for her to wait outside, the woman took a deep breath and composed herself.

Jenna threw her weight into a swivel chair, kicking up her large heeled boots on the nearby desk. Thankfully she rested a keyboard over her knees, leaving her with some modesty as her short skirt rode up her chunky thighs.

"So, what illegal cock up has Branden caused and how do you need me to fix it?" smirked the girl. Her incessant gum chomping picked up a gear as she pounded a few keys and a series of monitors, stacked across the cheap wooden surface, burst into life.

"Nothing like that," explained Minos, as he waved a beer mat with hand written details in the girl's face (they had all agreed that giving someone like Jenna the photos of the actual document would be a mistake), "I need the name on a bank account."

Fat fingers grabbed at the cardboard square and for a moment the spitefulness in the face faded, as the girl looked genuinely intrigued.

"Rather unique numbers – not your standard job..."

"Oh dear," Minos made a bit of a show as he snatched the details back. "Branden said it was probably out of your league."

"Oh, did the little dipshit?" growled the girl. Jenna grabbed at the details but the judge just manged to keep them out of her reach.

"Guess we better find someone else. A proper hacker..."

In a flash, and with more deftness than anyone would have expected, Jenna wrenched the mat out of the demi-god's hand and bashed at her keyboard.

"Done!" she proclaimed a few moments later. Minos, trying to keep up some level of pretence from his earlier words, sighed,

"I doubt it."

"Here..." Jenna started to turn the screen and then caught herself. She instead swivelled the monitor further away from the visitors. "If you want it, you're going to have to pay. And I mean serious moola."

Minos held the girl's dark stare for a full second and decided it was time for his prepared back up plan (the demi-god was finally starting to learn from his earlier mistakes).

"Do you know who I am?" he asked in a low tone.

The girl did not break the gaze between them,

"No, but I'd guess that you're one of the crazy branches that Branden's pathetic gene pool hit on its way down. Grandad, mad great-uncle, weird friend of the family who was secretly having it off with his Gran back in the day."

"Take a good look at me. Concentrate and think of everything you've learnt from that group of yours."

The girl lazily let her eyes run up and down the demi-god a couple of times and then she flinched. A light bulb of recognition seemed to pop on and she rapidly blinked her over-massacred eyelids.

"Nooo…." She let her mouth drop open, the gum falling out and making a light plop on the threadbare carpet.

The demi-god inclined his head ever so slightly. "It can't be. No way. Do you mean to tell me, you are one of 'His' trusted generals? A man of hell?"

"Even better," Minos said, with as much gusto as he could muster (whilst ignoring his least favourite word), "I'm a demi-god of the Underworld. The only person senior to me is the big man himself."

Jenna let her mouth bob up and down, as she stammered,

"Dev…Had…Sat…"

"Hades," confirmed Minos, before turning back to business, hoping that the new found respect Jenna had for him would make things easier, and cheaper. "Now, dark child of ours," he ran a finger under the girl's chin, with all the theatre of an old horror film, "I could pay you handsomely today or offer you something more in the life that comes after this. Your choice." He watched as the goth swallowed hard, her eyes glazing over as she considered the possibilities she thought the demi-god had just offered her.

"Ser...ser...seriously?" she stuttered, letting her chin drop back onto Minos' digit, as if the physical contact helped her take in what was going on.

"Oh, yes. There will be a very special place reserved for someone like you in the Underworld." Minos grinned, more to himself, than the girl.

Jenna greedily licked her lips, her breath coming in small pants. Without moving her head, the girl swung the computer monitor towards Minos. The demi-god was joined by Branden and Lucy, both having kept sensibly quiet during the exchange, to stare at the name of the account holder.

Persephone Kore.

"I don't get it," exclaimed Branden. Minos didn't say anything out loud but was agreeing with the youngster's sentiment. Deep within the demi-god's being, something stirred but he couldn't turn it into anything tangible.

"It's a very old account, if that's any help my dark lord?" threw in Jenna. Sweat was forming on her brow as reverence replaced her sullen look. "Possibly originating in Italy, if that means anything to you?" The girl tapped at a few keys, "I can't see any more details about the holder but there does seem to be a number of credits going in over the last six months. Not major, but we are talking hundreds or thousands in each transaction. Looks like it's coming from an online auction site."

Jenna turned her attention to one of the other screens, working to display a website called 'Ancient Antiquity Auctions.com'. Her mouse surged through a selection of the pages, displaying terms for sales, contact details and a list of current items up for sale. "I could try and hack them to find out something more, if it pleases you, malevolent one?"

Minos, his eye caught by one of the auction pieces, couldn't find the words to respond.

A picture.

A large one.

Depicting a master and his dog, a frisbee swinging between the pair.

At that moment, the room's door was pushed open and the young figure the judge had seen pictured towards the top of the stairs walked in. A set of small earphones hung out of the boy's t-shirt, a pop song buzzing out of them. Minos' mind twitched again but he couldn't place the lyrics about a thinner tree.

"Mum wants to know if you want garlic or ham and cheese Kiev for dinner?" The question was asked automatically and then the face brightened as it took in the assembled group, before it asked, in only the way that children can, "What you doing?"

"Get lost – I've got friends over ain't I!" screamed Jenna. "And tell Mum always garlic!!! She should know that by now, the stupid retard." The boy shrugged and used a small button on his earphones to increase the volume of the music. As the notes blared across the room, something went off in the judge's mind, but like the tail end of a happy dream on an early Sunday morning, he couldn't grab hold of it.

Before the child could disappear out of the room, Minos moved across to him. Uncertainty crossed the boy's face as he paused, the tune of the song now clearer in the demi-god's ears.

"Excuse me young man. What's that song you're listening too?"

"Oh god," wailed Jenna, "Will you get lost brat – you are embarrassing me!"

"No, it's fine," Minos shot the goth a look and she clamped her mouth shut. "Please, can you answer the question?"

The boy looked between the expectant faces, before shrugging and explaining,

"Dinner by the sea. It's been number one in the charts for the last two weeks. They reckon it will do it again tomorrow. I love it – brought it as soon as it came out. Even got the extended and gold editions. You wanna listen?"

"When you say it came out – what do you mean?"

The boy blinked, appearing a little perplexed,

"Released – available to buy. You couldn't get it before then."

"But that was a few months ago, right?"

"Oh no." The boy delved in his pocket and pulled out a little electric box. He flashed it at Minos, "See, released 19 days ago."

Minos did a quick calculation, thinking about the time he'd worked at Schneider, Schneider & Patterson, plus the days it'd taken him to cross Europe and, finally, recalled the last time he'd heard the poor excuse for music.

It was less than twenty days since he'd left the Underworld.

The judge looked over at the computer screen, which still showed the image of the familiar painting. His mind ticked over and he recalled when he'd last noticed that particular item. It had been at the same time he had been having a conversation about a lighter workload.

Suddenly, Minos had an almighty flash of comprehension, everything falling together like a giant jigsaw puzzle. He sucked in a breath, his wrinkly hand coming up to cover his mouth in dismay.

The demi-god's eyes went wide, as he realised that he knew exactly who Persephone Kore was.

Chapter 24

The group were all perplexed as Minos recoiled from his revelation.

No one spoke as they watched the demi-god's face twist and turn with emotions. Finally, Jenna's brother got bored of the fact no one was speaking and disappeared through the doorway.

Minos remained frozen to the spot, as he struggled to accept that the perpetrator had been known to him all along. She had pulled the wool over his, Cerebus', and, especially, Hades', eyes from the outset.

"But why did she want rid of me?" he asked aloud, no one else following his question.

Lucy rose and tenderly placed her hand on the judge's shoulder.

"Minos – what is it?"

"It's...well...I know..." was all the judge could get out. The mortal shook him gently,

"You know I like you Minos, but I swear to whichever other gods there are, I will hurt you if you don't explain what's going on right now."

The old figure sighed and dropped like a sack of potatoes onto Jenna's bed. He rubbed his hands over his face, grappling with the enormity of his discovery,

"It's Melinda," he started, and then realised that that meant little to the mortals. "She's Hades' wife and another member of the Underworld's management team. Before she was abducted from the Earth to marry Hades, she was known by the name Persephone Kore."

Lucy whistled, a long and low sound,

"So, Hades own wife is the one trying to take over his business?"

"Wait," Branden held his hands up in surrender. "What's that got to do with songs and auctions?"

Minos drew a tremendous breath, closed his eyes and tried to visualise the different clues. After a long moment of composing himself, he began to explain.

"The last time I heard that song was the day we were called in by Hades to talk about the consultants. Melinda was playing that tune and said she'd picked it up a few months ago but clearly that isn't the case. She must have been up here just days before – agreeing those instructions, I'm now guessing.

"Two days after, I bumped into a soul whose punishment involved cleaning all the items in Hades' palace. She told me that she had much less work to do these days. I think if we check the records on that website we'll find a lot more items that I recognise. I believe Melinda has engineered this whole situation and will be using money raised by selling off the artefacts from the palace to buy the Underworld."

"But that's ridiculous," stormed Lucy, "Surely she splits whatever Hades has, so his success is hers as well."

"That's some sort of ruthless takeover! Maybe Melinda's going to divorce Hades and have everything?" suggested Branden. Jenna, who had not quite followed the full conversation, chose to unhelpfully chime in,

"Why would anyone want to divorce the lord of death? I would give myself gladly to him..."

Minos ignored the girl's wistful look and moved on before that particularly disturbing thought took root in his brain.

"Whatever Melinda's plan — Hades needs to know what's going on. He has to understand that his wife had gone behind his back and is about to oust him. Wait..." he leapt up, feeling stupid for not having considered his next question sooner, "...could this have happened already? I mean — has the company been sold on your stock market thing?"

Jenna thrashed at her keyboard, flipping her attention between monitors.

"What would it be called, the company?"

"Beats me," Minos shrugged. He rattled off a few possible names for his home. At that moment it felt like such a horribly long way away. Minos missed the kingdom, his friends and co-workers.

Her eyes glued to the monitors, Jenna recounted her results,

"I'm checking through recent listings for stocks and shares but I'm not seeing anything. I think there may still be time for you to stop whatever is going on. And put a good word in for me," she fluttered her eyelids in a most disturbing way at the judge.

Faster than the quick brown fox that jumped over the lazy dog, Minos was heading for the door. Jenna continued to look longingly at him, as the others began to follow the demi-god.

On the landing, Lucy lunged at Minos' arm, stopping in him in his panicked tracks.

"What do we do now?"

"I don't know..." a sense of urgency pulled at the judge's whole frame, "...but I need to get back as quickly as I can. Come on." He struggled against the mortal, but her hold on him was rock solid. He looked into the woman's eyes, imploring her to let him go. Lucy, though, had one more thought on her mind,

"The epiphany you had in that pub – shades of grey and all that – it still stacks up right? So, if you make it through this and get your old job back, punishments become more about the outcome and the situation, rather than just actions."

Minos slowed his struggle against the vice-like grip,

"Yes, we'd have to start looking at the full tapestry of someone's life. Why?"

"Wait for me outside, will you?" And with that she had turned on her heel and rushed back past Branden. The young man spun on the spot, unsure whether he should be following Lucy or Minos, who was now taking the stairs two at a time.

Finding himself alone on the lovely landing, Branden decided to follow the judge, rather than try and understand what two women might be talking about, alone in a bedroom.

*

Out on the street, Minos looked this way and that, his mind focused on nothing but his desire to get home.

He just didn't know how to do it.

As the demi-god's head spun, he caught the sound of Lucy's voice wafting down from an open window on the top floor of the house. The judge couldn't catch many words but was certain he heard 'Don't', 'ever', 'Branden', 'or' and 'else'. A shrill yelp then floated down to the demi-god's ears.

Minos shook himself – his keenness to be on the move pushing his body into action. Without another moment of consideration, he set off along the pavement, not really knowing where he was headed. His legs strode out underneath him, his whole body easing as the forward motion soothed his stress.

Branden was following at the demi-god's heels and swiftly Lucy caught up. All of them slowed as they reached a busy crossroads. Traffic bustled across the intersection, each driver as concerned with getting somewhere as Minos was.

Again, the judge was uncertain which way to go.

Why didn't I think about getting back? his mind wailed, cursing his lack of foresight.

He was about to pick a course at random, when he caught sight of Lucy's hands. From her tightly curled fists, tufts of black and purple hair poked out. Minos stared quizzically at the blonde and she glanced down, starting as she suddenly realised that her knuckles were turning white. She relaxed her hands, letting the hair drift onto the breeze of a passing car. She shrugged,

"For the greater good."

"Hhhhmmmm," was all Minos could manage. His face tried to find an expression that gave the impression of scolding Lucy but his eyes gave him away. He knew the woman had done something to make Branden's life better, and the demi-god appreciated it. For his part, the young man was absorbed in his phone and didn't catch any of the unspoken exchange. Looking up from the display, he instead declared,

"There's a flight from Gatwick to Italy, leaving in five hours. We could get you there so you can get back home."

Minos, welcoming the effort, was immediately struck by the impracticality of his situation,

"That wouldn't help – the Exit Portal that I used was only one-way!"

"So how do people get to the Underworld? How would Melinda have done it?" Lucy asked.

Minos shrugged,

"I don't have a clue. Cerebus told me about some special portal at the palace that would take you anywhere on Earth, but I don't know how it works to return. I'm not sure if you have to go somewhere in particular or just say something specific."

"What about the souls we were with?" asked Branden. Minos shook his head vigorously,

"No, they wouldn't know. When they died, rather than arriving at the gates to the kingdom, they would have just have found themselves still here. Everyone else goes straight to the Underworld, but not them. Any correspondence about why they weren't accepted would have been posted to them after the event."

The threesome stood for a moment looking at the ground below them, uncertainty washed over each face as their hair and clothes flapped with each speeding vehicle that zoomed past. With a sudden sharp movement, Lucy cracked her head back and nudged Minos,

"Again – if you're successful when you get back to the Underworld, it's all about the ends justifying the means, right? Actions are considered against the motive?"

Minos nodded and started to form words but didn't get any further.

The almighty shove that Lucy gave the demi-god knocked the breath out of him. He stumbled back into the road, just keeping his feet. Gathering himself, he tried to speak but the car hit him before he could.

The pavement, and the feet of his mortal friends, was the last thing on Earth that Minos saw.

Chapter 25

Everything that mortals think they know about dying – the white light, life flashing before a person's eyes – it is all conjecture. No one who has passed away, arrived in the Underworld and ever returned to the Earth to tell their tale.

The souls that have gone through the process of death and still continue to exist on the planet have never had any luck trying to convey what happened, simply because the see-through look they develop puts the living off talking with them. Any attempt to sit down and have a decent conversation about what death involves, doesn't get any further than a lot of screaming, shouting and general running away. The only mortals who did speak to the souls were delivery drivers – and they were always more bothered about getting on to their next address, whilst being annoyed by how little they were tipped.

It is therefore more fluke than everything else, that what mortals believe about dying is spot on.

Minos tried to close his eyes against the blinding whiteness which was spreading across his vision. He found he couldn't and, while this was a mild inconvenience, the next thirty minutes spent watching a rerun of his life was even more irritating.

With his new found inspiration on how the Underworld should judge mortals, Minos was niggled at having to watch the playback of him sentencing souls over the centuries. He did offer up silent thanks to whoever had found the fast-forward button, although it was hard to process everything as it invaded his mind at high-speed. The only upside, the demi-god conceded, was that no one had considered selling the advertising rights to his life and, therefore, he wasn't presented with a series of wacky and inane commercials every ten to twelve minutes.

With his nerves well and truly jangled, Minos finally saw light at the end of the tunnel (metaphorically speaking, as the dazzling brightness shone round the edges of the whole experience) and, with a strange whooshing sensation, he passed through the gateway into his homeland.

The relief at finding himself back in the Underworld was intoxicating and the judge stood absolutely still, just taking everything in. The burning stench of the River Styx stung his nostrils, while he basked in the warm temperature of the whole kingdom. It was something he hadn't realised he had missed until that moment.

"Well, well – Minos. We heard that the going had got too tough for you and you'd hightailed it out of here." Hermes sniggered as he pushed up the brim of his Stetson hat, before drawling, "Never thought I'd see your face again – let alone watch it come onto my little ole' island."

"Can it, Hermes," warned Minos. He wasn't in the mood for any of the Guide to the Underworld's mischief making.

"Well that's a warm 'howdy doody' from an ex-colleague. How the heck are things? Found yourself a new job up on the Earth, did you? Obviously didn't go very well!" The statement was followed by a noise that sounded like a pack of hyenas and horses simultaneously having mental breakdowns.

Uninterested in what the welcome party had to say, Minos pushed forward, barging roughly past Hermes.

"Woooo there, little doggy. You got some place to be or did Mamma not teach ya' any manners?"

Minos ignored the question as he carried on towards the river crossing. There were surprisingly few souls on the island, yet Charon was already loading up the boat for his next trip. It looked like it wouldn't be long before the scruffy ferryman would cast off, and Minos upped his pace, slipping between the recently deceased as they aimlessly meandered along the shore. The judge was determined to board the boat – he had to get to Hades before it was too late.

The demi-god's progress was suddenly arrested as a hand clamped down hard on his shoulder. It squeezed tight, digging nails deep into the judge's skin. Minos yelped in discomfort and turned to face Hermes, who leered at him displaying nasty, yellow teeth. "I don't think you quite caught my drift partner! You better be telling me where you're going and what you're up to. Ain't no has-been going to arrive on my island without explaining their biziness."

Minos tried to wriggle away, attempting to break free of the cowboy's hand. Hermes just tightened his grip, causing the judge to drop to his knees, pain lancing through his shoulder blade. "It ain't that easy old one!

Your time is over. Gone. You're as spent as the coins in a tramp's collection cup. Life here is different now, and y'all don't fit into it anymore!"

The words were all the judge needed to hear.

Before Hermes knew what hit him, Minos hit him. His deft uppercut caught the guide in the chin, jarring the cowboy's jaw as the judge sent him flying backwards, the Stetson rocketing off into the dirt. The trickster crashed to the ground and rolled onto his side. Minos, not wanting to wait for a response, hot-footed it the short distance towards the ferry, which had just been set free from its mooring, a small sliver of water forming between it and the shore.

Despite its size, the boat rocked as Minos landed on it. He steadied himself and glared at Charon, ready to take on anyone else who stood in his way. The sailor, spotting the felled Hermes, raised his hands in surrender, clearly showing that he had no qualm with the judge.

On the island, Hermes staggered to his feet, grabbing at his ten-gallon hat and wiping a small trickle of blood from his mouth. He pulled out a pocket radio that would have surprised Minos – on the basis this sort of technology had never been employed in the Underworld before. "Hermes to Thantanos – better get yer best Kers out of their tower. We've got an unexpected, and definitely unfriendly, guest that needs taking down..."

*

Alone in the magnificent boardroom, Sandra Sparkes took a moment to savour how close she was to completing her latest project. Absently, the consultant stacked and restacked papers that didn't need any further organisation, and let her guard down just enough to allow a wicked smile to spread across her face. She was already relishing the large bonuses, official and unofficial, she would soon receive.

The work in the Underworld had become one of Sparkes' most enjoyable – and very soon, profitable – assignments. Recovery project after turnaround programme had started to wear thin on the self-confessed (and widely self-promoted) starlet. Before she had set foot in the kingdom her work had increasingly left her with a sense that she was just going through the motions. Even her sexual conquests and infidelities had failed to liven up her mood.

However, the Underworld had been a rare change, a project that had truly enthralled her. For Sparkes this had been an amazing opportunity to see a very unique operation in action. And, of course, who wouldn't want to be able to say on their CV that they had single-handedly rescued life-after-death (Branaghan, she conceded, was doing as he was told so didn't count one jot in the equation). The newfound success of the Underworld was, for Sparkes, the ultimate brag.

She let disappointment tug at her smile slightly, reflecting that there wasn't going to be many other opportunities like this one. Unless, she mused, she could convince Hades to recommend her to one of his brothers.

Despite herself, Sparkes shivered – the possibility of working for Zeus, was almost too pant-wettingly exciting for her. The consultant had heard a few of the demons make reference to Hades' older brother as something of a lover ('hung like Zeus' was one of the popular phrases thrown around the mess rooms) and she considered what it might be like to seduce the greatest god of all time. She took a long indulgent moment to wonder what sex with a supreme being would be like. She was certain she was up to the challenge of fulfilling a god's every desire. She imagined she could even teach him a thing or two.

With a yearning look in her eye, and a tiny bite of her lower lip, the woman returned her attention to the job at hand. Once more, she needlessly flicked through the neat documents in front of her. The movement of the paper wafted a soft breeze, which caused the top of her blouse to flap delicately, helping to cool her sexual desires.

As the final pages wafted together, the consultant was content that everything was in hand to start selling shares of the business. All she needed was a few signatures from Hades to seal the deal. She already had a team in the office ready to buy up the shares, as per the original instructions the firm had received.

Well, she grinned, *almost all of the shares*.

In addition to the lackeys back at headquarters, Sparkes' own personal broker was teed up and ready to go. She had transferred sufficient funds to him to ensure that she would be able to grab hold of ten percent of the total shares on offer, under an assumed name, of course. Because, as she would explain in the aftermath, once the shares were live, anyone could purchase them. What she wouldn't add was that this would include the person who knew exactly what was going on.

All the years in her chosen profession had blurred Sparkes ethics. It didn't matter to her that this sort of activity was decidedly illegal, immoral and, not forgetting, highly unprofessional. This didn't bother the consultant, who felt there was no harm in ensuring that she profited long term from her work. While her salary from her firm was well into six digit figures, and was being supplement by extra money for taking on an operational role in Hades' team, she yearned for more.

As far as Sparkes was concerned her tactics to supplement her income were justified by the actions, or lack thereof, of Schneider, Schneider & Patterson's board. If the male, pale and stale losers had wised up to the asset Sparkes was and promoted her to join the executives, she wouldn't need to keep finding ways to improve her own remuneration package.

Ten percent of the reformed Underworld's operations wasn't a big loss for anyone. It certainly wasn't enough to be considered a controlling partner or anything like that. Sparkes could just sit back and watch as her efforts continued to turn a profit for her, all towards a new holiday home. She was thinking somewhere warm, like the Bahamas.

The woman needlessly checked the papers again and glanced at the clock on her phone, letting the edge of her bright red lips tug wider. The small electronic display clearly indicated that the time was approaching for her to complete her business with the Underworld. She placed the device next to the documents, keeping it close to hand so that she could inform her broker as soon as the deed was done.

In fifteen minutes, Hades would arrive to sign over his empire for good.

Chapter 26

"Out of my way," stormed Minos, shoving past Charon as he scuttled down the boat. Without giving the judge a second look, the sailor headed towards the craft's rudder pole, steering the boat with a heave of his weight against the long stick.

Minos reached the front of the vessel, in a gruff panic. He was angry about having to fight Hermes but was now more determined than ever to get to Hades. He could not let the god sell the Underworld.

The judge's eyes widened as he stared past the ship's bow, suddenly realising that the river was much wider than he remembered. What had felt like a short lake, now seemed like an oceanic expanse that made the judge's sense of dread deepen. Looking back to the shore he had just come from, Minos' stomach tightened further as he saw Hermes barking into some sort of phone. The judge couldn't tell what was being said, but he got the impression it wasn't going to be in his favour.

Taking a second to track the slow progress of the ferry as it crossed the greater than expected distance, the demi-god pondered why he had never learned how to swim (it was one of those things he had always said he would get around to, but it had never moved off the bottom of his 'to do' list). Feeling useless, with no way to speed up his progress, Minos moved over to where Charon stood.

"Feel like a chat now, do we?" enquired the ferryman as he winked at the judge, a light-hearted look spreading across his face.

"Come on Charon – don't be like. This whole place is in real trouble!" blustered Minos. "I've got to get to Hades before it's too late."

"You know," wheezed Charon, as he leaned on the rudder, using his considerable weight to his advantage to steer the nose of the ship towards a new spot, "Everyone's got to be somewhere at some point."

"You surprise me – people on a boat, looking to get someplace," the judge's sour mood was reflected in his comments, "Next you'll be telling me that the mortals are still taking in oxygen."

"Tsk," chided the ferryman, "I thought that by this stage, you'd understand a bit more." Minos threw his arms up in the air, exasperation playing across his features,

"I understand plenty, mate – Melinda has been playing silly buggers with all our lives. She's the one who decided to sack me and Cerebus. She's about to take control of the whole operation. It's curtains for Hades."

"As I say, we're all trying to get somewhere," countered Charon, his relaxed tone starting to grate on the judge. "Sometimes the road is short, other times it's long. Often we can do it by ourselves. On other occasions, we need some help from our friends." The ex-navy officer pulled a short silver whistle from his pocket and blew into it. Minos could only assume that, like the rest of Charon, it had seen better days, because the piece of metal made no noise despite the sailor's face turning red through his efforts. The ferryman paused, regained his breath and then added, "And sometimes, what is hidden from one is obvious to others."

Minos started at the last remark,

"Do you mean to say you knew what was going on? Did you let me chase across Europe for nothing?"

Charon pulled at his steering pole as he shook his head from side to side, his unkempt hair and beard waving with the movement.

"A few weeks ago, if you had asked me the details, I could not have told you. Yet, it is amazing what you pick up in the expressions of others. Looks that ask for help, or ones that have set themselves on a certain course, that might, in turn, create a particular series of events."

"You're telling me that you know about everything that is going on?"

"Often, we hear more when we are not talking…" the sailor's voice trailed off as the boat scraped on the shore of the kingdom, grounding itself with a soft grating sound. "And sometimes we have to go the long way round but are richer for the experience."

Minos, giving up on the proverbs and vagueness, started to head towards dry land. He was conscious that the boat would have landed by the judging rooms and he would therefore have a long way to travel to the palace.

The small distraction of dealing with Charon over, the judge was already feeling concern grip at him once more

– how much time did he have left? Was he already too late to stop the sale?

As Minos looked out on the kingdom and slowed, taking in the sight of unexpected buildings. They were not at the spot where Charon was meant to drop off new souls. The judge let his head whip around, as he suddenly realised that they were, in fact, much further down the shoreline than they should be. As a result, the judge was significantly closer to the palace.

"But...what...how...?" Minos looked in confusion at the sailor.

"The kingdom is always under threat, in one way or another. This time it involves many factors, members of our own team, as well as mortals. Next time it will be smaller or bigger. The important thing is that we work together," chimed Charon.

Minos, deciding he wasn't going to get much more sense out of the demi-god, shrugged and threw a 'thank you' towards his companion. He made a mental note that the old sailor was more perceptive than anyone realised and hopped off the boat.

As the judge landed, he cursed slightly at the tide that lapped at his patterned trousers. As he pointlessly tried to shake his ankles dry, he looked up to find himself face to face with the first ally of his journey.

Cerebus beamed from floppy to pricked up ear, before slathering Minos in moist affection with his tongue. Even the creature's snake head nuzzled into the demi-god's side.

"Easy boy," was all Minos could manage as he embraced the pooch, oddly enjoying the wet sensation across his face.

Then a thought crossed the judge's mind, "How did you…?" Realisation dawned on his face and he looked back at the boat, where Charon was standing nodding in rhythmic motions. All Minos could do was beam and point his finger at the nautical demi-god. "You! You knew I'd need a quick way to get to the palace. But how did you know where to find him?"

"Who do you think has been keeping the hound hidden since the Kers started getting suspicious of each other?" called back Charon.

Minos was going to shout back with further appreciation, but he stopped as he spotted a black cloud forming, below the mist, in the distance. While the judge had grown accustomed to these phenomena on Earth (and all the words the British used for the various types of rain that came from them), the sight of a weather pattern in the kingdom was somewhat strange. Minos blinked a few times and then started to detect different parts within the darkness.

To his horror, the judge could suddenly pick out individual Kers swarming and writhing as part of the mass. Minos looked Cerebus in the eyes,

"I don't have time to explain what's going on, but can you get me to the palace pronto?"

"I'll do my best – hop on," Cerebus threw himself onto all fours, his fists curling up as his feet dug into the ground. The snake wound itself tightly into a coil and tucked itself down low onto the hound's back.

With some reluctance, the judge mounted the creature's back and immediately gripped his arms tightly around Cerebus' neck as the hound launched off at a fast 'four-legged' pace.

The menacing cloud drew closer and some of the harpies began to disentangle themselves from the pack, screeching and clicking their talons as they swooped low. Cerebus galloped on, attempting to keep as far away as he could from his old team. Minos wasn't sure how successful the animal was going to be.

*

Hades broke his brisk stride, joy spreading over his face as he spotted Melinda waiting for him at the end of the corridor. The god's heart skipped a beat at the sight of his lover.

"Hey you," he greeted, feeling his spirits lift at the sight of the gorgeous woman (others might have disagreed, but to Hades, Melinda was perfect). A crisp, white dress was wrapped around her lithe figure, accentuating her loveliness. It was a stark contrast to the god's pin stripe suit, with yet another overly colourful tie blaring out against his dark shirt.

"Hey yourself," the dainty demi-goddess fluttered her long eye lashes. "I had a bit of time between meetings so I thought I'd see if I could find you to say 'hi'".

"Hi," beamed Hades.

"Hi," grinned back his wife. "How's your day going?"

"Phew," breathed the god, no one knowing better than Melinda what was wrapped up and expressed in those four little letters. "It's been non-stop, but I'm starting to think I might be getting the hang of this meeting people thing. Knocked a couple out of the park this morning." The ruler swung his arms as if he if was a baseball player, a move he'd picked up from one of the mortals he met at some point in recent weeks. He quite liked both the metaphor and the movement.

"See – I said you were good when you were practising all your facts and figures at home," Melinda playfully reminded her husband.

The pair started walking and the god found his pace was suddenly lighter. He loved getting compliments, especially from his wife,

"It wasn't easy," he told her, "But I'm really getting into the swing of things now."

Melinda stared up into her husband's eyes and innocently enquired,

"Where are you headed now?"

"Boardroom, to see Sparkes. I'm signing the paperwork so we can start selling shares in the business. Then we can invest in other activities that will help make even more cash." Hades rubbed his hands together. His wife nodded, knowing how excited he was about further increasing the company's profits. The demi-goddess moved close to her husband, slipping her body into the nook between his arm and chest.

"I've not got anything in my diary for the next half an hour – why don't I come with you?" She purred slightly, rubbing her head into side of the great god's body, "It'd be nice to spend some time with you."

Hades turned and took Melinda's face in his massive hands, lovingly caressing her cheeks as he stared deep into her eyes.

"I am sorry darling – I know this has been rough on us, but very soon we'll have a proper company with shareholders and everything. We are very soon going to have more money than we know what to do with.

"Give it a few more days and then I promise – a magnificent holiday. Just you and me. No expense spared."

Melinda was almost giddy as Hades planted a deep and passionate kiss on her lips. She clasped his hands tightly,

"You are on. Let's get this signing stuff done and then why don't we clock off early and go for dinner? You can even choose where we go."

Hades brightened even further – knowing that meant he could pick his favourite steak restaurant. With delight, he asked,

"You want to grab a coffee? I'm sure the paperwork can wait five minutes."

"Oh no," chided Melinda, "Let's get on with it shall we. Work first, then we'll worry about what comes after. Besides I have a little present for you."

Hades was slightly taken aback, as the demi-goddess produced a small rectangular box, covered in soft felt. The ruler took it in his hands, which looked gigantic in comparison, and delicately flipped the lid open. Inside a beautiful fountain pen shone up at the god. Hades slipped the silver cylinder out of its home and felt the light weight of it in his palm. "I thought that someone of your stature, with all these important meetings you've been going to, could do with something more official to sign his paperwork with."

The happy expression on the god's face switched up to maximum wattage,

"That is so incredibly thoughtful of you. Thank you. You really are the best, especially after how much I've neglected you recently." Hades was so focused on the present, that he didn't notice the look that crossed Melinda's face.

It was the expression of someone who was about to see months of planning come to fruition.

Chapter 27

Minos howled as another onslaught of Kers swiped their talons at him and Cerebus. The judge tried to bat the winged harpies away with his right arm, while his left clung tightly to the hound's neck. Cerebus' snake head frequently sprung out from its position towards the base of the animal's back, snaping its fangs at anything that got close.

The judge genuinely couldn't tell how close they were to the palace – every building was a streak of colour, indistinguishable from the last. Cerebus galloped on, so fast that Minos could hear little above the shrill sound of the wind whooshing past his ears. The only noise which did punctuate the demi-god's ears was the screech of the Kers as they soared down, trying to halt the pair's progress.

Minos screamed as a winged beast attempted to grab his arm in its thick talons, missed, and sliced into the judge's skin instead.

Pain lanced across the demi-god's body as the assailants became more frantic in their efforts. He could sense blood flowing around him but was only vaguely aware that it was his own. The demi-god had no idea if the demons were inflicting the same level of damage on their former manager. If they were, Cerebus wasn't showing it, the mighty beast charging forward.

Another section of the darkness that hovered just above the demi-god's vision broke away and swiftly dropped down. Despite bracing himself, the judge could only wail in agony as his skin was again torn at. For the briefest of moments, his grip on Cerebus slipped. Flailing wildly, Minos managed to snag his friend again, grabbing tightly onto the hound with both hands as he just saved himself from a very painful fall. He felt a reassuring prod from the snake, as it tried to help in its own way.

Minos sensed, rather than saw, the next attack coming and, with his hands busy keeping him on top of Cerebus, tried to tuck himself into as small a target as possible.

It didn't work.

Without his arm creating a defensive barrier, the Kers' lunges dug deep into the demi-god's fleshy parts (that had only just started returning to their plump shape, thanks to Mrs Robert's cooking). The judge yelled out and even Cerebus faltered, stumbling and scuffing his hands against the hard ground. The beast immediately recovered and roared forward, as his passenger gripped on with what was left of his waning might.

Minos wasn't sure how much more he could take.

Without warning, the pair's forward momentum suddenly ceased. The whizzing lines that had tunnelled around Minos' vision turning back into familiar sights, and he just managed to make out the palace ahead of them.

With a controlled movement, Cerebus flipped Minos off his back, throwing the judge onto the ground close to the stairs up to Hades' home. The judge hit the pavement hard, expelling the air out of him in a heavy cough.

While Minos' battered body wanted to stay down, the urgency of the situation pulled the demi-god back to his feet. He looked up and watched with dismay as the Ker cloud drew in on itself, the creatures closing ranks. The harpies shrieked louder than Minos would have thought possible, the hairs on the back of his neck standing up.

Cerebus, his chiselled body almost sliced to smithereens, appeared between Minos and the dark sky. The former head of security kept his gaze fixed upwards, paying no attention to the blood that ran in deep lines from battered shoulders down to bruised feet.

"You go ahead – I'll hold them here," the hound roared. The snake hissed its agreement, but looked slightly more worried than the rest of Cerebus.

The judge staggered away from the palace, his wounds telling on his fragile frame.

"No way, they'll rip you to shreds."

For a brief second, the dog's head turned to meet Minos' concerned expression.

"I didn't get to be their boss by running away from them." Determination was clear across the creature's features, and as his focus returned upwards, he added, "Besides, I know a trick or two! Now go!"

The judge took one lingering look at his friend and then let his sense of duty to Hades take him onwards.

Minos ran like he never had before, his chest wheezing as he crossed the palace's entrance hall, surprisingly unopposed.

He could only reflect, as he bounded up the ivory stairs, that either the Kers had been overly confident about stopping him and Cerebus or, like the night the pair had drunkenly wandered the corridors, security had become very relaxed in Hades' home. A trio of demons did a double-take, but otherwise the demi-god passed deeper into the palace without any incident.

The demi-god pumped his arms as best as he could, forcing his legs to move faster. He was gripped by the same sense of terror a commuter experiences after they realise they've spent too long picking out which frothy coffee to have before madly dashing for their train.

As Minos ran, he caught sight of bare walls, display cabinets light on items to display and empty mantlepieces. He wondered how he hadn't noticed this before. Had he been so wrapped up in his own tiny problems that he'd ignored the clues that something was up? Or had Melinda stepped up her efforts once Cerebus and Minos had been dispatched?

Mentally pushing his questions to one side, the judge tried to up his pace. His legs ached in protest, the Kers' battering telling on the demi-god's form. The judge didn't know if he was too late to save Hades, but he was going to give it his all to find the ruler, just in case.

Minos finally arrived at the god's apartment and started pounding his fist on the door, but, like that night many weeks ago, no one answered. He slumped his face against the wooden door, almost in tears.

"Minos? What are you doing here?"

The squeaky voice was both extremely annoying and very familiar. Minos spun, batting at his moist eyes as he did.

"Gronix!" he screamed in delight at the pain in his backside that had been his Personal Assistant. He would have wrapped the little demon in his arms, if not for fear of the creature's spikes lacerating him even further.

The green pest was laden with multi-coloured folders which he hefted further up his body, in an attempt to stop any of the contents falling onto the floor.

"You look terrible – what's going on?"

"I'm looking for Hades! Do you know where he is?"

"Of course I do. I'm his Executive Assistant now." The demon drew itself up a few more millimetres as it proudly boosted of its achievement. "He's with Ms Sparkes in the boardroom. They are having a meeting regarding paperwork to sell shares. I think I've got copies of the meeting papers here." He bounced the stack of files and almost lost his grip on them.

"Oh god..."

"That's what he is and don't you wear it out," Gronix's attempts at humour had always fallen miserably flat and he didn't invoke any mirth this time, as Minos processed the fact that there was still a small window in which he could save Hades and the Underworld. The demon tried to cover over the cracks of his poor joke, with as much success as a bad decorator on a Friday afternoon when he's already three days behind schedule, by adding, "I mean he is the boss and all...Shouldn't you be somewhere else? Perhaps a hospital?"

Gronix got no response as Minos disappeared down the hall. The small demon shrugged and decided not to use any of his important paperwork to mop up the pool of blood on the floor.

"That sort of thing is definitely not in my job description," he muttered as he scurried off.

Chapter 28

"Stttttttttttooooooooooooooooppppppppppppppp!" Minos screamed at the top of his lungs as he zoomed past the empty reception desk (he wondered if he should raise the fact that it was rarely ever staffed with anyone?), and attracted three sets of quizzical looks as he crashed through the boardroom's door.

In front of the demi-god was his worst nightmare (well, second-worst, the one with the clowns and the helium balloons still haunted him in the early hours of the morning). Seated at the massive table Hades, flanked on either side by Melinda and Sparkes, was just completing the movement of signing his name on a sheet of paper, using a shiny pen. The mortal was already stretching out her hand, snatching at the freshly inked parchment.

Panicked by the thought that either of the women would try and stop him in his tracks, Minos let his pace carry him up onto the tabletop. He scrambled, stumbled and practically slid down the hard surface towards Hades, grabbing out at the pen and the associated paperwork (that had been so neatly stacked). Mistiming his snatches, the demi-god's hands closed around thin air and his momentum skidded him onwards.

Before the judge could regroup, he whizzed off the table, his whole body colliding into the tight embrace of Hades.

The demi-god's face was squeezed tightly against his old boss' shirt and tie (*???* Minos thought — he'd never seen Hades in such a getup, ever).

"Minos — I can't believe it's you! Where have you been?"

The judge gurgled a reply, which the god couldn't understand and then realised it was because he was smooshing Minos' bald head against his granite-like chest. Hades released the weary looking demi-god, who took several lungfuls of air as he was deposited onto shaky feet. "Wait — what's going on?" queried the ruler, standing as he noticed the blood that had smeared onto his designer outfit and the many wounds slashed across Minos' body.

"Pufff...don't...cough...sign...phlurrr..." was all the judge could manage.

Sparkes, momentarily taken back by the sight of a loose end she had thought didn't need dealing with (having Minos disappear had saved her a difficult conversation. It wasn't that she didn't enjoy firing people, it just saved her time if they left of their own accord), took in the words coming out of the demi-god's mouth and recovered with lightning speed,

"Security! Security — we have a trespasser," the mortal roared towards the empty corridor.

In the background, Melinda looked quietly from one face to another. Her expression suggested that she knew she had run out of moves.

Minos, having recovered somewhat from the sprint and being semi-crushed with affection, now snatched for Hades' pen.

"Don't sign anything – she's going to buy the whole business and oust you."

Hades ripped the writing implement away from Minos, distress crossing his face at his friend's attempt to take the gift from him. The god hoisted the cylinder high in the air, out of anyone else's reach. His facial features hardened as he stared down at his former colleague. Before the judge could speak again, Sparkes pushed her way into the middle of the confused chaos.

"Hades – why are you entertaining this ex-employee? He abandoned his post, without any word, and left you to pick up the pieces…"

"I did no such thing," yelped Minos, now turning the pent-up frustrations of his long journey on the mortal. "It's you! It's all your fault! You've been out to get me from day one!" He jabbed his finger at Sparkes, who responded with mock surprise that was meant to look genuine (and did to Hades, who wasn't following the subtext of the situation).

"See, Hades? He's absolutely mad. I mean look at the state of him," the woman stepped back with repulsion painted across her face. "This is a man who left you in the lurch. You definitely should not be listening to him now. Remember – he's not part of the solution, so he's definitely a problem." She once more looked towards the door and screamed at the top of her lungs for someone from the security team.

Words failed Minos, as the efforts of the late-night office robbery, his death, as well as the Kers attack, suddenly caught up with him. He stared straight at the bemused Hades, spluttering and flailing his arms,

"I…she…Earth…mortals…bad…plan…"

"He can't even string a sentence together!" wailed Sparkes, practically jumping up and down on the spot with glee. "He's probably high on drugs or something worse – we can't believe a word that falls out of that bloody mouth of his…"

"ENOUGH!"

It was Hades' turn to raise his voice, his body, which still held the pen aloft, trembling with the might of the roar. He voice was so loud it made the palace shake, and deep in the coffee shop at the front of the building, two cups of tea fell over, whilst the foam jumped off a latte. As the god drew another breath, he realised that his outburst had done the job, silencing Sparkes and Minos, freezing them both in their tracks. Behind the great god, Melinda slowly shrunk towards the corner of the room, her face pale.

Hades stared daggers at Sparkes, "You will be quiet until I have heard from my old friend. I owe him a lot – after all his years of service – and he shall have the opportunity to speak." With that, he turned to the battered demi-god. "I take it you have some sort of explanation for the fact you've been AWOL for the past few weeks, the state you're in and the fact that you are accusing my mortal of something that, right now, I am not quite following."

Minos tried to organise his thoughts. Failing, he started by addressing the points in reverse order,

"It's not her…" he tilted his head towards Sparkes, who was once more staring out of the room, looking for any soul (or demon, or mortal) to help her evict the judge.

Finding no one to assist her, the consultant started to cross towards Minos.

The judge, rightly picking up that the consultant was going to try and silence him, ducked behind Hades, positioning himself so that the god formed a physical shield that Minos could cower behind.

In the perceived safety of his old master's shadow, the judge turned to the other demi-god in the room, "Do you want to tell him, or shall I?"

Melinda kept an even gaze fixed on Minos, without saying anything. Hades gruffly cut in,

"Somebody better start telling me what's going on, right now, or I'm going to start breaking things – starting with necks!"

Minos jumped at the threat, and managed to focus his mind enough to implore,

"Look, I can explain everything, more than you believe, but please tell me you haven't signed anything to do with selling shares?"

Hades, becoming increasingly perplexed, grabbed at the set of documents that were still on the table (despite Minos' earlier antics) and waved them around.

"If you mean these, then no." He followed the judge's eyes to take in the piece of paper in Sparkes hand, before shrugging. "That was just me practising – I have a new fountain pen and wanted to try it out before I started using it for official paperwork." His eyes narrowed and his bushy brows dived low, "Now, start explaining."

And Minos did, the whole story, from drunken start to table-sliding end.

As the demi-god spoke, Hades sagged into his chair, a stunned look on his face, as he took in the actions he had been unaware of, the things that had happened in his name, as well as the ultimate deceit. Beside the god, his wife could do nothing but stand stock still, while Sparkes slowly, but surely, edged towards the doorway.

As Minos finished his tale, Hades leant back and scratched at his beard for a long time. The whole room was deadly quiet, except the occasional scuff of Sparke's heels against the carpet. Finally, the god stood and towered over Melinda. "Is this true, or do I need to consider doing horrible things to Minos for suggesting something like this is possible?"

Very meekly, the demi-goddess nodded her head up and then down, finishing the movement staring at her sandal covered feet. Using one of his massive fingers, Hades tilted the woman's delicate face up,

"Why?" sadness oozed into the god's words, "What possible motivation could you have for trying to remove me from the Underworld?" His whole body seemed to droop as he asked the question of the woman he loved.

Summoning up the inner courage that had set her on the path to deceive her husband, Melinda met Hades' stare.

"For us," she managed, "This was all for you and me."

The god leaned down, coming face to face with his partner.

"I don't understand how getting me fired is for us…" As Hades spoke the woman suddenly lashed out, striking his great chest. For all the effort she put in, it was a timid punch. There was no physical strength to the slip of a demi-goddess, and her soft attack was more a show of trying to knock sense into her husband. It was an outpouring of emotion against the one person she'd pledged her commitment to.

"How can you not get it? We've talked about this so much – it was meant to ensure you don't have the weight of a whole Underworld on your shoulders anymore.

"It was so we could have more quality time together!" Melinda snivelled and tried to compose herself, but it didn't work. Tiny tears streaked down her rosy cheeks, as she carried on, "Minos is wrong when he says I was trying to oust you. I still wanted you to be involved – I just needed someone else to take charge of the majority of decisions. It's time another person spent their evenings worrying about the kingdom.

"Everything I did was for you. So you could have a better life, and we…we could focus on having a little you." Melinda's resolve crumpled as the tears came thick and fast. She made the most pathetic noise, as Hades drew her to him, clasping her tightly to his chest.

"There, there," he cooed, holding the demi-goddess close. They stood, deep in an embrace, just two deities reminded about how much they cared for each other. Melinda's face finally emerged from the cuddle, her moist eyes meeting her husband's. Neither noticed the small streaks of Minos' blood that had rubbed off on her soft skin. Softly the demi-goddess explained,

"I didn't mean to hurt you. I just wanted what was best for us. I know you wouldn't take any action yourself and this seemed the best way to relieve you of your burden, while keeping everything running. The whole setup would ensure we still made money and would be in overall control, but someone else would do the hard work,"

Melinda paused, snivelling loudly as she rubbed at her eyes, "Are you going to divorce me?"

The question hung in the air between the pair, before the demi-goddess gave in to her fear and started balling once more. Any hint of anger Hades felt towards his wife dissolved, and his own eyes glistened. He drew his wife to him again, wrapping his strong arms around her petite frame.

"Not at all darling – how can I get rid of you for this? For going to such lengths to try and put my best interests first? You are by far the best wife ever." He squeezed her tightly, "We can sort this all out. Starting with me taking on board what's happened and really listening to what you've been saying to me.

"I vow to be better for you. For everyone."

Minos, who had been moved by the whole scene, couldn't help now voicing the one thing that still bothered him,

"What I don't get is, why did you have to pick on me and Cerebus?"

"Seriously? That's the bit you don't understand?" Melinda asked, as she detached herself from Hades and started dabbing at her eyes. "You're the only one around here with an ounce of intelligence, Minos. And for all his faults, that dumb dog always has Hades' back. I knew that if this was going to fall down anywhere, it would be one of you two stepping in to change Hades' mind."

Minos, despite the flattery, scowled as he processed the new information,

"So, I had to lose my job because I'm too smart…"

Hades, now trying to play peacekeeper, stepped between the pair and interjected,

"Now Minos, I'll be the first to accept that what my wife has done, and the way she has gone about it, aren't what I would have called the 'correct' approach to things." Melinda looked sheepishly at Minos as she mouthed 'sorry'. "But she had mine, and the kingdom's, best interests at heart. Didn't you say something about learning that it's the reason behind an action, and not the steps taken, that should determine whether it is right or not?"

The great god pushed on, not giving his friend a chance to reply to this observation, "It sounds like you've gained a lot from this experience. Skills and insight which could be useful to me, or to whoever is in charge…" he added, as he shared a look with his wife, "…in a new team. A new Underworld."

Before Minos could process his new found job security, Sparkes' phone, which was still on the desk (again, despite the judge's earlier trip across the top of it), started ringing. At the sound, the deities all turned to look at the consultant, who was half way out of the door. Panic sprang across the woman's face and she took two steps back towards the group. She ground to a halt as the judge grabbed at the device and pressed the green button in the way he'd seen Branden handle calls.

While Minos did this and spoke into the mouth piece, Melinda pulled herself close to Hades. Her eyes looked up into the deep pools of the god's, as she asked,

"Have I ruined everything? Are you mad?"

"A little. I know we've had our problems but I always thought that we could work them out. Discuss them.

"I never thought you'd feel compelled to do something like this to get your point across to me." Melinda sniffed loudly, as Hades stroked her hair. "It's not going to be easy but I think we can undo some of what you did and also embrace it. After the last few weeks, maybe running this place so we actually make money is more work than I can do by myself.

"Maybe now is the time for me to start taking it a bit easier – we did talk about a holiday, after all. Let's see what we can sort out with the others. After all, eventually I'll have a little one to worry about, won't I?"

He squeezed his wife and she hugged him back. Any division between the two was gone. They were now a combined might that no one would dare cross. Together they turned to face Minos, as he hung up the phone.

"That," the demi-god mused, "was a man called Ian, who is Ms Sparkes' personal broker. He wanted to know if the deal had gone through and he should start purchasing shares in the Underworld for her."

"That's not right," stated Melinda, her tiny hand wrapping into the god's. "I was meant to buy all of them." Hades scowled,

"Isn't that insider trading or something like that? I thought that sort of thing was illegal on Earth. Didn't we watch a film about it? You know the one I mean," he glanced at his wife for help, "The one with Martin Sheen,"

"Charlie," corrected Minos, not that it really mattered or added anything to the conversation. The demi-god mulled over the implications, before turning to Melinda. "If Sparkes bought some of the shares instead of you, you'd still have control. So why would she do that?"

"To make money," it's was the demi-goddess' turn to seethe, as she suddenly realised that she too had been deceived.

"She is a proper bad egg," observed Minos, attracting a strange look from his boss. "I'll explain later."

The threesome collectively turned towards to the boardroom's doorway.

Sparkes was gone.

As Hades sucked in a deep breath, preparing to shout the building down, the consultant suddenly reappeared, sinisterly flanked by two Kers. Cerebus followed, the creature even more bruised and battered than when Minos had left him. The judge also spotted ruffled feathers and bloody cuts on the harpies. Whatever had happened outside the palace, right at that moment both the Kers and hound were presenting a united front, as they marched Sparkes back into the room.

"Did someone call for security?" grinned Cerebus, as Hades made 'good dog' sounds at his best friend.

Chapter 29

With a flourish of his magnificent fountain pen, Hades signed the document.

With a soft sigh of contentment, the god eased back in his chair at the top of the boardroom table, adjusting his loose-fitting linen shirt as he did.

"There – all done."

"Thanks boss," beamed Minos, as he collected up the freshly endorsed Policy for Judgement and Punishment Administration.

It was two weeks since Hades had almost signed away the Underworld and Minos had spent most of that time working up the new set of operating procedures (alongside the occasional swimming lesson). The document had been a labour of love, reflecting the demi-god's varied experiences on Earth. Tucking the endorsed papers under his arm, Minos paused to smooth out a wrinkle in his new toga, purchased with the generous remuneration package he was now receiving as Chief Executive Officer.

It was a very new feeling for Minos – being in charge of everything. However, he had found it gave him the freedom to change the things that had previously frustrated him. Using the input of Branaghan, who had not known about Melinda's instructions or Sparkes' dubious share buying plan (and had been pre-paid until the end of the month, anyway), Minos was happily establishing a different way of working across the kingdom.

"Ah – man! Did I miss it?" called the freshly appointed Chief Operating Officer as he arrived in the doorway. The creature, who no longer showed any signs of his battle with the Kers, moved across to Hades' side and enjoyed receiving a good scratch behind the ears. His snake bobbed up for some attention and hissed appreciatively as the god's fingers found him too. "I thought we were all going to be present as we launched into the new era."

Although Minos had had a few reservations about Cerebus' appointment (his mind often wandering back to the disorganised moment they had shared by the Exit Portal), he had to concede that the animal had found a new lease of life. He was considerate and thoughtful, spotting potential flaws or opportunities in ideas before anyone else. It seems that the dog's time in hiding had been a good chance for him to reflect and consider what he'd do differently if he had his time again.

"Come on now," beamed Hades, who's own enthusiasm had been renewed since he had started as Chairman of the Underworld Board, "It's not a big thing – we're already embracing the new way of working. It's just that we now have the procedures properly signed off." The god rose, once more fiddling with the soft shirt, "And if you'll excuse me gentlemen – I have a date with my wife."

"Steakhouse?" asked Minos, raising an expectant eyebrow.

"No, we did that last week. I said Melinda could pick this time and we're going for something called tapas." Hades shrugged, but the grin on his face grew a few more inches. The god collected his silver pen and headed for the door. "Don't work too late," he called over his shoulder.

"Remind me again why he gets to sod off half way through the afternoon?" asked Cerebus, as he seated himself opposite Minos, his snake resting its head on the hard surface of the table, attentive rapture on its face.

"Because he and Melinda are now the major investors in the company," Minos again reminded his deputy. In the end, Branaghan has advised against bringing in outside investment, and instead using the funds the demi-goddess had raised to help the business move forward. "Basically, you and I get paid loads each month to try and make sure he gets a handsome return at the end of the year."

Cerebus shook his head, letting his tongue loll out and wag with the movement.

"I still don't get the finance side," he interjected.

"And that's why you look after operations and I handle the money, policies and staffing," shot back Minos. He glanced at his iPad, which he still hadn't quite got to grips with but had been assured by his new IT Consultant, Steve Jobs, that he would. "Now I've been thinking about the top team and I have a few ideas. I'm thinking Charon has the right stuff to become the Final Judge of Souls and what about Hermes to take on security? I know," he held up his hands in defence of the look Cerebus gave him, "But I'm thinking a bit of responsibility would do him good. With, of course, your support and input." The pair continued this way for the next few hours: playful, but serious, back and forth, until they had an agreed plan which built on the principles Hades had approved.

The way forward for the Underworld was underpinned on the total value of a soul's efforts in the mortal world, not just their best or worst act. This included a new set of rules around what constituted noble behaviour and would therefore be rewarded with a trip to the Island of Elysium.

The execution of this new way of afterlife was wide ranging and covered much, including a new financial model for the kingdom, with souls having to make a contribution to their keep by running essential demon services. It was Minos' intention that this would afford many of the souls the opportunity to pursue interests that they hadn't had the chance for in their lives (he fondly thought of Lucy every time he explained the principle to others).

Branaghan had given Minos a lot of help sorting out the finances for the Underworld going forward, however the demi-god was determined to get better at managing all the numbers. The consultant had paired the demi-god with a mortal Chief Finance Officer so he could continue this education. With the guidance of his new mentor, the demi-god had already introduced a cross-departmental training programme for demons, which included compulsory time in the finance team.

The other initiative that really excited Minos was the new soul-based mortal liaison programme. It offered work to the likes of Boleyn, Chopin, Richard and Robbie, and those who took up the roles would report to the demi-god on all-things-mortal. Not only would it provide the souls with a new sense of purpose on Earth, then could also claim a wage (which he was sure would be spent on a wide range of boardgames).

When Minos and Cerebus finally emerged from the office, light was fading and the evening was drawing in. The noise of demons at work was still clear though, as phone equipment, and the elaborate setup that came with it, was dismantled and packed up. Branaghan had done a superb job of unpicking negotiations and agreeing the return of devices. Minos had to concede he would slightly miss the chubby consultant, and his very thick glasses.

As the executives walked across the open space outside the palace (soon to be converted into a new set of restaurants and drinking establishments – including multiple coffee shops), they paused to look upon the final punishment Minos had dished out before his promotion. The demi-god had known that they were heading into a new world but he couldn't have missed out on the opportunity to invoke his old way of life one more time.

And as far as Minos was concerned, this one was thoroughly deserved.

Standing at the back of the large crowd, the Chief Executive watched as souls passed over coins in exchange for eggs. Each individual handled their purchase with care, knowing very well that the item had gone well past its sell-by date and, if dropped, would have been unpleasant to wash off their clothes.

"I have to say – this was by far one of your best punishments. I know it's all a bit different now, but we really should do more of this type of stuff in the future," Cerebus happily told his friend, "You having a go?"

"No, I think that would be adding insult to injury," retorted Minos, also mindful that he was now the head of the Underworld and may need to be seen to be above this sort of thing (even if he knew the souls and demons loved it). He wasn't going to ruin Cerebus' fun though and simply stood back as the hound slipped through the throng to part with his own hard-earned money.

A short wait and the dog found himself at the front of the queue, twirling his arm and snake head to launch two rotten eggs over the short distance. With a satisfying thunk the shells exploded on long blonde hair, further saturating it in gooey yolk.

Sparkes wriggled in the stocks, cursing at the mess across her hair and face. It would be a few more hours until she was released, for a quick wash and nap, before the punishment started afresh.

Cerebus returned to Minos' side,

"Bad egg," he chuckled. "I don't know how you came up with that!"

"It's all thanks to my time on Earth – you should try it sometime."

The dog and snake cleared their throats and spat,

"Nah, I think you can continue to worry about that stuff. Fancy a pint?"

Minos considered the amount of work he still wanted to get through that evening weighed it up against his longing to spend time with his friend. Finally, he gave in and agreed. The most important lesson he'd taken from everything that had happened was that sometimes you just have to go out of your way for the ones you care about.

Because, Minos reflected, *if you didn't, you never knew what they'd do to try and spend more time with you*.

With a contented stroke of his beard, the demi-god followed Cerebus towards one of their favourite pubs.

As they walked, Minos took in the sights, sounds and smells of a very content kingdom. It felt like his own new sense of purpose and direction was reflected straight back at him, as he passed souls and demons that seemed truly happy with their lot in afterlife.

The end...

...well, until Lucy arrived in the Underworld, six months later, to find no sign of the gods and all the demons running riot.

But that is another story.

Acknowledgements

I'd like to start by saying a big thanks to you, the reader. You've swapped your hard-earned cash and spent time reading the random things that have plopped out of my head onto the page. I really do appreciate it!

I hope that you enjoyed reading Underperforming Underworld as much as I did writing it. It's my first novel – and while it's been a real learning curve, I have loved every minute of it. Whatever you thought I'm definitely up for hearing from you – you can leave an online review, or drop me a message via Twitter or Instagram (both @harrowellandrew).

As an extra little something for you making it this far – I'd also like to offer you a freebie. Please just pop to my website (andrewharrowellwrites.co.uk) for more details about how you can get hold of a short story for absolutely nothing.

It wouldn't be right to finish this book without a few other words of thanks to those who helped get me to this stage.

Firstly, I want to say a huge thanks to my wonderful wife, Wendy, who when I said I wanted to spend an evening a week attending a creative writing course, didn't stomp her feet and point out that it would be nice if I spent some more time with her (although, on reflection, this may say more about how much I annoy her, than anything else...). She wholeheartedly backed me in this endeavour and even went out of her way to buy me every possible writing implement she could find – many of which were used in the notes for this novel.

Throughout the writing of this story, Wendy has continued to believe in me, and without her pushing me on, these words would most likely have continued to gather electronic dust on our laptop. She's been equal parts supportive and patient with me, never once complaining when I offered up my (now) infamous catchphrase: 'Do you mind if I just do a bit of writing?'. You wouldn't be reading this, if not for her (although she should share the positives, please don't send her any complaints – she only helped the horse get to the water, she cannot be held responsible for the way it bashed it's hoofs on a keyboard after that).

Equally, I could not have got this story beyond the initial draft (and there's been a few) without my first proof readers: my parents, Jeanette and Derek. This completely isn't the sort of book they'd pick up, but them taking the time to read it through and come back with notes was amazingly helpful. The fact they could see what I was getting at, could imagine the characters and follow the storyline gave me a real sense of belief at such an early stage.

Finally, I must make a quick mention of Ian St Peters from Watford College – who put up with my rough work during two writing courses. He helped me to no longer view a blank page as something to be feared, but relished! Thank you.

In case you are wondering...

This is not the book I thought I would write.

It's not the genre I grew up on (that was all detectives solving crimes and futuristic spaceships), nor the first piece of work I ever thought I would produce. It all really came about through being in a strange place, at an odd time.

The work was inspired by the Sistine Chapel, which I saw when we were on holiday in Italy in 2017. It was a few weeks before I started my second writing course and I was playing with a couple of novel ideas. I wanted to have something locked in, which I could focus on during the forthcoming sessions. I had been toying with a couple of possibilities but couldn't settle on anything.

That all changed the day we visited the Vatican City and I saw Minos for the first time. I probably should have been paying more attention to the overall beauty of the chapel's roof, but I couldn't help but be attracted to the contrastingly dark figure of the Final Judge of Souls.

I failed to shake that image and very quickly got to wondering what Minos would think of the twenty first century and how the Underworld would cope if it was forced to adapt to our way of life. One thing led to another and this story was born.

Whilst everything in this book is made up, I can share that a lot of the demi-gods and their home was based on actual research (again, not something I thought I'd ever do for a piece of writing).

A lot of the deities are based on what I learnt about them, but with my own twist. In some cases, I've kept close to the tales: Hades did take over the Underworld when he and his brothers overthrew the old gods. He was always focused on keeping souls in his kingdom, and he was married to the Goddess of Spring (who was known by a variety of names, including Melinda, Persephone and Kore). Other characters are much further away from the original versions. For example, I gave Rhadamanthus and Hermes more modern outfits and mannerism for a bit of variety and to help them contrast against Minos being stuck in his ways. Equally, Cerebus is a combination of the many different suggestions of what the beast looked like and I gave him the dog/man/snake combination for a little nod to the gods depicted by the Egyptians.

Elsewhere, the souls who were not allowed into the Underworld did all have their hearts removed after death. This practice wasn't picked for any reason other than the fact it wasn't a well-used practice, and therefore presented a small collection of potential assistants to the demi-god. Once I saw the list of famous figures who had had this done to them, I knew I had to go with it, my mind relishing the challenges of working up the rag tag band of misfits.

Everything else in this story just stems from an overactive imagination and a slightly too long commute by train! What happens in the afterlife, and how the judging works – well, I hope to give it a while until I find out! If anyone else gets there first, please don't feel under any pressure to come and tell me.

So, that's how this story came about, in a nutshell (I won't bore you with the tales of the early starts, the typing on my phone and the long arguments with myself over where to put the commas). For my next effort I'm aiming to be on more familiar ground for me. If everything goes as planned (and when does that really happen?), I hope to follow this with a detective novel, set in a bleak future, with a broken character who has some issues to work through. If that tempts you, do get in touch and I'll make sure you know when I think I've finished disagreeing with myself about all the punctuation!

Printed in Poland
by Amazon Fulfillment
Poland Sp. z o.o., Wrocław

61658054R00174